THE

GIVEN-UP

GIRL

The Given-Up Girl

A Novel

Ellen B. Rockmore

Sibylline
DIGITAL FIRST

For my parents, Martin and Shirley Bresler.
How did I get so lucky?

1

This story isn't about Amber, but her death set it all in motion. At least in my mind, it started on the day of her funeral, fittingly rainy and cold. I had assigned myself a list of tasks to cover for Amber's mother, Joyce, who was, understandably, immobilized by grief. Joyce is just a few years older than I am, and she's generally unflappable as my office manager—she keeps my law practice running smoothly and profitably, if only by the slimmest of margins—but, on the day of her daughter's funeral, it was my turn to make her life easier. I had ordered the flowers, and asked the florist to send the invoice to me, because bereaved parents don't need to be bothered with paying bills. Same with the platters of cold cuts that I had sent to their house, assuming there might be some relatives in town and that they might be hungry after the service. Probably the hardest thing I did was haggle with the funeral home over the price of the casket. I'm known as a reasonable negotiator, sometimes disarmingly so, because I am always calm and professional. I have even heard the word "disinterested" used to describe my style, which is a slight misuse of the word, but accurate enough that I don't bother correcting it. But believe me, I fell far short of my usual equilibrium when I was purchasing an Amber-sized coffin.

I had known Amber almost her whole life. She was a funny kid, a prankster and a daredevil. She was a terrible student, who charmed her teachers into giving her passing grades, usually for "independent projects" she made up and sometimes even did. By the time she hit her twenties, she was angry and aimless. She pierced her eyebrow and stole her grandmother's Percodan. Once she was a fiery and formidable young woman, who tormented Joyce by demanding money and blaming her for imaginary slights. But now Amber was a corpse in a box.

I also did everything necessary to close the office for the day of the funeral. I figured we could manage without Joyce for a few weeks, because my practice is a small one, and this was New Hampshire in 1990, after all. I don't even mean coastal New Hampshire, which is essentially a suburb of Boston for people who don't want to pay a state income tax. This is the other side of the state, where the horse farms and apple orchards are, just across the river from Vermont. I mostly draft wills and file deeds, and not much of it is ever urgent.

I also hoped, as I put on my raincoat and turned off the office light, that Lars, who had worked for me a year, would show up at the service. He had been surprised the day before when I told him that the office would be closed for the day out of respect for Joyce.

"I never met Amber, and I don't even know Joyce that well," he had said.

"But she works here. She is part of this family," I responded. It seemed so obvious to me that it didn't need explaining. But I shouldn't have been surprised that he needed it spelled out. Young people no longer thought a job was a life-long commitment or that a workplace was a community. I don't mean to sound critical; I'm just suggesting that a lack of trust can become a self-fulfilling prophecy. If you treat your employees like strangers, they will be strangers. If you treat them like family, they will be family. You learn at least that much when you have been running a viable, if not staggeringly successful, law practice for fifteen years.

"It will mean a lot to Joyce if you're there," I told him.

Joyce knew at the time I hired Lars that I hadn't brought him on because I was understaffed, or because of his stellar performance in law school. I had hired him because I owed his father—the most meticulous and generous accountant who ever lived—a favor. The man had been doing my books for all the time I'd been in business, and, in the early years, he did it for free. He told me I could start paying him when I began turning a profit, which took until the second quarter of 1979, my third year of practice. You never forget the people who were kind to you in the beginning, so when Lars passed the bar, I gave him a job. To my great relief, in the year since he joined my office, Lars had proven himself to be a quick learner and an able attorney.

Joyce had been with me a long time, and even though she is an even tighter-lipped New Englander than I am, I had heard quite a bit about Amber's troubles. Once, I even went to family court to get a restraining order against a particularly awful boyfriend who had locked his hand around Amber's neck and pinned her to a wall. I was relieved, almost happy, for the chance to do something useful for her. Amber never did seem to appreciate that I got that fellow out of her life for good, but I know Joyce did. And I know Joyce appreciated that I never asked, not even silently to myself, what Joyce herself had done wrong. That was our deal. I never questioned the kind of mother she had been, and she never questioned why I had not married and raised children of my own. I always suspected, actually, that it's precisely because I didn't have kids that Joyce could tell me the truth. When she talked about Amber to other women who were mothers themselves, Joyce once told me, she sensed they were only pretending to be sympathetic. They were secretly thanking God that their own children were married or in college or stationed on a base overseas, and that the troubled young addict was someone else's daughter.

I left the office in time to arrive early at the funeral home, in what had once been a Congregational church. Joyce and her husband Fred sat in a corner talking to their pastor and to a man I recognized as the funeral director. He had presided over the wake the night before, and he had a nice, soothing way about him. When I walked in, he was nodding his head thoughtfully at something Fred was saying. Joyce saw me come in and mustered a tiny smile of gratitude.

The building maintained its original austerity, though now, at least, there were some carpets that muffled the sounds of mourning. Eventually I made my way into the main sanctuary, where there were already many people sitting in the hard wooden pews. I recognized a lot of them, because Hopkins, New Hampshire, really is a very small town, and some of these folks were longstanding clients of my firm's. I was relieved to see Lars sitting by himself in the back row.

Joyce's brother spoke about Amber when she was a little girl who had loved gymnastics and butterflies. One of Amber's friends described a person who was nothing like the Amber that her mother and I saw. To her peers, Amber had been exciting, funny, and vivacious. Then the pastor recited Psalm twenty-three and, thankfully, didn't try to convince us that Amber's death was part of some divine plan or that Amber was "in a better place." I think I would have jumped out of my seat and called him a son-of-a-bitch at the top of my lungs if he had done that. At least, in my head I would have.

After the service, the crowd at the cemetery was much smaller. The rain hadn't let up, and it was miserable, the way March is always miserable here. Joyce and Fred stood together under an umbrella. I watched my friend cling to her husband and cry uncontrollably. There were belts and pulleys lowering Amber's casket into the ground, and, with each turn of the crank, the casket fell a few inches lower, and Joyce's sobs got a little bit louder. From now on, I knew, whenever she heard the sound of rain outside, she would think of Amber in this cemetery, alone and unprotected.

I had buried my father six years earlier and my mother four years before that, so I knew the finality of a coffin being lowered into the earth. But at least when you bury a parent, you don't feel that the universe has gone off course. I missed my parents a great deal, but I had been living without much parental guidance for a long time. When you bury a child, I imagine, you spend the rest of your life in a prison of grief. How much greater that grief must be when that child was so young, when her death was paradoxically surprising and inevitable, and when her final act hovered in the tragic and murky intersection between overdose and suicide.

I had never spent much time thinking about why a girl like Amber might turn out so differently from how her parents intended, any more than I thought about why one plant in my garden grew while another one didn't. Every fall I plant bulbs in my front yard, but I have no expectation that each and every one will bloom. Organisms are like that. Some thrive while others wither. I never asked for an explanation; I just planted a lot of bulbs. Why would children be any different?

As I stood in that cemetery, watching two men shovel heavy, wet dirt into Amber's grave, I finally allowed my thoughts to drift where they had been trying to go all day. The truth is that my focus on Joyce and her loss was not motivated entirely by altruism. I am not saying I am a false friend. Not at all. But pouring my energy into supporting Joyce had given me a welcome distraction from my own phantom limb, that presence-absence that hangs over my life at all times. What I have never told Joyce, or anyone else, is that I once had my own baby girl. Twenty years earlier, I held her for just a few minutes, before a nurse carried her away to some other woman's arms. This was where my mind always went when I was burdened with an idle moment. This was the background noise I could sometimes drown out but never silence.

I had not known it would be like this. I thought at the time that giving up a baby I did not want to raise would be liberating. I thought it would free me to become the grown-up I was ambitious to be. But I was young and stupid and unacquainted with abstract concepts like permanence and loss. I knew the meanings of the words, of course, and that they were features of the arrangement I had chosen. But I did not know the effect they would have. I had not predicted back then that, for the rest of my life, I would feel both connected to and completely cut off from the child I brought into the world. I did not know that every August 31 I would be consumed with memories of having been a mother for that one day. That every year, as summer ended, I would be paralyzed by aching and longing for her.

What's more, I had not known that it would get worse. I thought at the time that giving birth was a wound that would heal. Time would pass, I was told, and memory would fade. What I failed to predict was that, far from healing, the injury would recur. I was like that woman—perhaps you read about her too—who was thrown through the windshield in a car accident. Miraculously, she made a full recovery, except for one thing. Every few months, a small piece of glass embedded deep in her skin would work its way to the surface and remind her of the traumatic collision. Like her, I never knew when a tiny shard of grief would erupt.

I also assumed early on that each milestone I achieved in my own life would affirm that I had made the right choice. The graduations, the cases won, would be my assurance that what I gained was worth what I gave up. But my accomplishments, like the passage of time, had had the opposite effect. I found that whenever I reached a goal—being sworn into the bar, founding my firm, buying a house—I wanted her there to experience it with me. Every step forward felt incomplete if I couldn't share it with her. I wanted her to be proud of me. In the early years, I mistakenly thought that the problem was merely that I had not achieved enough. The next accolade, I told myself, would be the one that settled my conscience. And then the next. But instead I found that the more secure I became in my life, the more I wondered if I had paid too high a price. Maybe, I sometimes allowed myself to think, my success would have come even if I hadn't let her go. Maybe giving her up had not even been necessary.

But one thing I had never questioned was that my daughter was growing up happy. Whenever I conjured an image of her, she was smiling. I saw her as a baby blowing bubbles or a toddler smearing paint. I envisioned a girl playing volleyball or reading *Charlotte's Web*. I wondered how she would choose a prom date from among her many suitors. Until I watched Amber buried, I never thought to worry about my daughter. I had seen a photo of the handsome, smiling couple desperate to raise her, and I assumed they were giving her a good life. That had been the whole point of adopting her, hadn't it? But now, for the first time, I confronted the possibility that my baby—now a young woman—might not be happy, might not be well, might not even be alive. Not every bulb grows into a tulip.

2

WHEN I WALKED IN THE DOOR of my cozy house later that afternoon, I expected to feel relieved. I had successfully dispatched my obligations to Joyce, and to her out-of-town relatives and the funeral home, and I could finally be alone. I do love this house and everything in it. All of it—every watercolor on the walls, every glazed ceramic vase, every chair and matching ottoman— was picked out and paid for by me. I never had to compromise on whether the right shade for the dining room walls was *summer wheat* or *honeyed cream*. I never had to scour the house for someone else's car keys, never had to move aside someone else's book splayed spine-side up on the coffee table, never had to defend the hand-painted outlet covers and other useless knickknacks that I bought at craft fairs and farmers' markets.

I changed out of my gray wool suit, which had been damp since the morning, and into my comfortable green sweater dress. I made myself a nutritious dinner of scrambled eggs and scotch, and I ate it on the couch. I thought these familiar rituals would soothe me. But I was too agitated by the sight of Amber's coffin being lowered into the ground. I kept imagining my own daughter in that grave. It wasn't my usual longing that I was feeling. It was terror. And also helplessness. There was no way to calm my distress, because I had no information. I couldn't ask my daughter directly about her well-being, and I couldn't observe her from a distance. I needed a sign from her, and I would have to figure out how to get it.

As soon as I finished eating, I went upstairs to the third bedroom, the smallest one, not the one I sleep in and not the one I use as an office. It's the one used for storing all sorts of things that I want to keep but not necessarily look at regularly or display for visitors, like my framed diplomas and a quilt sewn by my mother. In the back of the top drawer of an old oak dresser, I kept a copy of my baby's birth certificate, along with the document I signed giving up all my rights to know her. For the first few years after she was born, I did not touch that folder. Instead, I tried to pretend she did not exist. When that did not work, there followed some years when I treated her birth certificate like a talisman that proved she was real. Every year, I spent the last day of August alone with my melancholy, reading and rereading that document, as if it were a portal to wherever she was, whispering to it, "Happy Birthday, sweet girl." Even in those years, though, I did not touch the relinquishment contract, in which my nineteen-year-old self had promised I would never look for or contact my baby. As time went on, I wondered if my attachment to her birth certificate might be stoking, not soothing, my sadness. These efforts to commune with a child by touching a piece of paper were futile, I concluded. And so, when I moved into this house in 1980, I put both documents in that drawer and hoped their power would fade. I had not looked at them in eleven years.

I took the papers out of the folder gingerly, as if they were an insect that might still have the power to sting. I brought them downstairs and put two more logs in the wood-burning stove. I sat on the couch and tucked my feet under my backside. Then, with the documents in my lap, I read them over, top to bottom, one more time. Even while I was doing it, I knew it was pointless. After all, there was nothing on the birth certificate I hadn't already memorized. On the line for *Mother* was my name—Bonnie Koller, age nineteen. But the baby herself did not have a name at that time. She was simply called *Female*. None of these details mattered, however, because she would have been issued a new birth certificate by now, with all new information. The infant once known as *Female* would have whatever name, first and last, her adoptive parents had given her. They would be listed on the birth certificate as her mother and father, as if they had been there all along. There would be no trace of my name or her father's, no indication that I had ever existed. These papers in my lap, far from being a portal, now seemed to me like a brick wall that separated me from her.

I had never seen my daughter's amended birth certificate, and I knew perfectly well that I was prohibited from seeing it. I had learned from my years practicing family law that there were strict rules about what I was and wasn't allowed to know. I might be able to get information that was generic, like, say, that my daughter's adoptive father was of German and Scottish descent. Details like that were so vague as to be useless. For a two-hundred-mile radius of my home, practically everyone is of German and Scottish descent. But I was not allowed to get a name or an address. That was what the state considered *identifying information*, and that was off limits to me. Maybe, just maybe, there would still be some useful details, like the baby's birth on August 31 in Grantham County, and maybe those details would lead somewhere.

The truth is that I had never thought about what steps I would take to locate her. I had often imagined a reunion—even assumed it was inevitable—but in my fantasy, it always came about in some fairy-tale way. I would see her in a group of young girls selling Tagalongs at the grocery or swinging on a rope at the lake. We would lock eyes and know each other instantly. The world would fall away as gravity pulled us together. We would not need to speak, because we could read each other's thoughts.

But now I had to think about logistics. There was, in fact, no magnetic force and no magical bridge that would bring the two of us together. I needed to come up with a first step that would lead to a second step that might eventually lead to a name, a place, a body. I knew the math. There were, on average, thirty children born every day of 1970 in New Hampshire. The number was daunting but not unmanageable. Could I get my hands on all those birth certificates? Would I immediately know which one was mine? How many of those children, who were now young adults, would I have to find in order to locate the one I wanted? I had no idea if my daughter lived one town over or on another continent.

And I had no idea if she wanted to be found. Maybe she did not feel the bond with me that I felt with her. Maybe she did not even know there was a me. Perhaps, I worried, even trying to locate her was asking too much of her. I couldn't expect her to cure my own loneliness and regret. That wouldn't be fair. And, of course, there was the terrifying possibility that she would want nothing to do with me. I anguished over this scenario, even though part of me knew that the best possible outcome of my search would be that I found a girl so happy and secure in her adoptive family that she had no interest in me. And surely her parents would consider me an unwelcome, even threatening, intruder. So I told myself that I was not looking for a meaningful reunion with my daughter. I simply wanted to check on her. Like any good lawyer, I was following up with a client to find out how she was. She just happened to be a tiny, pink, pointy-headed client I had briefly held and kissed.

3

MY SEARCH DIDN'T REALLY BEGIN UNTIL A few days later when I drove down to the capital. I explained my absence from the office—not that I needed to—by telling Lars that I was meeting my usual clique of lady lawyers for lunch. This particular group had been gathering several times a year for a decade. We began meeting early in our careers to talk about how miserable we all were. Back then we were outsiders in a very intimate club that was hostile to our entry. The female camaraderie, not to mention the Cobb salads, made us feel better and stronger. But ultimately, we had all been blessed with some degree of success. We found our way to comfortable lives in the law, and we might even have referred to ourselves as trailblazers, had that not seemed a little too much like self-congratulation. To toot your own horn in the jurisdiction of New England in the 1990's was practically a misdemeanor. When I told my office about the lunch, I had not been lying, exactly. We were in fact meeting today, and we had something to celebrate: one of our number, the brilliant Nora Wood, had recently been appointed a superior court judge.

We always met in the same restaurant, one of the oldest in Concord, a favorite of lawyers and legislators alike. They say that when Meldrim Thomson first ran for governor in 1968, he devised his "Ax the Tax" motto while sitting in this very establishment, and then memorialized it on one of their napkins. Since I was the one who travelled the farthest to get to these lunches, I was always the last to arrive. This day was no different. I took my seat on the oak bench in our regular booth and snapped off the end of a bread stick. My friend Frances caught me up on what I'd missed.

"First we talked about how everything has changed," she said. "But now we're talking about how nothing has changed."

We toasted the new Judge Wood, and reminisced about the man she would be replacing. Old Judge Richter had tried to hold Jean in contempt the first time she wore a pant suit in his courtroom, and for years he had refused to address a married woman by anything other than her husband's surname, whether it was her legal name or not.

"He tried that on me once," said Nora. "I kept insisting that there was no 'Nora Katchen' admitted to the state bar. Even though she didn't exist, I didn't want her charged with the unauthorized practice of law. He finally let up when the court reporter said that *she* was worried about losing her license for entering the wrong name into the record."

As we drank our Sankas and coffees, I finally told them about Amber's funeral the week before. While I had no intention of letting them in on my search for my daughter, I didn't want to be dishonest. Talking about Amber was a good way to almost talk about the truth.

"I'm worried that Joyce will never be the same," I admitted. "And I'm also worried that my office will never be the same. I know that sounds so selfish and terrible, and like the last thing I should be thinking about. But Joyce makes it all work. She is the only person who knows how to reboot the computer."

"I don't think it sounds terrible," Frances assured me. "You have to worry about uncertainty. That's what makes you a good lawyer."

"And, for what it's worth," said Nora, finishing off our communal slice of chocolate cake, "all you have to do is remember these three words: control, alt, delete."

By the time we paid our separate checks and agreed on how much to tip so that no one looked more generous or stingy than anyone else, I was ready to face my real errand in the capital. The Bureau of Vital Records was housed a few blocks from the gold-domed granite statehouse. I had not been to this particular building before. Though I had personally obtained many a birth and death certificate for countless matters in probate court, I had found those documents in various town clerks' offices. But pre-adoption birth certificates were kept in a central location, not accessible to the general public.

On the outside, the building was turn-of-the-century elegant, but inside it was post-war industrial. My heels percussed on the linoleum floor; my eyes were assaulted by a flickering fluorescent light. I checked the sign—white plastic letters pressed into black felt—which told me that the hall of records was down in the basement. The building had no elevator, so I walked down the concrete steps to the large open room underground. I saw a young couple coming up the stairs, and I guessed, by their smiles and their clasped hands, that they had just obtained a marriage license. They wore blue jeans and sweatshirts and made me feel overdressed in my wool skirt and houndstooth jacket. I was trying to look like I had come to the capital on important legal business, not self-interested sleuthing.

The large hall of records was windowless but for a few ceiling-level hoppers. The woman behind the tall counter looked stern. Near a small bell was a sign which admonished the public to ring *ONCE*, capitalized and underlined three times, for assistance. I was sure she had written it. I don't know what she was saying to the man in front of me, but her eyes were alert and focused. I tried to size her up and gauge the chances that, in fifteen minutes, I would walk out of that building in possession of my daughter's birth certificate. Not the one I had in my drawer at home, obviously, but the one with her given name and her adoptive parents' names on it. I considered the illegality of my mission to be only a minor obstacle. Because I am a lawyer, my whole job is to ask for things I know perfectly well I shouldn't get. Everything is a negotiation, and, in my experience, if you ask calmly and politely—for a larger insurance settlement, say, or the signature of a guarantor—you may very well receive it. So I tried to smile agreeably as I approached the counter, that protective parapet between myself and the files I wanted.

"Good afternoon," I said warmly. "Perhaps you can help me."

"Happy to try," the clerk said. "What is it you're looking for?" She leaned forward on her forearms and clasped her hands.

I relaxed a bit, because her response seemed courteous and professional enough.

"I'm doing some genealogical research," I said. I had learned the usefulness of this euphemism from magazine articles about mothers who found their adopted children. "And I'm looking for a young woman who was born in Grantham County on August thirty-first, 1970."

She waited for me to continue, but that was all I had to say. After an awkward moment, she pushed herself off of the counter and stood up straight.

"What's the young woman's name?" she asked. Was she asking because she wanted to help me, or because she wanted to test me? I couldn't tell.

"Well, that's the conundrum," I said. "I don't know this young woman's name, and I was hoping I could look through the birth certificates filed at around that time. I have a feeling that when I find the right one, I'll know it." I was trying to sound simultaneously reasonable and naïve.

It did not appear to be working, because the clerk looked at me just a beat too long before she asked suspiciously,

"What kind of genealogical research"—she stressed the words as if they just didn't sit right with her— "are you doing, exactly?"

I thought about telling her the truth. Maybe she was imagining something far worse than a mother trying to track down her own daughter. A social security scam, or a kidnapping plot, maybe. Perhaps with honesty I could convert her from a gatekeeper to a confidant. But just as I was trying to decide how much to divulge, an older man came into the room. He stood a little too close to me, radiating impatience, and I knew he would overhear everything. Even if I had been willing to share my story with the clerk when it was just the two of us in the room, I could not even imagine letting this strange man in on my secret. And I doubted that the clerk would violate protocol, even if she had been inclined to do so, now that there was a witness in the room.

"I am trying to find a lost relative," I said quietly. "A cousin I don't know."

And I knew immediately this had been the wrong thing to say, because the clerk narrowed her eyes.

"I wouldn't have birth certificates that old here on site. They're in the warehouse already," she said. "If you want one, you'll have to request it in writing. You'll need the name of the person you're looking for, and you have to tell us why you need it. You can't just look through a stack of birth certificates until you find one you like."

But I was not yet ready to give up. I focused on my need to win a battle of wits with this clerk, not on my yearning for my daughter.

"The problem is," I said, "that I don't know what my cousin's name was at birth. She took the name of her mother's second husband, and no one ever talked about it. Her mother was my father's sister, but they didn't get along." I waved my hand around in the air as if to say, that's a whole other story I'd love to tell you when we have more time. "I know just enough about her that I think I would recognize it when I see it."

The man standing behind me cleared his throat conspicuously. The clerk was not responding to my request, so I went on.

"Our grandmother would like to see her again," I said. "Before it's too late."

"What's your cousin's name now?" the clerk asked me, almost sneering.

She was not letting up. I've had quite a bit of practice questioning witnesses, and I had to admire the woman's technique. I tried to sound deferential, not flustered, and started to say that I wasn't sure of her name now either, when the clerk interrupted me.

"I can't help you if you don't know her name," she snapped. She looked at me pointedly and said, "You think I don't know what's going on here? You think you're the first woman to come sniffing around for *identifying information*"—I heard the italics in my head—"about a young woman you have never met? You have no right to that information, and I am not going to give it to you." She looked at the man behind me and gestured with her eyebrows that she was ready for her next customer.

And now I was mad. I had known all along that I might come up empty-handed, so I was prepared to accept failure. But I would not accept her accusation. She was insinuating that trying to find my daughter, just to know she was alive, was a form of cheating. As if it were terrible, even immoral, for a mother to want to look her daughter in the eyes and ask, how are you? What was this woman so righteous about? Why was she so determined to protect the fiction of my daughter's adoption? Though the clerk was beckoning with her hand for the older man to approach, I stood in place. I wasn't willing to beg, but I wasn't willing to concede either.

"Your tone is uncalled for," I said calmly but firmly. "I am merely trying to find a relative, my own flesh and blood. I am trying to make contact with her, not harm her, or anyone else, for that matter." I had said my piece, and I was ready to walk out. I pivoted toward the exit and saw a couple with an infant. They seemed confused by the tense exchange they had stumbled into, and I made a point of smiling at their baby to put them at ease.

I was shocked when, instead of just letting me leave, the clerk called loudly after me,

"You know what you are?" The sound of her voice spread around the room and seemed to emanate from every corner. "You're selfish. That's what." I was almost at the door, but I stopped, turned around and faced her. If she were going to yell at me, I wanted her to see in my face how unaffected I was by her insults. And she just kept going.

"You have no right to intrude on that family's privacy. You have no right to bother that girl, who's forgotten all about you, if she ever even knew you existed."

If she was still talking as I walked out into the stairwell, I didn't hear it. Until I got outside, I concentrated on maintaining my dignity, and then, as soon as I exited the building, I felt tears forming. I allowed myself to believe they were the unavoidable effect of late-winter wind. I sat in my car with the windows open to let the air cool my hot rage. What made me angriest wasn't that the clerk had tried to humiliate me. She hadn't succeeded, I thought, since I had kept my tears down until I was here, alone in my car. And it wasn't that she thought I was selfish. No, what made me angriest was the possibility that the clerk might, at this very moment, be holding my daughter's birth certificate in her own witchy fingers. The laws that prohibited me from learning my daughter's identity didn't apply to other people. Anyone who wasn't me was allowed to look at my daughter's new birth certificate. And the document might have been right there—I didn't believe that warehouse business for one second—on the shelves behind her. And she might have, for no reason other than curiosity, or boredom, or spite, pulled out the August 1970 box and found the one for my baby. At the very moment that I was staring at the salt stains on my windshield, that clerk might have been staring at my daughter's actual, legal name. It was the unfairness that angered me the most.

I felt aggrieved and also ashamed as I sat in my car and contemplated the wall I had just hit. Why didn't the world understand that my daughter and I were one soul, like in that John Donne valediction? We were like the legs of that poetic compass, always fastened at the top. When one leg moves, the other leans and straightens, keeping the point of connection. But that woman saw us instead like cesium and water, elements that need to be kept apart, prevented from making contact lest they cause an explosion.

Why had I let myself believe that my daughter could be conjured up through sheer will? She had seemed so present to me in the past few days. I imagined her walking through my front door, like a person coming home from a long vacation. It was hard to accept that at this moment she was as far away as she had ever been. I missed her so much. That might not sound like it makes any sense. You can't miss a person you never knew, some would say. But that's how I felt. There was a hole in my life where my daughter should be, and the only way for me to describe that feeling is to say that I missed her.

★ ★ ★

It is always easier to be angry than to be despondent, isn't it? I had enough rage to fuel my ride home from Concord that I probably didn't need gasoline. Luckily, I had a well-honed strategy for coping with the inexplicable hostility of strangers. I had learned it early on in my practice from a lawyer named Reed Masters. I met Reed on one of my first cases, the Mudge matter, in probably 1978 or so. It's hard to believe now, but I was pretty unsure of myself at that time. I had always been a good student, always had success in school. But learning the logistical details and mechanics of practicing law seemed so daunting that I spent a lot of time wondering what had ever made me think I could do it. I had loved law school, that Socratic salon where you ponder abstract ideas, like the limits of duty and the nature of justice. But once I graduated, I had to learn things like how to find a process server in the yellow pages.

The case where I met Reed was an orientation of sorts, and I've always felt grateful for the opportunity. The fellow who hired me, an old friend of my beloved accountant by the name of Luther Mudge, owned a lake house in the White Mountains. Only, he didn't just own it outright. He owned it together with his sister and three cousins, who had all inherited the house from their fathers, a pair of brothers who had in turn inherited it from their father. That patriarch was Orville Mudge, and he had built the house not long after the Civil War as a summer retreat for his family. In the century that followed, they had made only two changes: replacing the outhouse with an indoor bathroom in 1936, and purchasing a suite of GE kitchen appliances in 1951.

By the time Reed and I were on the case, a fourth generation of Mudge children had grown up spending at least part of every summer at the house. The various members of the extended family lived all over the country—Boston, Raleigh, Atlanta—but they still gathered there every year. The way they talked about their cricket and badminton matches, and their Parchesi and backgammon tournaments, you would think there was actually something at stake.

When Luther Mudge first called me, he was distraught. His younger sister, who was not just the baby of the family but also the only girl in her generation, had died at fifty-one, leaving them heartbroken.

"They cut her open, took one look at the cancer, and sewed her back up," he told me, as if he needed to hear himself say it in order to believe it. "She died at home a week later."

She had left behind a twenty-year-old son, Amos Crandall, but he claimed he wanted nothing to do with the Mudges or their lake house. What he wanted was to cash out his share of the property and move to San Miguel de Allende. Luther was willing to buy out his nephew for a nominal sum, but not, he was adamant, at the price the boy was demanding. Luther also thought that his cousins should pitch in. After a hundred years, the upkeep of the house was expensive, and Luther was tired of the escalating maintenance costs. The house was more of a liability than an asset, he claimed, and he didn't want to be responsible for more of it.

Luther's cousins were even more stubborn than he was. They referred to the nephew in question as the Mexican bandit, and they refused to pay him anything. Mudge Manor—yes, they actually called it that—belonged to the people who loved it, they said. If their hippie second cousin wanted to walk away from his birthright, that was his choice. They considered his ownership to be like a supermarket coupon with no cash value. The nephew filed a suit against Luther and his cousins, demanding to be bought out at full market value. Shortly after Luther hired me, his cousins hired Reed Masters.

I met Reed the first time we were called in for a status conference with Judge Hobart. Reed wasn't much older than I, but he was noticeably less nervous. What was even more noticeable was how handsome he was, with blue eyes and a bright smile. He must have picked up on how new to the practice I was, because as we walked into the judge's chambers, he said, "Hobart can get off track sometimes. Just try to keep the conversation focused on the matter at hand. We'll be fine."

It was clear as soon as we sat down that His Honor was in a terrible mood.

"Where is Mr. Crandall's attorney?" he barked at me.

That really caught me off-guard. How was I supposed to know where the attorney for another party was? Had I screwed up this conference already? I did not yet know, but I would soon learn, that when you are the only woman working on a case, people often assume that you will be the one to keep it all running smoothly, to manage the other participants, to keep track of unruly details, and, of course, to keep the coffee and Danish fresh. I was too young to know how unreasonable Judge Hobart's expectations were. I opened my mouth to apologize for having so carelessly misplaced my opposing counsel, but before I could answer, Reed jumped in.

"I don't believe Mr. Crandall has an attorney, Your Honor."

"Then he ought to be here," the judge insisted. "Where is he?"

"I understand he currently resides in Mexico, Your Honor," Reed replied.

"Mexico?" Hobart sneered. His mood did not improve at the prospect of an ex-pat plaintiff.

"Yes, Your Honor," I said, trying to keep the conversation from leaving the continental United States. "Amos—Mr. Crandall—has moved out of the country. That's why he is trying to force a sale of the Mudge property. He has no known plans to return to New Hampshire."

"Perhaps he'd better not," said the judge, "given the incomprehensible complaint he filed."

"He is hoping to force a sale," I continued, "in order to maximize his share, but he has drastically overvalued the property."

As Hobart looked down at the case file on his desk, Reed smiled at me. *See?* his perfect white teeth seemed to say, *you're doing great.* I almost smiled back, but I was sure that, if I did, Hobart would look up at exactly that moment.

"It seems to me, Miss Koller, that you and Mr. Masters ought to be able to settle this right here right now."

I had assumed the purpose of the conference was to set a schedule for the case. We would pull out our calendars and talk about when discovery would start, and when we would take Mr. Crandall's deposition, and when the first hearing would take place. I had no idea I would be asked to come up with a settlement proposal on the spot. This was another thing I didn't yet know but would learn soon enough: whenever you are in the presence of a judge who presides over one of your matters, even if the meeting is social or accidental, the judge will demand to know why you haven't settled the damn case and cleared it from his docket.

But at that time, I sat dumbstruck until Reed spoke up again. "Your Honor, Ms. Koller and I have been actively pursuing a compromise. It is Amos Crandall who won't cooperate."

"Well, what do the documents say?" demanded Hobart.

I looked to Reed for guidance, but this time he seemed confused too. I noticed that my palms were sticking to my legal pad.

"I'm sorry, Your Honor," I said. "Which documents do you mean?"

"Isn't this property in some kind of trust by now?" asked Hobart. "There must be an agreement that governs the trust. I'm asking what, according to the agreement, is the procedure for dealing with an owner who doesn't want his share?"

I honestly had no idea what he was talking about. Maybe we covered it in Trusts and Estates, but it had already been four years since I took that class. I wasn't sure whether to ask the judge what he meant or to pretend I knew. Even Reed did not seem to know how to answer. He was silent, and then he offered weakly, "They're family, Your Honor. They work out their issues as they come up."

"So you haven't bothered to write up an agreement regarding the rights of the individual owners?" He shifted his eyes from Reed to me. "Miss Koller, your client has owned this property since 1956. Yes, I read the pleadings. And, Mr. Masters, your clients inherited it in 1953. You've had twenty years to come up with a procedure for handling a situation like this. An entirely predictable situation.

I wouldn't have to suffer the incoherent demands of a countercultural nincompoop, if you two had done your jobs."

Reed, to his credit, responded apologetically, and not at all defensively. "You're certainly right about that, Your Honor," he said. He might even have said "golly" at some point in that sentence. "Ms. Koller and I will talk to our respective clients and get to work on that trust."

"Perhaps you should let your father handle this one," said Hobart to Reed. Then he moved his eyes to me. "You two don't seem like you're up to the task."

His assessment stung me painfully, probably because it came so close to what I had been thinking myself. If I heard it today, I would shrug it off. If nothing else, I would recognize how unfair it was for Hobart to blame us for the annoyance of this case. But at the time, I thought I deserved it. I had been anxious all morning, and it had taken great effort to be as cool a cucumber as I was, even if I had not fooled anyone. All the stress of having to act more competent than I felt started to leak out in the form of hot, angry tears. I was terribly embarrassed, and I put my head down at an awkward angle, hoping my hair would fall in such a way as to obscure my face. Then I heard Reed asking the judge to take a look at some exhibit, Chester Mudge's will or something equally unimportant, just to get Hobart's eyes off of me. I could not have been more grateful.

When the conference with Judge Hobart finally ended, Reed offered to take me out for coffee and there was nothing I wanted to do more. We went to a diner in town and right away I admitted how embarrassing it was that I almost cried at my first judicial conference.

"Hobart can be awful," Reed said, almost dismissively. We sat down on adjacent vinyl counter stools. "That was my third time meeting with him, and that was the worst he's been. What he said to you was out of line."

"I'm not sure it was," I confessed. "Maybe I'm not really up to the task."

He shook his head.

"You just started. All you need is experience. Every lawyer is in over their head at the beginning. Finally, after four years in this business, I don't feel like a complete fraud anymore."

"I'm not sure I'll last four years if I have to go through more conferences like that." It wasn't hyperbole. I really meant it.

Reed loosened his plaid tie, and the motion made his stool swivel. "Let me tell you what to do whenever a judge is being an asshole," he offered, rubbing his knees. I enjoyed observing how Reed shifted from the deferential way he talked to Hobart in conference to the irreverent way he talked to me in the coffee shop.

I was pretty sure I'd heard this one before. "I know. I know," I said eagerly, "Picture them in their underwear."

"No," said Reed. "Don't ever picture Judge Hobart in his underwear. I'm trying to help you maintain your composure, not go permanently blind."

I laughed, and for a second I worried that coffee was going to come out of my nose. Sneezing coffee in front of a handsome man would be a much higher order of humiliation than tearing up in front of a judge.

"You're laughing," he continued, "but I'm serious. This actually works. And not just with judges. It works with other lawyers, anyone who's rude to you, really. Have you had to deal with any lawyers from New York yet?"

I said I hadn't.

"Well, eventually you will, and this technique will come in especially handy."

"Okay, I'm listening," I said, still smiling. I took a bite of my cinnamon toast.

"First, you step back. Try to mentally check out for a few seconds."

"So you imagine yourself on a beach, watching the sunset or something?" I asked.

"Not exactly. While you're sitting there, pretending to listen, you tell yourself all the reasons why this person might be angry, reasons that have nothing to do with you, and why you would not want to trade places with him. You try to come up with some other explanation for why he's yelling. Maybe his son just got kicked out of St. Paul's. Maybe his wife is an alcoholic. Maybe he hasn't had sex in two years. You never know."

"Okay. I'll try it." I took a sip of coffee and noticed that Reed was watching me closely. I offered, "Maybe Hobart was angry because *his* parents left *their* lake house to his younger brother."

"See?" Reed smiled broadly. "You're getting the hang of it. Don't worry about Hobart. I'll go back to the office and ask my old man about this trust business. You'll talk to . . ." He stopped when he realized he didn't know how to continue. "Who's the senior partner in your firm?"

He was quite surprised when I told him that I was the senior partner in my firm, as well as the junior partner, the secretary and the janitor. He made a face of exaggerated shock, eyes wide and mouth open. Reed could be a ham, the Jerry Lewis to my Dean Martin.

"You're kidding," he said, as if he were floored by the revelation.

"You're appalled," I said, apologetically.

"No, I'm impressed. I don't think I would've had the nerve to strike out on my own." He tilted his head in thought. "No," he said, "I'm sure I wouldn't."

I left that diner quite certain that I was in love with Reed Masters, but now, looking back, I would say merely that, for a short time in my late twenties, I had a powerful crush on him. And there were some signs that my feelings were reciprocated. We always met in person to negotiate the Mudge Manor trust and operating agreement, and, really, he was driving those face-to-face meetings every bit as much as I was. He was very entertaining, distracting me with stories of his years at Bates and his strategies for working with an older generation of lawyers without becoming exactly like them. Reed wanted to please his father but be his own person. They argued frequently about Reed's refusal to wear a bowtie, which his father considered essential. Without one, he insisted, a lawyer might as well be wearing a clown suit.

Reed was affable and generous, and one of the most social people I knew. He seemed to have a lot of friends, mostly married couples, and he occasionally asked me to come along with them to the movies or the bowling alley. He was solicitous and attentive when I was with him, though never forthcoming about his feelings or his intentions. Sometimes I couldn't tell if I was his wingman or his date. But then one night he kissed me, and I was thrilled. He kissed me the same way he talked to me back in that diner, instructing me, drawing me toward a more confident version of myself. For the first time in many years, I felt desire for someone I saw as a partner and ally. Perhaps, I thought briefly, my investment in my work would pay a dividend in love. Perhaps the choices I had made a few years earlier would not, after all, consign me to live my life without a companion. Wouldn't it be perfect if those choices had even led me to that companion?

But then Reed chose someone else. He never called me again after that kiss, and I did not see him until we ran into each other at a campaign event for Ted Kennedy. Reed was with a beautiful woman, and he introduced her as his fiancée, Cass. She was a Bennington graduate, and she talked with quiet passion about her plans to open a Montessori school in Manchester. Reed was visibly in love. He confided to me, as if we were old friends, that the argument with his father about the bowtie had been eclipsed several times over by the row over Reed and Cass's decision to leave the Episcopal Church and become Unitarian.

I didn't see Reed much after that, and eventually I came to believe that it was just as well. He seemed to like me, and even admire me a little, and it was unlikely that he would maintain that opinion if he knew the truth. I couldn't imagine telling Reed about what I had done or who I really was. If he knew I had a secret child, he would never again see me as the capable, trustworthy professional I wanted to be in his eyes. He would think I was irresponsible and deceitful. But then again if Reed and I had become a couple, I couldn't imagine not telling him. I couldn't make a life with someone who didn't understand me, who didn't know where my mind and heart went in those quiet moments. How could he and I build a family if he didn't know that I already had a family, that she was out there somewhere, that I would always want to lay one more place setting at our table? It was a trap that seemed impossible to escape.

4

I GREW UP ON A DAIRY FARM, but I was always good at school, and my parents made it clear that they wanted a different life for me. We weren't sure what that life would be, but we were confident that it would not entail milk or manure. Maybe I would be a secretary or librarian, we thought. And then, after I won a statewide contest for a term paper on McCarthyism, my principal called me into his office to suggest that I might want to be a teacher. He was the one who encouraged me to apply to two of the most selective women's colleges in Massachusetts. I was nervous about asking my father to pay the fifteen-dollar application fee at not one but two schools, but when I got into both, he said it was the best thirty dollars he'd ever spent. I chose to matriculate in the 113th class at Halstead College, and we began the process of cobbling together the scholarships, loans and campus jobs that would, hopefully, cover the 3000-dollar tuition.

I set off for my new life on the first Sunday in September, 1969. My parents drove me the two-and-a-half hours in the truck, the three of us shoulder to shoulder. My father was quiet the whole drive, preferring to express his pride the old-fashioned way—by cleaning the truck to a shine and securing my luggage in the bed. My mother tried to stifle her tears by exclaiming continually how wonderful it would all be. We knew that I would never be coming home again.

We entered the campus through a wrought-iron gate, marked by a hand-painted sign. "Welcome Sisters of '73," it said in uneven blue letters. The road wound through a small arboretum, which opened up onto a perfect green quad. We were overwhelmed by its beauty. It wasn't rustic and rocky like our farm; it had the manicured symmetry of an English garden.

We arrived at some kind of check-in, and my father rolled down his window. A smiling young woman in a short green dress that appeared to have been hand-crocheted approached our truck.

"Welcome to Halstead!" she said cheerfully, as if I were the day's most anticipated arrival. She leaned forward to talk around my father at me.

"Do you know what dorm you're in, or do you want me to look it up?" She gestured to her clipboard.

"We're looking for Coffett Hall," I said, pleased that I already knew those two words in the Halstead lexicon.

"Coffett is that one over there." She pointed across the quad to a squat brick building, four stories high. I thought it resembled a sleeping woods animal, with ivy for fur and windows for eyes. I loved it instantly. On the short approach, I took in the magnificent campus and the eager students, all of us marveling that this was our new home. As soon as we parked, I jumped over my mother's lap and out of the truck. I had only two suitcases of clothes, so I carried one and my father carried the other. My mother tucked a neat pile of linens under her arm. My father, like Cinderella's footman, held the door open and, with a tilt of his chin, told me to enter first. I found myself in a generous-sized foyer, being greeted by a bosomy woman who introduced herself as Mrs. Crutchmeier. She was the dorm mother, she told us with pride, who lived on the first floor.

"I'm just thrilled to meet you," she said, "and to welcome you to Coffett."

Just behind her was a reception desk, a boundary between the entrance to the dorm and the staircase to its rooms. The young woman sitting at the desk looked cool and sophisticated to me, with long, straight hair and a loose, embroidered blouse. Mrs. Crutchmeier called to her.

"Marcia, can you find the name tag for Bonnie Koller, please?"

As Mrs. Crutchmeier handed me the laminated card, she said, "That's Marcia, sitting bells. She's one of the juniors helping out with orientation. When we come back from the tour, she'll explain to you how sitting bells works."

As I pinned the nametag to my blouse—the clean white cotton one I had selected for my first day—Mrs. Crutchmeier spoke to my parents.

"Bonnie is in good hands, Mr. and Mrs. Koller. She's going to love living here, and we're going to take good care of her. You'll see." She gestured down the hall with her hand. "Let me show you the dining room first," she said. "The Coffett girls eat together family style, and they each have to wait tables one shift a week."

My mother and I looked at each other. I would be doing a lot more than that, we both knew. To pay my tuition, I would be working in the kitchen on Mondays and Wednesdays.

The oak-paneled dining room had a vaulted ceiling and tall lead-paned windows. There were four long tables lined with high-backed wooden chairs.

"Skirts are required on Thursday and Sunday nights," Mrs. Crutchmeier informed us, "but you can wear what you like on the other days. Tea is served every day at four."

She showed us the communal pay phone and the smoking lounge before we headed back to the reception area.

"There is absolutely no smoking in the rooms," said Mrs. Crutchmeier sternly. "Of any kind," she emphasized, and I thought I saw Marcia smirk. "That goes for candles, too," she continued. "There'll be no fires on my watch, thank you very much."

By now, there was another freshman girl and her family in the reception area, and Marcia was handing her a name tag. *Diane Hendel.*

"Marcia," Mrs. Crutchmeier said, "would you be so kind as to explain the rules to Bonnie and Diane?"

Marcia moved her long brown hair away from her eyes and began to speak with the flat affect of a person who has read the same script a dozen times in one morning.

"Assuming you've been given permission to leave campus,"—she looked at my father with suspicion, as if he might be just the type to deprive me of this most basic human right— "you have to sign out when you leave and sign back in when you return," she said. She was as annoyed by the constraint as I was excited by the freedom it enabled.

"You always have to be back by eleven p.m. on Sundays, no matter what," she continued. "Men are allowed in this reception area, but the only times they can go above the first floor are between the hours of two and four on Sundays."

At this point Mrs. Crutchmeier seemed to conclude that Marcia was not presenting the parietal rules with the requisite enthusiasm. She took it upon herself to finish the explanation with a tone of wholehearted endorsement.

"The girl sitting bells will announce all male visitors, and we count on everyone to holler 'man on the floor,' so that no one gets surprised in her skivvies." Then she got more serious. "If you do have a gentleman caller on a Sunday afternoon, you must keep your door open, and there must be three feet on the floor at all times."

She looked at me and then at Diane, as if seeking acknowledgment. We nodded our assent just as another new girl was coming in the door.

"I'll leave you to get settled," she suggested. "And perhaps you'll find each other when it's time to make your way to the amphitheater at four."

My dorm room was quite elegant by my standards. The two bedrooms were tiny, but they shared a common room with a fireplace and windows eight feet tall. The fireplace didn't work, but the carved mantle made the room feel both homey and posh. My bedroom had a desk, a chair, a small bookcase, and a narrow bed. I had brought two books with me, a dictionary and a thesaurus, and I set them on the shelf. I noted all the empty space that remained and thought about how exciting it would be to fill it. My mother unpacked the quilt she had sewn for just this occasion. There was a remnant of my baby blanket, a rendering of our farm, of my high school, and, finally the insignia of Halstead, the alma mater where I now stood.

"It's still summer, really," she said. "Maybe you want to put it away for now."

I insisted that it was my only decorative item, my sole *object d'art*, and I wanted to be able to look at it. We spread it out together, and briefly allowed ourselves a moment of quiet. Then we heard the sounds of people entering the room and of heavy objects being set on the floor. The syncopated thuds of suitcases, boxes, and furniture went on for what seemed like a long time. I turned and saw a beautiful young woman, in a light blue jumper with buttons down the front, knee socks and clogs. She had long blond hair, fastened with a barrette at the base of her neck, and she fixed her luminous blue eyes on my quilt.

"I love it," she exclaimed. "It's so authentic." She swiveled her head behind her. "Mother, come look at this."

Her mother appeared behind her and agreed. "Exquisite," she said. And then to my mother, "Are you the artisan?"

"Yes, I am," said my mother, proudly. "Annette Koller." She held out her hand. "How do you do?"

While our mothers shook hands, my new roommate turned to me.

"You must be Bonnie," she said. "I'm Hollis. Hollis Locke."

We didn't shake hands; that was something that parents did. Before we could decide on what kind of gesture might mark our introduction, we heard an irascible, paternal voice outside the room demanding,

"How do you plan to get those record albums up this staircase? Do you think I'm going back down there to get them?"

The man standing in the living room must have been Hollis's father. He was holding on tight to a tall floor lamp. I assumed he had just carried it up the stairs, and now he was demanding that it return the favor. No one looking in that room would question which man worked at a desk and which man worked on the land. Mr. Locke continued to scold his daughter with excessive theatrical bombast, "I told you you were packing too much. You want to be independent, you can start by carrying those records."

He looked at my father, hoping to recruit him into the fraternity of men who spoil their daughters then mock them for their entitlement. But thankfully, my father would not wink or nod or join Mr. Locke in bemoaning the heavy load carried by a doting father. Mr. Locke was on his own.

"Don't worry about it, Dad. I'll manage." Hollis said patiently.

When Hollis's father realized he would not get affirmation from mine, he agreed to fetch the first box of albums. "I can see I'm still needed," he said.

"Thank you," Hollis said, with a slightly condescending pat on his shoulder, "You are the dearest moving man a girl could ask for."

I tried to discern who was patronizing whom, but the Locke family dynamics were too complex for me. I wasn't surprised, though, that Hollis could talk so self-assuredly to her father. A girl that pretty, I thought, must be completely at home in the world. Nothing, not a heavy box, not an irritable parent, not a strange new school, could shake or disturb her placid, comfortable demeanor.

Hollis and I were not, at that moment, complete strangers to each other. We had received each other's names and addresses from Halstead over the summer, so I knew that she was from a place called Sewickley Heights, Ohio. Since my family could not afford the long-distance call, I had written Hollis a short introductory letter. I told her a bit about myself, but I made a point of not providing my phone number. I didn't want her to think I was foisting the cost of the call onto her. She wrote back and told me she knew the campus well because her own mother had attended Halstead. ("If it's my mater's *alma mater*," she wrote, "does that make it my *alma grand-mater*?") She mentioned that she would be bringing to school her blue Smith Corona, which I was welcome to use. She apologized that it was not the newest model, as she had bought it when she was in the fifth form at the Sewickley Academy. I was thankful for her generosity, because I didn't have my own typewriter. The one we had seen in the Sears catalogue was over 200 dollars, and therefore completely out of our reach. Hollis had not mentioned that she would also be bringing a lamp, a collection of posters, a phonograph, and thirty of her favorite LP's.

Once introductions had been made, Mr. and Mrs. Locke began their visual inspection of the room. Hollis's mother turned her head up—every strand of hair maintained the position into which it had been rolled and sprayed—to look at the ceiling, and Mr. Locke scrutinized the floorboards.

"This place looks ready for an upgrade," he said, poking his toe at a small buckle in the wood floor.

"I think it has charm," said Hollis.

"It's a shame you didn't get one of those new dorms with the elevators," her mother said, touching the cast iron radiator.

"I'm with Hollis," I said, though I hadn't been asked. "I'm very happy with this room."

My mother put her arm around me and squeezed my shoulder in agreement, but the Lockes did not respond.

Hollis's father half-sat, half-leaned on our windowsill and watched the activity down below.

"Look at all these girls lugging valises around like a bunch of teamsters," he said, though I couldn't tell if he was admiring or criticizing. "Incredible. Maybe *they* should be fighting the Viet Cong." He chuckled.

We could hear doors opening and closing all throughout our dorm and the voices of women meeting each other for the first time. I could tell that Hollis was as eager as I was to chase our parents out so we could begin the important business of making lifelong friends.

Hollis's mother, who was, of the four parents in the room, probably the most reluctant to leave, tried to prolong our interaction. She looked at me,

"Bonnie, dear, what are you planning to study?" She was warmer than her husband, and probably well-practiced at letting him blow off steam before she joined the conversation.

I told her that I planned to study English or History, because those had been my favorite subjects in high school.

Mr. Locke looked at my father. "You're a lucky man to have such a practical daughter," he said. "Hollis vacillates between wanting to study sociology, whatever that is, and wanting to major in Classics, like her mother."

At this point my mother decided we needed to finish setting up my room. She turned to my father and nodded toward my door.

"Sigfried, honey, all hands on deck," she said.

He followed us into my bedroom though the three of us could barely fit, let alone putter around productively.

A few minutes later, Mrs. Locke leaned her head in and asked us if we would like a tour of the campus. The three of them were going to meet up with one of her classmates, a woman who was also dropping off a daughter. We declined as politely as we could, and I was surprised that Mr. Locke addressed me directly before they left.

"Bonnie, I want you to look after my Hollis, okay? You seem to have a good head on your shoulders, and she could learn a thing or two from you. She's a good kid, and she'll make sure you find your people."

★ ★ ★

Later in the day, when Hollis and I were finally alone in our room together, she apologized for her father.

"It's a wonder my-mother-the-Classics-major hasn't pulled a Socrates by now," she mused. "You'd think a nice tall glass of hemlock would look pretty good compared to thirty more years with him." As she spoke, she unbuttoned her jumper and lifted it over her head. "And that crack about finding your people!" Now she was donning a pair of jean shorts. "He's such a snob. Don't pay any attention to him."

Was this her way of saying that she wouldn't waste her time on me?

"He probably just meant that you'll help me make friends. Which I wouldn't mind, to tell you the truth," I confessed. "I don't know a soul here."

"Right." She tossed the crumpled jumper in the general direction of her bedroom door. "Which means you *earned* your spot here. You didn't inherit it the moment you were born. I'll probably be the one leaning on you."

Now she was unrolling her posters and holding them up to the walls.

"Who do you like better," she asked, "the Rolling Stones or the Beatles?" She had a poster of each.

"Honestly?" I said. "My ears like the Beatles, but my eyes prefer the Rolling Stones."

She showed me some of her record albums, and had just put on Laura Nyro when the girl I'd met in the lobby, Diane Hendel, knocked on our door.

"It's almost four o'clock," she said. "Are you walking to the assembly? Can I walk with you? My roommate's not here yet."

We spilled out of our dorms all at the same time, in lines like ants, making our way to the corner of the quad that led to the amphitheater. I saw Hollis wave to one or two women she recognized, but she stuck with us.

"So," she said, as if she had important information to impart. "You know we're not allowed to walk on the grass, right?"

Diane and I looked at each other, confused.

"What do you mean?" Off to our left, I could see three girls, one with a guitar, sitting on the lawn in the shade. "What about those girls over there? Are they not supposed to be there?"

"When I came to visit last spring," added Diane, "I saw a whole class sitting on the grass in the quad with their books. The professor was there too, so they couldn't have been breaking the rules."

"Yes," explained Hollis, "you can sit on the grass, but you can't cut across it on your way to class. They don't want us to make ugly brown footpaths on the perfect lawn. Mother thinks this is a very important rule." I detected a hint that Hollis did not share Mrs. Locke's view.

"Diane," I asked, "is your mother a Halstead alumna too?"

"Oh, gosh, no," she said. "No one in my family went here."

"Well, then," said Hollis, "it's about time. Where are you from, Diane?"

"I'm from Eastchester. It's a suburb of New York City."

I didn't want to admit that I wasn't sure what the term "suburb of New York City" meant, so I asked her what Eastchester was like.

"It's like New Rochelle, the town where Rob and Laura from

The Dick Van Dyke Show live," she explained. "My dad takes the train into the city every morning, just like Dick Van Dyke, only less funny. How about you?"

"I'm from New Hampshire. About two hours north of here."

I didn't have to say any more, because we had arrived at the amphitheater carved into the hillside, where the welcoming ceremony would take place. The day had cooled enough for the late afternoon sun to feel good on our bare shoulders. We continued to chirp questions at each other like cicadas as we took our seats on the grassy steps. I didn't notice Marcia, our jaded guide to the parietal rules, slip in next to me until her leg brushed the side of mine.

"Linda Sweeny is delivering the address this year," she said. "I wanted to hear her speak before she graduates, because she's going to be president some day."

A woman in a navy shirtwaist dress walked to the lectern on the stage below us. She carried no notes.

"That's her," Marcia whispered to me. "You'll see."

I could certainly see that Linda Sweeny beamed confidence with her purposeful gait and toothy smile. She stood at the edge of the stage and moved her head slowly around the arc of the amphitheater. She seemed to make eye contact with every single one of us. Her gaze quieted us like a blanket settles a baby. She stood regal and radiant for a moment before belting,

"Welcome to Halstead!" in an explosion of joy.

We cheered together, releasing all the tension of being strangers to each other and becoming, instantly, friends.

"You have chosen and been chosen by an institution that will nurture your mind and your spirit. You will not only study science and literature in the classrooms, but you will discover your own character in your hearts."

I had never before heard anyone so genuine and yet so polished.

"Today you join a sisterhood that will sustain you throughout your lives. And you do so at a critical time in human history. For the world is about to discover what we here at Halstead have known for generations: that women always have been and always will be the equals of men."

Marcia clapped her hands, but most of us were too mesmerized to react.

"Or perhaps not 'equal,' not really. For it is we women who in ancient times built houses, developed agriculture, and invented language while the men did nothing but hunt. Why should we pretend we are merely 'equal' if everyone knows we live longer than men? That we survive better under duress? That there are more of us than there are of them? But let's not play that game. Let's not waste our time on who's better. Let's instead improve the world for everyone."

Now there were heads nodding, and a woman in a billowy floral dress called out,

"Right on, Sister."

"First," our speaker continued, "we will reject the status quo, in which women are treated as second class, turned away by landlords, employers, restaurants and banks. We will reject the elitism and racism that pit rich women against poor women, white women against Black. We will reject the myth of inferiority that has been used by generations of white men to justify treating women and Blacks like chattel."

I noticed that my heart was beating faster, because this Linda Sweeny had abraded a recent wound to my pride that was still raw. I graduated first in my high school class, and this distinction should have earned me a seventy-five-dollar prize, endowed by the local lumber company. But two weeks before commencement, I was told that the prize would be given to our salutatorian, Roger Bishop. He needed it more than I did, I was told. I had already won that term paper prize and been accepted to Halstead, so the honor would be wasted on me. Roger was applying to the Marine Corps Officer Candidates School at Parris Island. The award might not only get him admitted, but also ultimately save his life, I was told. The principal offered to pay me the seventy-five dollars out of his own pocket, if I would keep quiet and allow him to present the plaque and prize to Roger at commencement. I was sure that Linda Sweeny would never have agreed to such a humiliation.

"Here at Halstead," she continued, "you will become the women who will lead us to this better world."

Her voice dropped slightly, and her audience, like a jellyfish pulled by a wave, leaned forward to hear her.

"But not as wives or homemakers. Not as helpmeets to men. With this education, with this family of women to support you"— here she began her crescendo— "you will become whatever it is you dream of being, be it artisan or aviator, doctor or decathlete, linguist or lawyer."

And that's when it hit me. I'm going to be a lawyer, I decided. I am going to make my living by thinking. And I am going to do it in a clean, painted office, while wearing a skirt. When I win awards, I will hang them on the walls. People will respect me and pay me to solve their problems.

"So," she continued, and she began walking the stage, as if she wanted to be closer to us, "You're probably thinking, shouldn't the men be worried? And my answer is emphatically, 'No.' Because this world will be better for them too. I say this to the men who are frightened by feminism: If your wife is a partner, not an albatross, won't that be better? If you are present to raise and love your children, won't that be better? If you let go of the power that corrupts you and seduces you into foreign wars, won't that be better?"

We were on our feet now, clapping and cheering. Hollis put her arm around me, and then Diane joined our chain.

"Daughters of Halstead," Sweeny called to us, "I welcome you, and I invite you to join me in the movement toward progress and peace."

I saw a few girls quietly say, "Amen," and I heard at least one loud, "Hell, yeah." But mostly I heard the sounds of applause. It took several minutes for us to settle back down and give our attention to the next speaker. It was the woman who had been sitting on the lawn with the guitar, and she was there to teach us the lyrics to Halstead's alma mater. I was able to pick it up fairly quickly, because I had Hollis next to me, and she already kind of knew it. The smell of hamburgers being grilled for a post-assembly cookout was all the motivation we needed to master a performance-worthy rendition of the song. To this day, I can never forget these words:

Where Labor 'twines with Honor,
Where Truth be ne'er denied,
Where seekers yearn for Knowledge,
Brave Halstead is our guide

Where sisters ride together
Four journeys 'round the sun,
We rear the weave of friendship
For Halstead makes us one.

When mem'ry of our Halstead years,
By tempus distant grown,
with jubilation fills our hearts,
Still Halstead is our home.

The final speaker was the president of Halstead, Dr. Aline Spofford Hewitt. She knew she could not match Linda Sweeney's rhetorical flourishes, and, based on the brevity of her speech,

I guessed she also knew we were hungry. She congratulated us on the accomplishments that had brought us to Halstead, and she welcomed us. She told us a little bit about ourselves as a cohort. We came from nine countries and forty-three states, she said proudly. We had more Black members than any class in the history of Halstead. And then she got to her point.

"You have come to Halstead at a time in history when it may seem that what is happening outside this cloister is more urgent than what is happening inside. There is conflict in the jungles of Vietnam, and there is conflict in the streets of our inner cities. But I exhort you to be patient. Halstead offers you four years of tranquility, four years to get lost in books, paintings, and microscopes. My advice to you is that you use this respite from our national turmoil to learn, to grow, to discover yourselves and each other. The world will still be there in four years, and you will be better equipped to embrace it or to change it however you see fit."

We applauded Dr. Hewitt politely, but without much conviction. The ceremony was over. We stood and smoothed our skirts, wiped the grass off the backs of our thighs.

"What did you think?" Marcia asked, not to any one of us in particular.

We began to walk back to the quad, following the cookout smells.

"That was amazing," Diane said.

"Which part?" I asked. I had thought so too, but I wasn't sure even for myself which piece of our orientation had been most meaningful to me.

"All of it," she said.

I said, "Yeah, all of it."

And then Hollis turned to Marcia, "Any suggestions for how we get around Mrs. Crutchmeier?"

Marcia laughed lightly and tossed her head. "Oh, don't worry about Crutch. Her heart is good, but her eyesight isn't."

What I remember about the rest of that evening was that I kept expecting Hollis to ditch me. I figured she would go off with the other girls she seemed to know through her mother or through Sewickley Academy. There was even a classmate she recognized from her annual trip to the Breakers in Palm Beach. But instead, she stayed by my side, met all the women I met. She was good at asking friendly questions like, *What's your favorite movie?* And, *Do you play any instruments?* Or, *How many siblings do you have?* She seemed to think it was cool—exotic, even—that I grew up on a dairy farm in New Hampshire. I heard her tell someone she was rooming with a cheesemonger, as if I hailed from the Scottish moors.

And that's how it went that fall. We were a team. Hollis introduced me to breakup songs by Joni Mitchell, and also to blue jeans and peasant blouses. All those skirts I thought I would wear to class took up semi-permanent residence on my closet floor, to be picked up and shaken out only for the two dinners a week when they were required. And I, on a few occasions, had to wake up Hollis for class or remind her where she'd parked her bicycle. People gravitated to Hollis, and she made friends easily. But she liked our quiet time in our room, too. We took two courses together that semester, Studies in Religion and Classical Mythology. We loved those classes, and we often stayed up late just talking about the readings. Hollis thought she was particularly profound when she was high, which, thankfully, wasn't all that often. She would say things like, "Us and the North Vietnamese, we're all *the same*. We all subscribe to *the same revelations*. You know what I mean?" I would smile, not because she made any sense, but because I liked to hear her talk.

We did our smoking on the roof of our dorm, as per Marcia's instructions, as long as the weather stayed warm. We were amazed at how boldly the juniors and seniors defied the Coffett House rules. I remember a fire drill at around eleven o'clock one Friday night, and as we stood outside in our nightgowns and clogs, our hair brushed out and our retainers in, we saw a figure running between the basement door of Coffett and the hedges that rimmed the quad. For a split second, as the figure passed under a lamp, we saw a whirl of naked limbs, more like a cartwheel than a sprint. But in that split second it was obvious that those hairy muscled thighs did not belong to a daughter of Halstead. Crutch was so busy counting us and checking names against the sign-out sheet that she didn't notice a thing. Hollis and I scanned the faces of the upperclassmen to suss out the female half of this clandestine couple, but they were all deadpan.

I loved the nights when Hollis and I would return home from the library to find that Crutch had made popcorn in the kitchen.

"You girls are working so hard," she would say affectionately. "You deserve a treat."

I didn't even mind my job waiting tables. I shared most of my shifts with Althea Washington, whose father was a chemistry professor at Howard University.

"He wanted me to go to Spelman," she told me, "but I said that Washington D.C. was as far south as I would ever set foot, thank you very much."

Althea liked to ask the cook a lot of questions, and together we learned how to spatchcock a chicken and make tuna-noodle casserole. (The essential ingredient, for those who may be wondering, is one can of Campbell's Cream of Mushroom Soup for each pound of dry macaroni.) From one vantage point, I had nothing in common with Althea. She was a Black woman who grew up among intellectuals in our nation's capital city. And I hailed from New England, the daughter of uneducated farmers. But sprinkled with Halstead's magic pixie dust, we didn't seem so different. We took the same classes and read the same books. We ate the same food and breathed the same Berkshire mountain air. When I told her I wanted to be a lawyer, she told me she knew Thurgood Marshall and would be happy to introduce me.

Marcia was right that Crutch didn't bother us much. She was mostly our booster, and her naivete about what was actually going on within the walls of Coffett Hall was kind of endearing. There was one Saturday night in late October when about seven of us convinced her we were going into town to see *The Love Bug*, which was a kids' movie about a talking car. We were actually going to a one-night-only showing of *Bob & Carol & Ted & Alice*. The film's plotline—two married couples grow increasingly tolerant of their respective spouses' infidelity, until all four end up in bed together—was well-known, and most of the adults we knew considered it positively degenerate.

As we made our way back to campus afterward, it was clear that the only one who liked the film was Marcia. "The whole point," she seemed certain, "is that a relationship should be built on love, not jealousy or possession."

Later that night, I admitted to Hollis that I didn't understand the movie at all.

"At the end, when the husbands are holding their wives' hands," I said, "what were we supposed to think? That they all realized those affairs were mistakes? Or was the movie trying to say that infidelity somehow made their marriages better?"

"It's hard to know. You can't always tell if the real message is the stuff that happens at the end, or the stuff that happens in the middle." Sometimes Hollis made good points without even knowing it. "Kind of how Shakespeare always sends his characters into the forest to go crazy. Girls turn into their twin brothers and all that. But then at the end everything is back to normal. Everybody ends up with the right lover, and all that chaos in the middle is forgotten."

"Now that you mention it, *The Graduate* is kind of like that too," I said. "It's funny, you know? In the end he runs away with a nice girl his own age, but no one even remembers that."

"That is so true, Bonnie." I loved it when Hollis agreed with me. "The thing everyone talks about is the affair with Ann Bancroft. That's why I had to sneak out of the house to see it. My father thought it was 'an affront to decency.'" She imitated Mr. Locke's deep voice, as she always did when she was presenting his comically backward views. "I can't wait to tell him what we saw tonight."

"Are you going to say you liked it?" I asked.

"Yeah," she said, "just to rile him up. But I'll tell him you thought it was tasteless. Then I'll tell him that after the movie I lent you ten dollars to buy a pair of Levi's in town. He'll want to reward you for being such a good influence on me, so he'll say that we should forget the ten dollars and consider the jeans a gift. I've got it all figured out."

5

M Y AWFUL CONFRONTATION WITH the clerk at the Bureau didn't stop me from setting up my next meeting, with a social worker at the Department of Health and Human Services. I was nowhere near ready to give up, and I certainly had not come to believe that I was doing something immoral. To the contrary, I became even more convinced that my daughter and I had a right to know each other, and that government bureaucrats shouldn't have the final word on a matter that affected me so much and them so little. Especially not in a state that printed *live free or die* on its license plates. Why wasn't I free to form a relationship with the girl I brought into the world?

On the way to my appointment, I distracted myself with a story on the radio about the antics of New Hampshire's official state embarrassment, Lyndon LaRouche, and his latest presidential bid. By that time he was in prison in Minnesota, serving a sentence for stealing money, either from his campaign supporters or from the IRS; no one was sure which. From his cell, he was accepting more donations and making his usual promises to colonize Mars. But soon enough the story, instead of distracting me, made me feel indignant. LaRouche didn't show a hint of shame about his paranoia and Ponzi schemes, and everyone else seemed to find him amusing. His incorrigibility was practically a point of state pride. But for some reason the idea of a mother wanting to know her own child was an offense to community morals.

I was scheduled to meet with a woman named Elizabeth, and she greeted me just inside the oversized front door of the former mill that now housed her department. I was immediately hopeful. Elizabeth was young and seemed relaxed as she led me to her office. Her hair was long and loose, and she wore an unhemmed denim skirt embroidered with vines and flowers. We walked to her cubicle, one wall of which looked out over the river. The walls of Elizabeth's workspace were a bulletin board of calendars, newspaper clippings, photographs, children's drawings, thank you cards, and even a few album covers. Elizabeth sat down in her desk chair and gestured for me to sit in the chair opposite her. She offered me a stick of licorice and said, "What can I do for you, Ms. Koller?"

Elizabeth seemed like a person one could talk to. Yes, she worked for the state government, but her job was to help people, not to guard documents. I had a hunch that the best strategy with Elizabeth would be to tell her the truth. But I was surprised by my own sudden inability to speak. I was about to say to Elizabeth sentences I had never before spoken aloud, and it felt momentous. An old legal rule, one I had learned almost twenty years earlier, popped into my head. It's a rule of evidence that applies to statements that can alter reality simply by virtue of having been spoken. The sentence "I now pronounce you man and wife," for example, isn't just words. It has legal consequences, in that it effects a marriage that didn't exist before. Telling my story to Elizabeth, I thought, would not be just words. It would be an action that could cause the ground to shift.

"I'm looking for some information," I began. This was the kind of sentence I said all the time. So far, this was easy. I was composed, for the moment. Elizabeth watched me earnestly and patiently.

And then I just blurted it out. "I had a baby twenty years ago," I said. I looked at Elizabeth, waiting for her face to change from acceptance to judgment. Surely she would know where this was going, and her offer of assistance would be revoked. I braced for a lecture or a rebuke. But Elizabeth was simply waiting for me to continue, giving me her full attention.

"I gave birth in St. Gabriel's Hospital," I went on, "but I gave the baby up for adoption because I was in college." I tried to sound detached, as if I were describing the facts of one of my cases.

Elizabeth nodded slightly, encouragingly, and said, "I understand."

"I haven't had any contact with her since," I said, and just hearing my own words frayed my composure.

"Of course," said Elizabeth. She swiveled toward her desk to pick up a box of tissues and swung back to offer it to me.

"I just want to know she's okay," I said, and I could hear my own voice cracking. I took the tissue box from Elizabeth's extended arm, and I continued.

"I'm not going to bother her, or her family. I won't push to see her if she doesn't want to see me." And now I was really crying, because that part wasn't really true. I couldn't bear the possibility that my daughter might not want to see me. I had said that to Elizabeth only because I knew it was something I had to say. "I just want to know how she is," I pleaded.

Elizabeth put her hand on my shoulder.

"I know," she said quietly.

I felt hopeful for the first time.

"Lately I've been thinking about her a lot," I admitted. I imagined myself telling Elizabeth all about Amber's death. I wanted her to know that it was anguish and concern that had brought me here, not selfish curiosity. But Elizabeth did not seem to need a convincing explanation. She was nodding with empathy already. So I said one more time, my throat tight with the effort not to sob, "I just want to know she has a good life."

That was when Elizabeth's face slowly changed. She had been looking at me openly, encouraging me to unburden myself. But now she looked sad, aware that she was about to disappoint me.

"I'm not sure how I can help you," she said apologetically.

I was almost relieved at the opportunity to negotiate with her. Arguing about how to proceed would be so much easier, more familiar, than putting my weakness on display.

"Don't you have a record of the adoption?" I said, though it was more a statement than a question. "It all happened here, in state. The papers must be somewhere."

Elizabeth paused and dropped her head for a moment. She did not want to say what we both knew she had to say.

"I wish I could help you."

She was genuine, as pained by our predicament as I was.

"I really do," she continued. "I don't know why we still have these outdated laws. They're stupid and cruel. Believe me, you're not the first birthmother who has come into my office looking for her child. And I know your heart is in the right place." Elizabeth touched her own heart. "You feel like a piece of you is missing, and it's out there. You just want to find that missing piece and feel whole."

I was amazed at how well Elizabeth was describing the thoughts that I had never articulated to anyone.

"I hate saying no," she continued. "But I have to. I could lose my job if I let you see those records."

I stopped haggling. In the short time I had been sitting in Elizabeth's office, I had come to like her enough that I did not want her to lose her job. But at this point I had no other plan. That was the problem. There was no legitimate process for finding an adopted daughter. The only way to get the records I wanted was to beg someone to break the law and give them to me. I had no idea what I could try next.

Elizabeth folded her hands in her lap.

"I'll tell you what I can do," she offered. "Give me the information you have, and I'll see if I can find the file. If there's anything in there I can tell you without getting in trouble, I will."

"Thank you," I said, as appreciatively as I could. At least it was something.

"In the meantime, don't give up. If you find any leads, come back and see me. I might know something I can't exactly share, but I can, you know, wink if you're on the right track."

"I don't know what kind of leads to look for at this point," I said.

"I assume you've already signed up with the registries?"

I admitted that I did not know what she meant, and she got very excited about the chance to educate me.

"You don't know about the registries? They're essential if you're looking for a relinquished child, or any family member you've been separated from, actually. They've united a lot of adoptees with their birth parents. But it only works if both parties register."

I took a legal pad out of my brief case and started taking notes. This familiar exercise calmed me even more as I listened to Elizabeth's explanation.

"Some states have their own registries, but not New Hampshire." She rolled her eyes just a little. She leaned forward and put her elbows on her knees. "The closest one is in Massachusetts. It's called the Concerned United Birthparents Reunion Registry. Come to think of it, if your daughter is still in the area, that one's the best bet. They can match people based on just a birthday. There are some other good ones I recommend, too. There's the Adoptees' Liberty Movement Association. They're in Harlem. And then there's one called the International Soundex Reunion Registry. That one is unusual. They use a coding system, so let's say your daughter overheard your name once. But she doesn't know the right spelling. It's k-o-l-l-e-r, right?"

"Right," I said, though I did not need to. Nothing was likely to stop Elizabeth at this point.

"But let's say your daughter doesn't know that, and she thinks it could be k-o-*h*-l-e-r. In the Soundex system, it doesn't matter, because Kohler with an h and Koller with a double-l are coded the same way, phonetically. How old did you say your daughter is?"

"She is twenty now."

"Okay, good, because you have to be at least eighteen to register. I'll give you the addresses for all these places. Soundex is in Nevada. Some of them ask for a small fee to register. Some just ask for a self-addressed stamped envelope. Or what I call a SASE." She pronounced it say-zee. "And, of course, we should put a letter in the file. You know, in case she comes looking for you. Something that says you're okay with being contacted."

I was intrigued by Elizabeth's mention of "the file," and the ease with which she assumed it could be accessed. Maybe once she saw that file, she would be more forthcoming with the information in it.

By the time I left her office, I had regained some of the optimism I had lost during the early parts of our conversation. With a little more gumshoeing, I might eventually find what I was looking for. And for the first time, I felt like I had an advocate, someone who wanted me to succeed. Elizabeth's description of how the registries worked had tapped into a hope I had not been willing to indulge: While I was wrestling with the state bureaucracy, trying to solve the mystery of who and where my daughter was, maybe she was navigating the very same maze from the other side, trying to locate me. Perhaps, just as I felt the weight of her absence, she felt the weight of mine. Maybe she, too, scanned the faces of strangers in movie theaters and supermarkets looking for a resemblance. If I found my daughter through one of these registries, then I would know that this search was mutual. I would not be faced with what

I had recently concluded was the worst possible outcome of this quest—that my daughter, once found, might never forgive me for the distant sin of giving her up.

★ ★ ★

A few days later, Joyce came back to the office earlier than any of us expected.

"I couldn't sit around the house anymore," she told me. "I wanted to be where there are people, and I'm needed."

"You are very needed, Joyce," I assured her. "We are starting to fall apart here." This was not exactly true, but it was close enough, and it was the right thing to say.

Lars looked nervous, like he didn't know how to be around her. The best way to handle this would be to force an interaction between them that was entirely work-related. I directed Lars to catch Joyce up on everything she had missed, and give her a preview of all the tasks that were coming her way. Joyce didn't really need that kind of handholding to do her job, but she did need to talk about something other than her loss. Lars was about to file two actions on behalf of a client who had a ground pollution claim, one against his insurer for indemnification and one against the former owner of the property. Joyce offered to start preparing the affidavits of service, which was exactly the kind of busy work I wanted her doing.

By the afternoon, Joyce seemed to be her regular efficient self. Don't get me wrong; I knew she wasn't done grieving. But I was confident that putting her to work was the right way to help her, and everyone around her, feel normal. When, late in the afternoon, she leaned into my office to let me know I had a call, she sounded so placid that I momentarily forgot she was still deep in recent mourning.

It was Elizabeth on the line, though I could tell by the apologetic tone with which she identified herself that she didn't have good news.

I reported to her that in the days since we had met, I had signed up with all three registries.

"I'll let you know if I hear anything," I promised her. "I don't have any new leads yet, but I wouldn't be able to tell if you're winking anyway."

"I don't think I'll be able to answer your questions," she said, with sad finality.

I wondered if, in fact, she had gotten in trouble. I imagined her being dragged before some hostile tribunal and forced to denounce me.

"I couldn't find your papers," Elizabeth said, now sounding anguished. "I searched everywhere, and we have no record of your relinquishment or your daughter's adoption."

I was stunned.

"What does that mean?" was all I could ask.

"It probably means your adoption wasn't handled by the state. At first, I thought it must have gone through the private agency. There was only one that was operating in the state in 1970."

"I'll call them, then." It was half a statement, half a question.

"Well, no, I already did that for you. I called a friend who works there—let's just say she's a good soul—and she was willing to pull your file. But they don't have it either."

"I don't understand."

"I think your adoption must have been done privately. *Really* privately. By a lawyer or a doctor, not an agency. Do you remember anything about it?"

To say I "remembered" the experience of giving birth was not accurate. The misery of being alone in the hospital, the pain of labor, the humiliation inflicted by the brusque hospital staff, were all still with me. They were elements that formed the core of my character, not temporally distant events. But the details, especially the details of what I had been told—other than that it would all be taken care of—had been sealed off and written over by time.

I didn't say all that to Elizabeth. But I did relay my impression that the doctors and nurses at St. Gabriel's had seemed far more interested in the baby than in me. They fawned over her like she was found treasure, and I was just the map with an X.

Elizabeth considered this information useful.

"That fits with my theory that they already had a family picked out. I think you want to start with the OB who did the delivery. It's not unheard of for a doctor to place a baby in a home without all the proper paperwork. This isn't necessarily a dead end, Bonnie. Do you have your medical records from the hospital where you delivered?"

I admitted that I did not, but this did not slow her down.

"It shouldn't be hard to get those, unless the hospital has destroyed them. You're entitled to your own records, but I recommend you don't say why you want them." She barely paused before saying, "Ooh. I have an idea."

Just as she had when describing the registries, Elizabeth was getting excited.

"You can say you're pregnant and your doctor wants to know if there were any complications the first time you gave birth." Elizabeth sounded very pleased with this plan. "They'll definitely send them to you for that reason. Some information may be blacked out, but I bet the doctor's name is there."

I dismissed this suggestion.

"They'll never believe I'm pregnant," I said, perhaps more exasperatedly than was necessary.

"Why not?" Elizabeth sounded defensive.

"Because of my age."

Elizabeth was quiet for a second.

"Bonnie," she said, no longer excited. "If you are going to do this, you have to become a believer. You have to be willing to try anything and everything. Just keep telling yourself that eventually something will work, and don't ever assume defeat."

I smiled to myself, because I often spoke to my own clients this way.

"Besides," she continued, "what are you, like, forty?"

"Not quite."

"Well, they're not going to bother doing the arithmetic. And even if they did, no one would think twice about a pregnant thirty-nine-year-old. It happens."

★ ★ ★

When I called St. Gabriel's, it turned out that Elizabeth was right. The woman in the records department did not question my proffered reason for wanting to know my delivery history.

"At your age, you want to be prepared for anything," she said approvingly.

I allowed myself to enjoy the ruse, and even invented the fiction that my older daughter was eager to help with the new baby. It gave me a chance to imagine my daughter, to conjure in my mind's eye a young woman who was gentle and generous, eager to please and support me.

"You're a lucky woman," said the clerk at St. Gabriel's, and I so wished it were true.

The file arrived two long weeks later, and I finally, after so many false starts, felt that I was making progress. When I opened the envelope at my dining room table, I could see that, sure enough, parts of it had been struck through with a black Sharpie. All the information about the baby, like her weight, her appearance, even her pulse, was covered up. But the one detail Elizabeth had told me to look for, the name of the doctor who supervised the delivery, was there. Robert Hauptman. I had no memory of his face and was sure

I could not recognize him. I did recall that there had been a man in charge, and that he had been aloof and old. Looking back, however, I couldn't trust my nineteen-year-old self's opinion about what constituted "old." I wondered if this Robert Hauptman were the right age to be delivering babies at St. Gabriel's still, or to be living in a retirement village in Florida, or to be long gone from this world.

I called the obstetrics department at the hospital and said I was trying to reach Dr. Hauptman.

"Well, now, let's see," said the woman who answered the phone. She sounded like she was looking for something. "We used to have his number tacked up here on a yellow sticky. So many of his patients wanted to stay in touch, you know. But he's retired a while already, and I think we must have thrown it away the last time it fell off."

"Is he still in the area? Do you ever see him?" I tried not to sound desperate.

"No, dear. We do miss him. Once his wife passed, he moved to Massachusetts. One of those towns outside Boston, to be near his sister."

That was all she could tell me, but I thought I could make do with what I had: a name, a town, and the universal phone number for the information operator: 555-1212. I tried calling it with 617- at the beginning, punching the numbers with a pencil eraser. But the woman who answered had no listing for Robert Hauptman. The Boston suburbs had recently been issued a new area code, so, with diminished enthusiasm, I tried 508-555-1212. Again, no listing for a Robert Hauptman. How quickly my big lead was going nowhere. I wondered if there were any Massachusetts phone books at the library, and I thought about going over there on Saturday morning. I remembered Elizabeth's advice, that I had to try anything and everything. I had a few books to return anyway, and I had to thank my favorite librarian, Dorothy, for recommending *A Thousand Acres*.

And there was one other option. I could call Carol, an old college friend, who lived in one of those towns, and who probably had the relevant telephone book in her kitchen. She lived in a big house that was constantly being renovated, with two teenage children and a lawyer husband who, unlike me, worked all the time. I hadn't talked to Carol in a few months, and it would be nice to catch up.

But of course I couldn't tell her the real reason for my call. Carol had known me since our first year of college and, though she teased me on occasion for being a country mouse, I knew she actually respected me. In her eyes, I was strong, self-reliant, and accomplished. I could not jeopardize her good opinion by telling her about the baby. I would be revealing how weak I was twenty years earlier, and, worse, how deceptive. She would figure out that I was not the courageous and honorable professional she thought me, but rather a coward and a liar. And, if she thought about it long enough, she would eventually realize that she had seen me pregnant without knowing it. She would feel betrayed, as if I weren't the person she thought she knew. As if that person had never existed.

All of this is to say that I decided to ask Carol to look in her phone book for Robert Hauptman, and I devised a plausible story in the unlikely event that she asked for an explanation.

I dialed her number and made my request.

"Why do you want it?" she queried.

A good lawyer is always prepared, I thought.

"I have a malpractice case against a doctor he supervised. I'd like to know his opinion of my opponent."

"Sure," she said gamely, "I'll be your girl Friday . . . You said there's a T in the middle?"

"Right. H-a-u-p-t-m-a-n."

I imagined her licking a finger and turning the pages.

"I see a Bernard and Ethel Hauptman," she said. "But no Robert."

"I'll take it, though I doubt that's it."

Carol read the number to me, and I wrote it down.

"Anyone else?" I asked, trying to sound like I was just being thorough.

"No, that's the only Hauptman."

"Are you sure?"

"Bonnie, I'm sure. I'm looking right at the page."

"Hmm," I said, trying to sound like I wasn't too invested. "Do you think he could be dead?"

"I suppose that's possible," she said, as if it were no big deal. "Or maybe he moved into an old folks' home. He might still be in the area but not listed."

I realized she was right, and I asked her to read me the numbers of the retirement homes in the area.

"No way, José," she said, "as my kids would put it. According to the Yellow Pages, there are at least nine old age homes in my town, and a couple more in the next one over. If you want them, you have to come here and get them. Come have brunch on Saturday. You can call around from my house. If you find him in a home nearby, you'll go see him in the afternoon. It's not like he'll have other plans."

★ ★ ★

I went to visit Carol over the weekend and was struck, as I often am, by the way driving south from my home in early April is so much like time travel. I left a town that was cold and barren, encrusted in a layer of snow blackened by tailpipe soot. After traversing a distance of a few inches on a road map, I arrived at Carol's house to find pink rhododendron already in bloom.

When Carol opened the door, I saw that I was dressed for winter, and she was dressed for spring.

"How is the working girl?" she said with affection. "Come in. Come in." And she waved me inside with her hand. "You have to see what we've done since the last time you were here." She took me into the kitchen and showed me her new granite countertops and a refrigerator she described as *subzero*, which I thought was a reference to its cooling capacity but was actually, she told me, a brand name.

"I know it seems like a crazy time to invest in home improvements, but I've always wanted a beautiful kitchen."

It was all gleaming white, and I wondered if she were ever unable to find the refrigerator.

"And now you have one," I said, admiringly.

"Thank you," she said. "I was thinking that this would be a good time to learn to cook."

A voice from the sitting room off the kitchen called,

"Please don't."

It was Carol's daughter Emily, sounding much more petulant than the last time I saw her. If I remembered correctly, Emily had turned fifteen over the winter.

"Pay no attention to her," said Carol. "She won't forgive me because she converted to vegetarianism two days ago, and I've already violated her constitutional rights, apparently, by putting Worcestershire sauce on her rice. Honestly, I don't even know what I did wrong, but she hasn't spoken to me since."

"I think Worcestershire sauce has anchovies in it," I offered, hoping that this would sound helpful, not critical.

"Really?" said Carol. "I thought it was just salt and brown food coloring. And besides, she's not even a real vegetarian. She just wants to eat the starchy side dishes. God forbid she should eat an actual vegetable."

I asked after her husband and son, and was told that Randy had gone into the office for a few hours, and Topher was unaccounted for.

"Seventeen-year-old boys don't tell their mothers where they're going. It's just you and me for brunch, unless we can convince Emily to join us."

Emily's voice, again from the other room, called out, "Not a chance. You probably put baby seal in the quiche."

Carol looked at me. *You see what I have to put up with?* she said with her eyes.

"Don't be ridiculous, Emily," Carol called back. Her voice sounded nonchalant, but her expression looked annoyed. "Baby seal is just for bouillabaisse."

"You made the quiche?" I asked, a little surprised.

"Don't be ridiculous, Bonnie. I got it at the Stop & Shop."

We sat down in Carol's dining room, which had been beautifully set with dishes I recognized as her Wedgwood wedding china. We ate the store-bought quiche and swapped gossip about our classmates. I told her about some of the matters I had been handling lately, but nothing was very interesting. Honestly, I was finding it hard to make conversation, given that I had already decided not to talk about the one thing that was most prominent in my mind. It took a lot of energy, I realized, to construct a public version of myself, to perform the part of the good citizen, good colleague, and good friend. Maybe this was why I liked being alone so much. The alternative was exhausting.

I was grateful when Carol had a story she was dying to tell me.

"You know how you're always saying you would hate to work at a big firm like Randy's?" she said. I acknowledged that it was true and pointed out that here I was having brunch with her on a Saturday afternoon while her husband was billing hours.

"Listen to this," she said. "They just fired a brand-new associate, a girl who worked there for five days." She held her hand up with her fingers splayed. "Five," she repeated. I didn't need the visual aid, but I loved that Carol was such an expressive storyteller. "All the young lawyers are on edge about it."

"What happened?" I asked, my interest piqued. I was genuinely curious about what it took to get dismissed from a big Boston law firm before you'd been there a week.

"This young woman had just started, just passed the bar. For her first assignment, she's supposed to accompany Randy in court for some kind of hearing. Of course, she's not supposed to do anything at this hearing. She's just there to take notes or fish papers out of Randy's briefcase. You know."

"Not really," I said. "I can't afford a caddy when I go to court."

"Fair enough." Carol smiled. "Well, anyway, the girl gets to the courthouse first thing in the morning and can't find Randy. He's stuck in traffic on 495. The judge starts calling cases, and when he gets to theirs, she has no idea what she's supposed to do. So she just sits there. Doesn't say a word. Doesn't even stand up and acknowledge her existence. So the judge goes ahead and makes a ruling, against their client, of course. Just denies their motion and moves on to the next case. The whole thing was over in a minute. The client was furious, and said the girl had to be fired."

I wasn't sure how I was supposed to react, but it didn't matter. Emily responded first.

"Mom!" she yelled, still in the other room, but now even angrier than before. "Stop telling that awful story. I don't know why you think it's amusing."

Carol turned her head slightly and said over her shoulder, "Em, if you want to contribute, you can come sit in here with us. But you can't eavesdrop from the other room and then yell out a score on the quality of the conversation." Carol turned back to me. "At least your Joyce doesn't screw things up for you. How are things going in your office?"

The conversation turned somber as I told Carol about Amber's death. Joyce and Amber were familiar names to Carol, but she had never met either of them. I was surprised by how stricken she looked. She had the expression of a person who had just been informed of the death of a child she had known since birth. Carol slowly, blankly put her fork down and patted her lips with her napkin. Her hands were shaking slightly. She mumbled "excuse me," as she pushed her chair away from the table. She walked to the doorway of the sitting room and, with her back to me, spoke softly to Emily.

"Sweetheart, I'm sorry that I didn't prepare your rice properly. Truly, I am." Carol's dormant southern accent began to awaken.

"You made me eat fish," I heard Emily say, still a little defiant.

"I know, and I'm sorry. I should have been more respectful of your principles."

"Yes, you should have."

"I promise you there is nothing in the quiche that ever had eyes or lungs. Please come join me and Auntie Bonnie in the dining room."

"Please, Emily," I chimed in. "I want to catch up with you. Tell me what's going on. Are you still doing gymnastics?"

Somehow Carol and I cajoled her daughter to join us, and I learned about the big changes in her life. In addition to giving up meat, she had traded in gymnastics for long jump. She was no longer enamored with the popular boyband whose concert she and Carol had attended the year before. This event was now, apparently, a source of great embarrassment, because she had come to recognize both that her earlier musical tastes were juvenile and that her mother's company was insufferable. She was now fixated on one particular member of that band, a performer with the redundant name Marky Mark, who was pursuing a solo career in which his sculpted abdominal muscles played a prominent role.

I was impressed with Carol's equanimity in the face of Emily's scorn. Carol took in her daughter's criticism and her fickleness with detached bemusement, while Emily showed little tolerance for the woman who gave her life. I wondered if I could muster Carol's strength or humor in the face of relentless filial censure, and I thought I probably could not. I felt anxious just thinking about the rebukes that might await me if I found my daughter. I was sure I would crumble in the face of her disapproval. I surmised that Carol derived her strength from the knowledge that she, unlike me, had been a good mother. She knew she gave everything to her children, even when Emily's hormones said otherwise. But I had no such record of maternal devotion to fall back on. If my daughter hated me for what I did to her, I would know she wasn't wrong.

"Emily," I said, because I needed a change of subject, "when is it time for you to start looking at colleges?"

She looked at me oddly.

"Not for a couple of years," she said, but in a much more forgiving tone than she used with her mother.

"That's still a long way away," I agreed. "But promise me that when you and your mom visit Halstead, you'll let me tag along. It's a beautiful campus, and we can show you our old haunts."

Emily glanced at her mother nervously, and said, almost like an apology she had prepared ahead of time, "I know Halstead is a great school, Auntie Bonnie, but I'm pretty sure I want to go co-ed. No offense. I know you and my mom loved the whole all-women thing."

"No offense taken, Emily," I assured her. "You should do what's right for you."

Emily seemed concerned that she had hurt my feelings, though there was no need.

"It's fine, sweetie," Carol assured her. "We know that not everyone wants to go to a single-sex school." She turned to me, "You had that roommate freshman year, right? I called her Gidget so many times that I don't remember her real name. Didn't she transfer to Yale after one semester?"

"Yes, that's right," I lied.

"There you go," said Carol to Emily brightly. "Different strokes for different folks." Then Carol turned back to me.

"Do you ever hear from her?" she asked.

I told her, truthfully, that I had not spoken to her since January, 1970.

★ ★ ★

After the dishes had been cleared and Emily had gone off to meet a friend, Carol handed me the phone book.

"You've earned this," she said, "by giving me twenty minutes of pleasant conversation with my daughter. I'll leave you alone and let you do your research."

I sat on the leather couch in Carol's den, with its floor-to-ceiling bookshelves, every surface holding a silver ashtray, or a framed photo of Emily and Topher, dressed for Easter, or walking the flats of Cape Cod Bay. I began dialing retirement homes in alphabetical order. In the span of half an hour I learned that Friendship Valley had no Robert Hauptman, nor did Grandview Terrace or Little Sisters of Compassion. Stalling to avoid the disappointment of reaching the end of the list without success, I looked idly at Carol's shelves for a minute and noted all the titles we had read together and talked about over the years: *Circle of Friends*, *The Joy Luck Club*, *The Cider House Rules*.

My friendship with Carol went back to our first year at Halstead. She was funny and full of life, and I liked her instantly. It was she who taught me the alternative words to Halstead's alma mater:

Where labor yields to leisure,
And tonic 'twines with gin,
When Amherst's finest come to call,
Fair Halstead lets them in.

Carol was always nice to me, and at first, I chalked it up to nothing but school spirit. But at the end of freshman year, she asked me if I would room with her the following fall. Her current roommate was Althea Washington, my partner in the kitchen, but Althea had made other arrangements for sophomore housing. It turned out that none of the Black women in our class chose to stay with their white roommates for a second year; they preferred instead to live with each other.

I sat in Carol's den all these years later, straightened my back—not an easy feat in that leather couch—and resumed my dialing. And then, it was as if the invocation of memories of Halstead had changed my luck. The woman who answered the phone at Sunrise Gardens said that Dr. Hauptman was one of her favorite residents and would be delighted to receive a visitor this afternoon. In fact, I was told my call was fortuitous, as Dr. Hauptman's nephew had given word that he might be unable to make his usual Saturday appearance. I hung up the phone and breathed. In a half hour I would be face-to-face with the man who sent my daughter out into the world. For almost twenty years I had hoped never to see him again, as he had not been kind to me. I remembered him as cold and patronizing, except when he was talking about my plans for the baby. Then he was solicitous, in a way that struck me, even in my compromised state, as calculated and manipulative. But I would have to put those memories aside if I hoped to pry information from him. For one afternoon, I would have to play the part of the grateful patient.

★ ★ ★

Sunrise Gardens had a cheerful milieu, despite its dated décor. The carpets were green, with gold fleur-de-lis, and there was a ficus tree in every corner. It was clean and well-lit. The receptionist smiled at me and thanked me for taking the time to visit Dr. Hauptman.

"He's such a gentleman," she said. "We just love him. Are you a family friend?"

"No, actually," I said, "I was a patient of his many years ago."

This made her even happier.

"Of course," she said. "He does have several patients who stay in touch. I'll ask Casey to bring him into the lounge."

The receptionist pointed me to a large room off the lobby, and I took a seat by one of the windows. There were a few other families in this common area, each cluster anchored by an elderly relative. The adults spoke loudly but dully, and I overheard various reports of the traffic, the weather, and the price of gas. The children occupied themselves with coloring books and word searches and occasionally asked with their eyes when it would be time to leave. After a few minutes, I saw a young man in scrubs who was gently leading an older gentleman in gray slacks and a yellow cardigan. It would not be true to say that I recognized him, but based on the receptionist's description, it seemed reasonable to conclude that the shuffling man talking jovially with his escort was Dr. Hauptman. I saw the younger man point in my direction, and the two made their way toward me, slowed by the doctor's salutations to each small group he passed. When he was close to me, I rose and held out my hand. He clasped it and said, "Well, now, this is a treat. How nice to see you."

Casey held Dr. Hauptman's elbow and lowered him into the chair beside me.

"I'm the one who should be thanking you," I said. "I appreciate your making time for me."

He waved his hand.

"Nonsense. Any day of the week I'll take an intelligent conversation over the parlor games in the activity room."

I noticed a table in the corner with juice and coffee, and I offered to get Dr. Hauptman a drink.

"I'll take a Bloody Mary, thank you very much." He winked at me and laughed.

"Will you settle for ginger ale?"

"If I have to, I have to."

I fetched us two paper cups of room temperature soda.

When I sat back down, he asked, "Tell me, to what do I owe the pleasure of your visit today?"

I had practiced this conversation in the car, and had done it once with Elizabeth, so I was able to look Dr. Hauptman in the eye and say, "I was once a patient of yours."

This announcement delighted him, as if there could be no more meaningful connection between us.

"Yes, yes, of course. I thought you looked familiar," he said, with enthusiasm. "I delivered your children?"

He was much warmer than I had remembered, and I was having difficulty reconciling my ingratiating host with the disdainful doctor I had encountered decades earlier. Had I misremembered, or had he changed?

"Just one child," I said. "You delivered my baby girl twenty years ago."

This was clearly happy news to Dr. Hauptman.

"You know, dear," he said, leaning in as if to tell me a secret, "I delivered ten thousand babies." He sat back with satisfaction.

"That's very impressive," I said.

"And rewarding. Extremely rewarding. But enough about me. Tell me a bit about yourself."

Back when he was my doctor, I had barely exchanged a word with him, and now I wondered if that had been a lost opportunity. Had he been this curious and considerate when I knew him, and had I simply not seen it? I might not have felt so frightened and alone if he had asked this simple question twenty years ago.

I explained that I was a lawyer and had a small practice in New Hampshire. I tried to emulate his conspicuous professional pride, but my attempt fell flat. I was fixated in that moment on the daughter I did not have. My occupation seemed like a wan substitute.

"Good for you," he said. He reached out and gave my arm an affirming tap. "That's just wonderful. Do you derive great satisfaction from your work?"

"I do," I said. "I enjoy it, and I think I do it well."

"Anything worth doing is worth doing well," he said, approvingly.

He looked at me expectantly, but I wasn't sure what to say next. The conversation paused for an awkward beat, until I realized it was time for me to get to the reason I was there.

"I came here to ask you some questions about the baby you delivered, about my daughter," I said.

The look on his face suggested he thought this was a wonderful choice of topic, and that he had not noticed my obvious hesitation.

"How *is* your daughter?" he asked, with interest.

How much easier this conversation would be, I thought, if I could be like those other mothers, who recite their children's milestones with maternal pride. I wished I could simply tell him that she was an equestrian or ballet dancer or flight attendant. Clearly, he was accustomed to hearing gratified mothers report on their accomplished children and implicitly offer him some of the credit. But I knew this was where the conversation would take a turn.

"I don't know my daughter," I said, as matter-of-factly as I could. "I gave her up for adoption as soon as she was born."

At my cracking voice, Doctor Hauptman's expression remained soft and calm, not judgmental, not angry. Or perhaps he was too blindsided to speak. Either way, I was grateful that he was still listening, not trying to prevent me from revisiting an outcome that could not be undone. I pressed on.

"That's the reason for my visit," I said. "Maybe you were the one who found a home for her. I wanted to ask what you remembered about the adoption. If you know where she is. If you ever knew."

Dr. Hauptman remained placid. His face was inquisitive, expectant, as if he hoped I would say more. And suddenly I had a different concern from the fear that he would be yet another sentry guarding the secret of my daughter's identity. Perhaps I would meet an entirely different obstacle, one I had not foreseen. Now that I knew the sheer number of births he had attended, it seemed unlikely that he might remember a specific one. The event I had asked him to remember had been monumental in my life, traumatic and shameful. Burying those emotions inside me, under layers of more palatable qualities like competence, patience and generosity, had been exhausting emotional work. But in the story of his life, putting my daughter up for adoption had probably been mundane, barely worth noting.

And then Doctor Hauptman's face lit up with recognition. It seemed that the information had just come to him. But he said nothing, and I soon realized he was looking up over my shoulder at someone else. I turned my head and saw that he was smiling at a man with a reddish trim beard who was approaching us.

"Here's Theo," Dr. Hauptman said, as both an explanation to me and a greeting to the bearded man.

Theo, who seemed to be in his forties, fit but not tall, pulled a third chair up to make a small circle and sat down. He placed his hand on the doctor's shoulder affectionately.

"You've got some company, Uncle Robert?" Theo seemed pleased and not surprised at finding a stranger by his uncle's side.

"We were just waiting for you," Hauptman answered.

I introduced myself to Theo and reached my hand out. He shook it readily and firmly, which I appreciated. A lot of men avoid shaking hands with a woman, I had noticed, because they mistakenly believe it is entirely unlike shaking hands with a man.

"Theo Boal," he said. "Nice to meet you. You know my uncle from . . .?

"I was a patient of his many years ago."

Theo turned to Dr. Hauptman and spoke at the slightly elevated volume people tend to use with the elderly.

"Your patients still come to visit you after all these years." His cheer struck me as exaggerated, possibly condescending. But when he spoke to me, his tone was more authentic.

"You're very kind to spend time with Robert. It really means a lot." Then, loudly, to his uncle, "You've even delivered babies for patients you delivered, haven't you?"

"I've delivered ten thousand babies," Doctor Hauptman replied.

"You had a wonderful career, Uncle Robert," said Theo, but now he sounded less cheerful, a bit more wistful. He placed his hand on the doctor's back.

"And rewarding," said the doctor. "Very rewarding."

"I didn't mean to interrupt," said Theo, and he urged us to continue our conversation.

"You didn't interrupt," said Doctor Hauptman. "We were just catching up."

Doctor Hauptman turned back to me and asked, "So tell me, to what do I owe the pleasure of your visit today?"

Was he giving me a chance to change the subject? Perhaps he thought I would not want to talk about the adoption in front of his nephew. But I had come all this way, and I was willing to plow ahead. I wouldn't have another opportunity to probe Hauptman's memory.

"Well, as I mentioned," I continued, "I wanted to ask you some questions about my daughter."

"Of course," he said. His face brightened, as if he were remembering. He looked at me expectantly. "Tell me," he said, "how *is* your daughter?"

Confused, I started again.

"That's why I'm here. Soon after you delivered her . . ."

"I've delivered ten thousand babies," he interjected, as if I would be pleased to hear this yet again.

I looked nervously at Theo, and then I understood. There was sadness and forbearance in Theo's eyes. He had accepted his uncle's limitations, and, he told me silently, I should do the same.

"You had a wonderful career, Uncle Robert," he said, with resignation.

It had all been a waste of time, I realized. All of it. The effort to get my medical records, the drive down east, the telephone calls from Carol's den. None of it would lead to the answers I wanted. The old doctor could barely follow the thread of our exchange, let alone bridge a twenty-year gap of memory. I had exhausted the three sentences in his repertoire. So I smiled weakly and said,

"She's quite well, thank you."

"Tell her to work hard," he said, proud of his insight. "Anything worth doing is worth doing well."

"I will."

"And what about you? Tell me a bit about yourself," he requested.

I told him once again about my work back in Hopkins, and he asked me once again if I found it very satisfying. I wanted to extricate myself, but Theo clearly liked having a new participant, a circuit breaker of sorts, in this repetitive loop of conversation.

"Did you grow up near St. Gabriel's?" he asked me.

"No," I told him, "I was raised about an hour north of the hospital. On a small dairy farm."

"Tough business," Theo said, and I wondered how he knew that.

"It was," I agreed. "Even with all the subsidies, my parents couldn't make it work in the last few years. Though for all I know, there's still cheese from our cows in a USDA warehouse somewhere in Kansas."

Dr. Hauptman laughed, though I'm not sure what he found funny.

"Do you visit this area often?" Theo asked.

I told him that I make the trip a few times a year, to shop and visit friends. I wrapped up with a reference to my brunch with Carol earlier in the day.

"So you're here by yourself?" he said. It sounded like more of an observation than a question.

"Yes," I said, "it's just me."

He smiled as if I had answered correctly.

Making small talk with Theo for his uncle's entertainment wasn't terrible. It gave me a distraction from my own disappointment. And Theo was easy company. He was curious and well-informed, and he listened as well as he spoke. He occasionally tried to bring Dr. Hauptman into the conversation with a *Remember that summer you took me to Tanglewood?* or a *You would find that article really interesting, Uncle Robert.* But for the most part we just chatted with each other and allowed the elderly doctor to follow along or not. I learned that Theo was also a physician, and that he was recently divorced. When his uncle was momentarily distracted by the task of giving his dinner order to Casey, Theo leaned in toward me and said, "Robert doesn't always remember the divorce. Don't be surprised if he calls you Jill."

"I won't let it phase me," I promised.

Eventually, I felt I had remained longer than is appropriate for a mere acquaintance paying a courtesy call. We had run out of topics for a superficial interaction, and it was clearly time to go. There was a part of me that dreaded leaving. I remembered the despondency that came over me when I left the Bureau of Vital Records with nothing but a scolding from the clerk, and how hard it had been, on the car ride home, to control my rage. Reluctantly, I said goodbye as graciously as I could. I thanked Dr. Hauptman for the visit, complimented him on how well he looked. But I'm sure my dismay was palpable, because

Theo stood up just after me and offered to accompany me to the door. As soon as we were out of the room, he said sympathetically, almost conspiratorially, "He's not quite what you expected, is he?"

There was no point in complaining to Theo—the devoted nephew who engaged in this painful parody of conversation every Saturday afternoon—that his uncle's dementia had crushed my hopes of finding my daughter. Instead I said, "Your uncle is very charming. He was an excellent host."

"Yes," Theo said ruefully, "he is very charming. He always was. He also used to be brilliant and a little imperious. Now I would settle for coherent. But at least he's easy to be around, not like the residents here who curse at their own families."

"You're very good with him," I said, which was true. "He's lucky to have you."

Even in my state of disappointment, I recognized that Theo's was deeper. He clearly loved his uncle, and had to endure watching him succumb to a disordered brain.

"He's been very good to me," Theo said, as much to himself as to me, I'm sure. "All my life. So, whatever I give him, he's earned." He looked down at his feet, but when he looked up again at me, he seemed cheered. He had the look on his face of a person who had just had a great idea.

"You shouldn't drive home on an empty stomach. Let's get an early dinner before you hit the road. I've already spent more time than usual with my uncle. He gets tired. I know a nice place very close to here. It wouldn't take you out of your way at all."

I said yes because I needed to eat. And because I didn't want to go home alone to stare again at my baby's birth certificate. I needed something else to do, and Theo seemed decent and companionable. These are not great reasons for saying yes, I acknowledge, but, to this day, I am glad I did.

* * *

The restaurant was sort of Italian, sort of Greek, with a menu the length of a Russian novel, even though all there really was to decide was whether you wanted your pasta straight or curly, your fish sautéed or grilled, your side a potato or salad. Theo greeted our server by name, and moments later a plate of fried calamari appeared on our table without having been noticeably ordered. Theo doused it with lemon and began telling me about his uncle.

I learned that Dr. Hauptman's only child, a son named Erik, had died of leukemia when he was twenty-three.

"He was in medical school when he was diagnosed," Theo said. "His big dream was to take over his father's practice."

It had not occurred to me that Dr. Hauptman might have his own longings for a child he could not see or hold. I had known nothing about him, I realized, and certainly had never imagined that he too might have borne the weight of parental love that has no object on which to rest.

"Were you close with your cousin?" I asked.

"I was a little kid, but I looked up to him, for sure. And he's the reason I chose hematology and oncology. All these years later, I'm still trying to find a therapy that could save him."

I was touched by this poignant admission, so I asked more questions about what that therapy might look like.

"Bone marrow transplants," he said, definitively. "The problem I work on is that patients sometimes reject their donor marrow, because of antigens, you know. My lab is studying one antigen in particular, trying to figure out how to control it. We're focusing on leukemia patients, but ultimately, we hope to improve the chances of people who need kidneys and hearts too."

To my surprise, I enjoyed listening to Theo talk about his research, since he wasn't didactic or condescending.

"Maybe someday you'll say you did ten-thousand transplants," I offered.

Theo flashed an appreciative smile.

"I love that idea," he said. "What a great description of a life well-lived."

Then he got thoughtful, and I realized that I had unintention-ally brought his mind back to Dr. Hauptman.

"Uncle Robert was a great mentor to me, even though I chose working with blood over delivering babies. He was always support-ive." He pulled a piece of garlic bread from the loaf and said, "How about you? Who was the mentor who helped you the most?"

I forgave him for sounding like an interviewer reading pre-pared questions, because I thought it was a good one. He seemed genuinely interested in learning more about me. The question even got me thinking about my early career, but no one came to mind. Most of my college professors were men, and none of them had been very nurturing. Some were committed to fostering our academic development, but not to helping us with the larger task of building cohesive lives once we left Halstead. Some professors saw us as aco-lytes in their anti-war activism. Still others treated us like nymphets to be bedded in open secrecy.

"Not really," I said, though I was still thinking. "Though maybe I should give Professor Hollander a little credit. I was a research assistant for him, and he wrote me a recommendation for law school. I talked to him about where to apply. Some of my classmates were aiming for big name schools like Yale or Harvard. We were the first generation of women to think those schools were within our reach. But New Hampshire had a brand-new public law school. It was practically free, and I had no money. I thought this was a terrible quandary, and he said something I still remember. He told me, 'You ladies want to find the secret door that the men have been walking through, because you think they all know something you don't know. But lots of doors can lead to a good life. Just pick one.' It was very helpful for me to hear. Though I can see from your squint that you're skeptical."

Theo cocked his head to the side and thought.

"I think it's good advice for a bright student choosing a law school. But I'm not sure it's true that there are no right and wrong choices in life. I can tell you that marrying Jill turned out to be one clearly very wrong choice."

I was impressed that he could be argumentative and self-deprecating at the same time.

"Yes, but you were able to get out of the marriage. Hollander might say you proved his point."

Theo seemed perfectly content to have his assertion challenged.

"Okay, so maybe that isn't the best example. Let me try to think of a life decision that really can't be undone. Like, say, suicide. But that's too obvious. I'll think of a better one. Maybe going to war?"

He appeared to be thinking while he was eating.

I had started the evening with no intention of telling Theo the real reason for my visit. But he was so open with me, telling me about divorcing his first wife and losing his older cousin. I enjoyed Theo's candor, and it seemed stingy not to reciprocate. Also, in the days leading up to this trip to Boston, I had practiced and repeated my story many times over, preparing myself to lay it out for Dr. Hauptman. The anticipation of unburdening myself had been building, and now I needed to release the pressure.

"I have an example," I said. "It's actually perfect." I steeled myself with a deep breath and told him the truth. "The baby girl your uncle delivered . . ."

Theo nodded, waiting for me to finish the sentence.

"I gave her up for adoption. I was in college. I couldn't imagine raising a baby myself, so I gave her up."

Theo looked like something had clicked into place, like this was the explanation he had been waiting for.

"I sensed there was a reason you didn't want to talk about your daughter," he said. "I didn't want to pry." To my relief, he seemed simply gratified that the mystery was solved. It was much easier, I concluded, to tell the truth to someone who barely knew me. I wasn't terrified that I was chipping away at an already solid sense of my character. With Theo, I was starting from scratch.

"That's the reason I went to visit your uncle." I spoke with momentum, now that there was nothing left to lose. "I think your uncle may have been involved in placing her, and I had hoped he would remember something about it."

He waited, and when I didn't continue, he said, "I'm sorry your trip was a waste, Bonnie. I wish my uncle could have helped you."

"It wasn't a waste," I assured him. "It was disappointing. But not a waste." I could feel myself starting to cry.

"If I had known that's why you were coming, I would have saved you the trip."

Theo waited patiently for me to blot my eyes with a tissue.

"You could be right," he said. "I wouldn't be surprised at all if Robert occasionally got involved in private adoptions. Out of ten thousand babies, there must have been at least a few who needed homes. Robert knew a lot of people, and it was just like him to help anyone he could."

The waiter cleared our dessert plates while I tried not to cry. When he was no longer in earshot, and I was composed enough to speak, I said, "I just want to know she has a good family, that she has a good life."

I didn't tell Theo that, in truth, I wanted so much more. He reached across the table and placed his fingers on my arm. Then he said, "If my uncle had anything to do with it, you can be sure she went to a family that was stable and loving. He would never have trifled with a baby's life, if that's what you're worried about. If I know him, he probably placed the baby with a couple from his church."

"Thank you," I said, weakly. "That's reassuring."

"I'm sorry I can't tell you any more," he said.

He signed the check in its faux leather holder, and then snapped it shut, as if to close the book on this topic.

I wasn't sorry I had told him, and I wasn't sorry I had stayed for dinner with him. But the day had been long and draining, and I was ready to go home to my quiet house in my sleepy town.

Theo ordered me a coffee to go, and then he walked me to my car. We stood in the restaurant's parking lot, where diners were just arriving. I opened my car door and sensed that he was about to ask another question.

"So this all happened how many years ago? If you don't mind my asking."

"She was born on August thirty-first, 1970."

He nodded.

"At St. Gabriel's?"

"At St. Gabriel's."

He looked as if this meant something to him, but he didn't say any more about it. He thanked me for having dinner with him, said how much he enjoyed meeting me, and then shut my car door. He seemed to be thinking about something else, and our conversation felt unfinished.

When Carol called me the next day to ask about my witness, she was tickled to learn that the fiasco had ended in a halfway decent dinner with an eligible divorced doctor.

"Don't you think it's a sign from God?" she asked, sounding more like her own teenage daughter than the grownup she was.

"Sure," I said, humoring her. "Now that God got Nelson Mandela released from prison, he has lots of time to focus on my dating life."

6

IT WAS JUST BEFORE THANKSGIVING of our freshman year when Hollis proposed a road trip.

"How would you feel about going to Yale this weekend?" she asked.

"Is there a mixer there on Saturday?" I asked. It seemed unlikely, since I knew there had been one just a few weeks earlier in October. Some of our classmates had taken the bus down to New Haven for the football game and the party, and the reports were that the weekend was good but not great. At first it was fun, they said. The young men at the dance were friendly. But a sophomore named Andrea Bockhaus drank too much and had to be dragged outside by her friends to vomit on the ground. After that, none of the guys would talk to them, or even find them a comfortable place to rest. The women had to ride all the way back to Halstead with Andrea lying across two seats, begging the driver to pull over so she could retch.

"We can do better than a mixer," Hollis said. "I know a fellow there, a senior. He's my cousin's cousin on the other side. He told me I could come see him any time, and that I should bring a friend. He's got a roommate, and we can just get some beers."

This all sounded fine to me. Hollis was right that I had been cocooned at Halstead all fall, with just a few trips into town to see a movie or go to a bar, and Saturday nights were getting boring. The prospect of venturing out to meet a couple of Yale men was not entirely unappealing, so I agreed. It would have been simpler to take the bus to Amherst or Williams with all the other girls, but Hollis had made a plan for us to catch a ride to New Haven with a senior named Shelby.

I was at a loss when it came to deciding what to wear. When I first presented myself to Hollis for inspection, I was sporting a ribbed turtleneck sweater, a navy tartan skirt, which I had regularly been wearing to our Thursday and Sunday dinners, and a pair of perfectly matching blue Pappagallo flats I had fished out of her closet. She shook her head, but not unkindly.

"Wear the Levi's," she said, as if it were the obvious choice.

"Really?" I asked. She herself was wearing blue jeans, but on her they looked fashionable. I was sure that on me they would look like farm clothes.

"Yes, really," she said. "They're perfect. We'll dress you up just a little with this." She found a paisley silk scarf and handed it to me.

I tied it loosely around my neck. She stepped back, cocked her head and hummed her approval. She wore a white blouse with embroidered flowers. It looked beautiful on her, though it was hardly ideal for the November weather.

I wasn't sure how Hollis knew Shelby, but they were obviously well enough acquainted that Hollis slid confidently into the passenger seat without a word. I didn't mind sitting in the back and listening to them talk. It sounded to me like they were resuming a conversation whose first half I had missed.

"I think you're very smart to start with Yale," Shelby said. "It's really the best place to meet men. I wasted a lot of time my freshman and sophomore years going to different schools and didn't meet anyone suitable. I finally met Charles at Yale in my junior year. He was a senior then, but now he's in his first year at the medical school."

"Have you ever been to Dartmouth?" I asked. It was the only men's school that was in my orbit.

"Too cold," said Shelby, definitively. "And I've heard rumors that they put drugs in the punch. Not just booze, like all the guys do, but actual LSD. I don't know if the rumors are true, but I wouldn't risk it. Anyway, the men there seem more interested in getting drunk with each other than getting to know us. Like they were relieved when we went home, and they could get back to their competitions over who can pee the farthest. The men at Columbia and Brown are much more sociable, but you have all those Barnard and Pembroke women to compete with."

Hollis gave me a look over her shoulder. It was downright amusing that Shelby thought we were out to find husbands. Of course marriage would happen eventually, we assumed, but it was hardly an immediate goal. We were after some weekend fun and had no aspirations to be engaged by graduation. We were certainly not looking to Shelby for guidance on how to be just like her.

Shelby noticed our silent communication but didn't seem offended.

"What are you two giving each other secret looks about?" she asked. "You think I'm old-fashioned; is that it? You think I won the hoop rolling contest?"

"The what?" I asked. If this was some ancient Halstead tradition, Hollis had neglected to fill me in.

"You don't know about that?" Shelby asked, slightly incredulous. "The seniors used to hold a hoop rolling contest on alumnae day to see who would be the first in the class to get married. You might think that's insane, but I've heard the competition was pretty fierce."

She was trying to discern our reactions while still keeping an eye on the road.

"We're not thinking marriage just yet," Hollis finally admitted for the both of us. "We have other things we want to do first."

Shelby was quiet for a moment, as if passing the truck on our right took all her concentration.

"Like what?" she finally asked. I was as curious as Shelby to hear Hollis's answer, as I had known her to vacillate among various career choices, including poet, social worker, art appraiser, beatnik, and model.

"I'm not sure," Hollis said, more meekly than I expected. "I was thinking about the Peace Corps and then doing some graduate work in anthropology."

Interesting, I thought.

"How about you, Bonnie?" Shelby asked, looking at me in her rearview mirror.

"I'd like to go to law school," I answered, and Shelby nodded in thoughtful approval.

"Good for you," she said. "When I was a freshman, I didn't even know what lawyers do."

"Bonnie doesn't know what lawyers do, either," said Hollis. "Right, Bonnie?"

Okay, so she was ribbing me for Shelby's entertainment, but it didn't bother me. Her teasing revealed that she actually knew me pretty well.

"I know they don't milk cows," I said, and that made Shelby smile.

"Suit yourselves," she said. "But I feel lucky to have met Charles. He is a great guy, and he's not expecting me to vacuum the curtains all day long. I'm not going to be his housekeeper, if that's what you're worried about."

Hollis, ever the peacemaker, asked Shelby to tell us more about Charles. This proved to be an inexhaustible topic, and we heard more than we needed to know about him and his family. He had two older sisters, one of whom was in the Halstead class of '65, and one of whom had just graduated from Smith. His father was an accomplished sailor and "so witty" according to Shelby. His mother was a generous woman who had given Charles her grandmother's diamond ring for his own marriage proposal. Shelby lifted her left hand from the steering wheel and wiggled her fingers so we could get a better look.

"It's beautiful," we said in unison, even though it was actually a little fusty.

Then she told us all the plans for her wedding, which was to take place two weeks after her graduation, a mere seven months away. The church and the band had been booked. The only open question was whether Charles's nine-month-old niece would learn to walk in time to be a flower girl.

Before Shelby dropped us at the campus, she told us the address where she would be.

"If you need a place to stay, for *any* reason,"—the stress on *any* was meant to communicate something— "you can crash with us. Call first or just ring the doorbell. It doesn't matter. Really, Charles won't mind."

★ ★ ★

The men we were planning to meet—I didn't think of them as "dates"—were waiting for us under an ornate gothic archway. It led to an expansive central courtyard, which, they told us, was the heart of what they called Branford College, a dormitory that was grander and more beautiful than any building at Halstead. Hollis introduced me to our host, Colton Bingham, who, in turn, introduced us both to his friend and roommate, Marshall Eckstein. Hollis and Colton looked similar though not necessarily related, and had the easy familiarity of people who had known each other since childhood. I sensed, as Colton's eyes widened at the sight of Hollis, that he had not remembered her being so pretty. Marshall had dark hair and eyes, and an appealingly craggy face. The pair of them made me think of Jon Voigt and Dustin Hoffman—not as the down-and-out hustlers on the *Midnight Cowboy* poster, but as the movie stars they were, all cleaned up for the talk show circuit.

"We thought we'd start with a tour," Colton said. "We live off-campus now, but this was our dorm for a couple of years. It's a more suitable locale for meeting up with respectable women from good families."

Was he making fun of us? If Hollis thought so, she didn't show it.

"I'll keep an eye out," she said, "in case any show up."

The comment achieved its desired effect of making Colton and Marshall smile.

"Have you ever been to Yale before?" Marshall asked us politely, perfunctorily.

"I know this is Hollis's first visit," Colton said. "Though I don't know what took you so long." He was practically leering at her.

"I've never been here either," I said. "It's even prettier than Halstead." I hoped I didn't sound as unsophisticated to them as I did to myself. "I feel like I'm in Europe." It was true. Halstead's architecture had seemed so grand to me when I first arrived, but in comparison to these cathedrals, our buildings looked like railroad depots.

"That's intentional," said Marshall. "You're supposed to think you're at Oxford."

"Come," Colton said. "We'll show you around. Let's start with Old Campus."

It was dusk as Marshall and Colton led us through their enchanted fairy-tale city. We admired statues and oak trees and an imposing tower of filigreed stone. Then there was something Colton insisted we needed to see inside a small courtyard of one of the more modest residences, which he and Marshall called "colleges."

"Come on," he said, "you'll love this."

He led us through a gate, across a plain but pleasant quadrangle and into a small stone courtyard, where he instructed us to look up and observe the gargoyle at the top.

I was confused by what I saw.

"It looks like a man sitting on a toilet," I said.

"That's because it *is* a man sitting on a toilet," Colton said gleefully. "It's Rodin's *Thinker*, taking a crap!" He thought it was hilarious. "Pretty funny, isn't it?"

"I guess," I said, though I actually thought it was more crass than amusing.

"Oh, Colton," Hollis said, shaking her head. There was pity in her voice. "You really are a boor."

He gave her a guilty-as-charged grin, and Marshall proposed that we move on.

"I bet they'd like to see Sterling," he said, and ushered us out the way we came.

The aptly named Sterling Memorial Library did indeed seem to be the architectural equivalent of expensive jewelry, complete with stained glass windows the colors of precious gems.

"They're building a more modern library right under the grass where we're standing," Marshall informed us.

"It's basically going to be a bomb shelter with books," Colton added. "You can read up on your Nietzsche during a nuclear attack."

I was starting to wonder if I could keep up with these two fellows. They were so confident and comfortable, as if they had been initiated into all of the world's inside jokes. They also, I could see, had a strangely competitive approach to each other. Each was intent on winning whatever conversation he participated in, Colton by means of rakish humor, Marshall by means of deference and manners. Hollis made it clear that she appreciated both approaches by flirting equally with both of our hosts.

It was dark, but not yet dinnertime, when we finished our informal tour. At the edge of campus, Marshall and Colton led us down a few steps into a bar that offered, according to a chalkboard on the wall, three beers for a dollar. The tables were made of thick wood, tacky with grease, and mottled with generations of carved initials. Hollis sat down first, then pointed to the seat diagonal to her.

"Colton, you're there," she said, authoritatively. Then she patted the chair to her left. "Bonnie, you're next to me."

From the configuration of our seating, an observer might have concluded that I was on a date with Colton, and Hollis was on a date with Marshall. No one objected to this arrangement, and Marshall, I noticed, looked downright thrilled. Colton called over the waitress and ordered our beers and two plates of fries. Hollis requested a screwdriver, which prompted Marshall to ask for the same. Then he began asking Hollis earnest questions about her family and her classes.

I wasn't sure how to get the conversation off the ground with Colton.

"So you're Hollis's cousin?" I asked.

"No, not really." He seemed perfectly happy to explain. "I have an uncle who's married to her aunt," he said. "We have cousins in common, so Hol and I see each other at weddings and christenings. If you can follow all that, you're several steps ahead of most people."

For a few minutes, there were two separate conversations happening at the table. Marshall and Hollis were animatedly engaged in learning everything about each other, while Colton and I tried to think of polite questions. When we got to the part about my interest in going to law school, Colton saw a way to unify our foursome.

"Like Marshall," he said, as he elbowed his friend in the arm. "Right?"

Marshall did not welcome the interruption but nevertheless obliged his friend.

"Yup, that's right," he said. "I'm planning to start at Columbia next fall. If they'll take me." He sipped his beer.

"They'll take you." Colton said. Then, to us he said,

"And he's not just doing it for the deferment. He actually wants to be a lawyer."

Hollis looked at Marshall as if she had an urgent question that only he could answer.

"Do you think you could represent murderers?" she asked him. "I don't think I could, but I admire people who do."

"Oh, Hollis," Colton sighed obviously. "You had to open that can of worms, didn't you? Marshall here is a regular Hubert Humphrey. I should have warned you."

Hollis looked at Colton.

"Don't tell me you're still a Nixon man?" Again, that note of pity in her voice.

"I am who I am." Colton shrugged. "But you, Hol, you seem to have changed a lot."

The ambiguity of that statement hung for a moment, before Marshall gave Colton a sideways look of annoyance and said,

"To answer your question, or maybe to avoid your question, I don't plan to practice criminal law. I'm interested in taxation, or maybe bankruptcy."

Colton took Marshall's chin in his fingers and turned his friend's face to the side.

"Look at that profile," Colton said. "Does this guy have a nose for tax law, or what?" Colton laughed, but no one else did. Marshall seemed more bored by the joke than offended.

"How about you, Colton?" I asked. "What are you planning after you graduate?"

He looked happy that the conversation had now turned to him.

"I thought you'd never ask. In fact, things are looking up for me. As of this week, congratulations are in order. I just lined up a job at Manny Hanny."

"Wow," said Hollis. "Manufacturers Hanover. Congratulations indeed."

She said that for my benefit, I was sure. She had to have known I didn't have a clue what Manny Hanny was.

Hollis raised her glass, though there was nothing left of her screwdriver.

"To the pursuit of filthy lucre," she said.

Colton did not raise his beer.

"I'll never get rich if you toast me with an empty glass," he said, and he waved the waitress over.

As soon as we had ordered another round, Hollis had more questions.

"So you're going to live in New York City?" she asked.

"Of course. That's the whole point," he answered.

"Can my girlfriends and I come visit you?"

"It's okay by me," he said, "But do you think Papa Locke will approve?"

"I'm eighteen," she reminded him. "He doesn't get to approve or disapprove."

Lately, Hollis had been complaining a lot about her parents. They called too often, she thought, and she was embarrassed at how frequently we heard the phrase, "Phone call for Hollis Locke!" relayed up the stairwell.

"Tell them I'm in the library," Hollis would call out, and the message would be sent back down.

Just two nights ago, Marcia popped her head in our door.

"Your parents know the library closes at 9:30," she said to Hollis. "They said you never call them back."

"Did you tell them I'm busy studying?" Hollis asked.

"No," said Marcia, "I told them you took a job as a Playboy bunny, and we haven't seen you in weeks."

Even though Hollis bristled against her parents' oversight, I was a little bit envious of her. My parents had taken the opposite approach, treating me as if I had outgrown them the minute I was accepted to Halstead. They deferred to me, as if I knew things they didn't. They thought my work was too important to be interrupted, and they called me only once, in early October, at 11:03 pm, minutes after the cost of a long-distance call dropped to its lowest. They wrote to me twice a week, taking pains not to ask too many questions, lest I feel obligated to take the time to write them back.

"Well, then, it's settled," Colton said. "You and your cute friend will come see me in New York. Though, of course, nothing is really settled until I know what my draft number is."

Colton's reference to the upcoming lottery brought down the mood at the table. We were all aware that Uncle Sam was worried about a troop shortage in Vietnam. The impending lottery, which would assign a draft number to each birthday, had put a lot of young men's plans on hold. Until you knew what your number was, you didn't know your chances of being sent off to war. And even after the lottery, no one knew how many men the government would have to call up in order to meet its needs. Even when you got your number, you could still be in limbo for a very long time. My mother had told me in a recent letter about the effect the lottery was having back home.

"The boys talk about it non-stop," my mother had said, "but there is never anything new to say."

"Are you really worried about that?" I asked Colton.

"Of course he's worried," Marshall spoke up for his friend. They were considerably more in sync on this topic than they had seemed at any point earlier in the evening. "We all are. I think about it less than he does, because I'll still be a student. But it's on all of our minds."

"What are you going to do if you get a low number?" I wanted to know.

"I'm not going to enlist, if that's what you're asking," answered Colton. "And that's a point of principle as much as it's a point of self-preservation. The best way to fight communism is to be a good capitalist. That's how I see it."

Marshall shook his head at his friend's comment, but with obvious fondness.

"No, my plan," continued Colton, "is to convince Hollis here to marry me if I get drafted." Hollis seemed to think this was a very flattering joke, and I wondered if she were drunk.

"I thought there was no more marriage deferral," I said.

Colton leaned toward me from across the table and said in a stage whisper, "Shhh. Don't tell that to Hollis." He winked at me, and then smiled at his not-quite-cousin.

"That's enough," she said. "You're not getting drafted, and we're not getting married." She finished her second screwdriver. "I want to talk about pleasanter things. Marshall was telling me about his class on Freud and Jung, so let's get back to that. That's kind of heady stuff for an aspiring tax attorney, isn't it?"

"I like to take esoteric courses. It's intense, but,"—he shrugged his shoulders slightly— "that's why I'm here."

"I think that's great," said Hollis.

"It's made Marshall quite adept at dream interpretation," Colton interjected. "Try him."

"You start," Hollis said to me.

"Okay. I had a dream the other night that I had a German test," I said, "but I hadn't studied at all because I thought I had dropped the course."

Colton rolled his eyes.

"That's too easy," he said. "Try another one."

"I have that dream, only it's real life," said Hollis. "I have to write a paper about *Tristram Shandy,* and I *wish* I'd dropped the course. I don't understand the book, and I have absolutely zilch to say."

"That's funny," said Colton. "I wrote a paper on *Tristram Shandy* my freshman year. I guess it's kind of a rite of passage."

"I remember that paper," said Marshall. "You didn't understand the book either."

"I know," Colton agreed. "I had no idea what I was talking about. But I think I got a B-plus."

Hollis perked up. She was visibly tipsy, and was hatching a plan.

"How much do you want for that paper?" she asked, with a big grin.

Colton put down his beer and looked at Hollis sternly and disapprovingly.

"Hollis," he scolded.

She bit her lip coyly, like a person hoping that her cuteness could get her out of a jam.

"We're practically family," he said. "You don't have to offer me money."

For the first time that evening, I saw why Hollis liked Colton. He was a bit of a throwback, but he could make people laugh. And once he saw that his charm was working on me, he began to look at me differently.

"I can't believe you still have a dorm mother," Marshall said at one point. "You're not children. Don't they know it's 1969?"

"It's silly," I agreed. "But luckily ours is kind of old. She doesn't see or hear very well."

"It's true," Hollis said. "Caitlin McKelligan climbs down the fire escape after curfew all the time, and Crutch never notices."

"Still," said Colton, "How are you supposed to have any fun?"

"Don't worry," said Hollis. "We have plenty of fun."

This was true, but also misleading. I really did think college was fun, but not in the way Hollis was suggesting. I didn't have to flout the rules to enjoy myself. With or without a dorm mother, college was a net gain in independence and opportunity for me.

"The idea of a dorm mother seems so quaint compared to what's going on here," Colton said. "Bobby Seale on trial. The Black Panthers moving in. There are students talking about letting these criminals—"

Marshall interjected, "We don't know that they're criminals. Innocent until proven guilty, remember?"

Colton was annoyed at the interruption. He shook his head.

"You always say that, but the evidence is pretty clear. They executed one of their so-called brothers because they thought he was an informant."

"It's also clear that they're being tried for their political views, not just for the shooting," said Marshall. "And that they're not going to get a fair trial."

Unlike me, Marshall already sounded like a lawyer.

"My point isn't about the Panthers," insisted Colton. "What I'm getting at is that there are students here at Yale who want to invite these criminals—you can call them radicals, if that makes you happy—to stay in the dorms. With the students. In their rooms. Can you believe it? And at Halstead they're worried that a phi beta kappa from Williams might sneak in."

There was an edge of anger in Colton's voice. Perhaps he was annoyed at Marshall, who had tried to derail his rant. Or perhaps it irked him that his college years, which should have been placid, were turning out to be tumultuous. Or maybe he was peeved at us, at Hollis and me, for our immunity from the looming draft. Either way, I wasn't unsympathetic, because I knew there was truth to what he was saying. At Halstead we talked and worried about the war and about the country's epidemic of political assassinations. But they were abstractions taking place outside our gates. The women of Halstead were nowhere near the bullets.

I could have told Colton I understood him, but I didn't bother. It was Marshall, not me, he was trying to sway. There was a tense pause in the conversation, until Hollis announced an intention to use the ladies room. She asked me to join her, but her request wasn't necessary. I understood that my company was the whole point.

As soon as we had squeezed ourselves into the unheated bathroom, she asked, "What do you think of Colton?" Her tone was surprisingly business-like for a woman as buzzed as she was.

"I'm not sure," I said. "He's not exactly the Musak of men."

Hollis laughed.

"I know. He's kind of abrasive," she conceded. "But he's funny, don't you think? And interesting."

I had to agree that he was both those things. I had concluded, also, that Colton exaggerated his rough edges for comic effect, and was probably more decent than he let on.

She put on lipstick in the metal mirror, then turned and looked at me.

"I think his friend is really sweet," she said. "He's different from the guys I usually meet."

She said it innocently enough, but I knew what she really meant. She was relishing the prospect of introducing a Jewish Yale man to her parents and daring them to say he was unsuitable. And then she got pouty-faced.

"Could you put up with Colton for a few more hours?" she asked. "Or would that be too much to ask? I'd like to see how things go with me and Marshall."

The truth was that, by that time, I was enjoying myself. I had discovered in the course of the evening that I could hold my own well enough with Colton and Marshall, despite the differences in our ages and upbringings. Sure, I had grown up outside their clubby world. But I read books and watched the news every night. I wasn't ignorant about what was going on in the world. I had high school classmates serving in the Marines, and I cared about what happened to them. And I liked Colton more than I was willing to acknowledge to Hollis. I was intrigued by his gruffness and his over-familiarity. I appreciated that he didn't hold back his commentary for the sake of decorum, as most people I knew had been trained to do. And he did not talk down to me or exclude me, as if I were hopelessly unsophisticated.

"Just for you," I fibbed. "I'll do it, but just for you."

"Thank you, Bonnie." She actually clapped her hands in gratitude. And then, out of nowhere, she said, "You know what would be fun?"

I couldn't even guess what she had in mind.

"Let's run a little experiment," she said, getting excited. "Let's swap outfits, and see if they notice."

It was precisely the kind of idea that made life with Hollis entertaining, and I agreed. I wriggled out of the turtleneck sweater and gave it to her with the paisley scarf. She pulled off her peasant blouse, and I put it on. It took effort to retain our poker faces as we walked back to the table, but we pulled it off. Marshall saw us approach, and he did look slightly puzzled, but neither of our dates mentioned the switch.

We made a plan to walk to their apartment and pick up dinner along the way.

"There are three options in our neighborhood," Colton said. "Pizza, pasta, and Italian."

Their apartment was on the second floor of a blue clapboard house. Colton led us into the living room and motioned for us to sit anywhere on the mismatched secondhand furniture.

"Make yourself at home," he said. "We have some beers in the refrigerator. Or would you prefer a glass of Cold Duck?"

I didn't know how to answer until Marshall explained, without condescension, "It's a sweet red wine. It's fizzy. You'll like it."

Hollis sat down on their scratchy old couch, and I took a seat in an overstuffed chair. Marshall set the pizza down on the coffee table then sat next to Hollis on the couch. When Colton returned from the kitchen with drinks, he sat down on the rug at my feet.

"So," Hollis said, "Do you think the days of mixers are coming to an end? Isn't Yale going co-ed?" She half-said it, half-asked it.

"I think there will always be mixers," Marshall said.

"The freshmen and sophomores love them," added Colton, "though we haven't been to one in years. Besides, there are only a few women here. Not nearly enough to go around."

"I feel bad for those women, actually," said Marshall. "I don't think it's easy."

I asked him why he said that.

"Think about it. The alumni were clear that they didn't want women. They even said that going co-ed would bring down the caliber of a Yale education. So they let a few women transfer in, like human guinea pigs. But those women have missed out on their chance to live on Old Campus with the other freshman and to make friends on day one."

"Still," said Colton, "they get to be Yale men. I think they're pretty lucky."

Marshall wasn't giving up. It was becoming clear to me that Colton wasted his time trying to tell Marshall what to think.

"There are four women in my economics class," he said. "The professor never calls on them. Ever. By now they've stopped even bothering to raise their hands. And one day back in September I was sitting at a table in the dining hall with two of these women. There were about eight of us at the table, and we were having a perfectly nice conversation. But then along comes Hugh Dunning." Marshall paused to ask Colton, "You know him, don't you?"

"Of course I know him," said Colton. "I believe he's what your people would call a 'putz.' Did I say that right?"

"Perfect. I've taught you well," said Marshall. "Anyway, Hugh leans over and tells these girls that it's not fair that there are two of them at this table and he just had to eat dinner at a table where there were none. He told them they should be more gracious next time and spread themselves around."

Hollis sat up. "He didn't actually use the word spread, did he?" she asked, tickled by the double entendre.

"Yes, I swear he did," said Marshall, smiling back at Hollis.

"I assume those two women ignored him?" I asked.

"Bonnie, you're going to think this is crazy, but I never saw those women sitting together again."

"I don't think you need to worry about those two," said Colton. "Every one of these women is tough and ambitious. They're here to be rocket-propelled into the professional stratosphere, and they probably will be, so boola boola for them. And I don't know what's wrong with your economics professor, but there are women in all my classes this semester, and my professors couldn't be nicer. They are practically fawning all over the gals, especially the pretty ones." When he finished, he leaned back against my legs. All I could think about was the feeling of his weight on my shins.

"Ugh," said Hollis. "Who wants to be at a college where the professors only care about your looks?"

Though such a system would not disadvantage Hollis, I understood her objection.

"I completely agree," said Marshall, and he nodded at Hollis.

Colton turned his head all the way around to look at me.

"What do you think?" he asked. I contemplated the question for a moment and said, "I know I wouldn't want to be in a place where I felt unwelcome. I'm glad I chose a college that exists just to educate women. It sounds like Yale is using its female students mainly as a way to recruit men."

Colton nodded his approval of my answer, though I shouldn't have cared what he thought. It is paradoxical, I know, to express a desire to be liberated from men's opinions and then to seek a man's approval for that desire. But that nod made me feel like I had passed a test. I looked over at Hollis to make sure she had observed the way Colton had just affirmed my good judgment.

This was the point at which I first noticed that Hollis had put her head on Marshall's shoulder. When she saw me looking at her, she smiled and closed her eyes, as if she had found the perfect place to rest. Marshall put an arm around her and touched her hair. He leaned over and kissed her forehead. It seemed chaste, but also bold, and I watched for a second too long.

"Bonnie," Colton said, and I startled. "Remember that tower we looked at on Old Campus?"

"Uh huh," I said, though I didn't follow.

"There's a great view of it from the roof. Do you want to see?"

It was the only way I could think of to get away from the awkwardness of watching Hollis and Marshall, so I agreed. In fact, I was grateful that Colton had thought of it. We put our jackets back on, and Colton tossed me a blue and white wool hat.

"Here. You'll want this," he said. "The wind comes off the sound at night."

We walked up another flight, and Colton opened the door to the roof with a key. The air was cold, but the sky was beautiful. Sure enough, we could see the illuminated spire, and it dominated the view of the city.

"It's not exactly the Eiffel Tower," Colton said, "but it makes an impression."

"It's pretty up here," I said, though he was right about the change in the weather. It had seemed like a mild autumn day when we did our campus tour. But now it felt like winter. I crossed my arms and tucked my hands into the opposite sleeves of my coat.

"You're cold," Colton observed.

"A little," I admitted.

"You probably shouldn't have changed into Hollis's blouse. The sweater you were wearing before looked much warmer."

He was very pleased with himself, like a hustler finally revealing his pool prowess.

"It was Hollis's idea," I said, though I didn't need to mount a defense. He clearly thought it was funny.

"I'm sure," he said. "It's not even the first time she's done it. She swapped dresses with one of the bridesmaids at our cousin Lydia's wedding. Then she thought the dress would be improved by the addition of Aunt Ivey's emerald brooch, and she dared me to pilfer it from her bosom."

"Sounds like an exciting wedding."

"Well, no, actually. It was a very boring wedding. Except for Hollis."

"She is a great roommate," I agreed, "Though now I'll know to keep an eye on my jewelry."

"Her old man has a pretty tight grip, so I'm glad she has a roommate who lets her be herself."

I didn't know how to respond, so I just stood and shivered. Finally he said, "It would be a shame if that roommate froze to death. Let's get you back inside."

I hadn't expected him to be so attuned to my comfort. He took my hand and led me back downstairs into the apartment. By this time, the living room was empty.

"I guess Marshall is showing Hollis his etchings," Colton said with a wink. "At least now we can sit more comfortably." Still holding my hand, he led me to the couch. He sat down next to me, closer than I expected.

"How about you?" he probed. "Are your parents like Hol's? Or do they let you have fun?"

The truth was that, unlike the Lockes, my mother and father did not presume to have any say in whether I had fun. They never expressed doubt of my good sense and judgment. But I didn't tell Colton any of that, because I understood that the question was not really about my parents.

"I'm allowed to have fun," I said, because I understood that to be the right answer.

"Good." He ran a finger down my forearm, from my elbow to my wrist. "A pretty girl can't be well behaved all the time."

I reeled from the compliment. It had not occurred to me that I was the kind of girl Colton would come on to. I thought that only girls who could be carefree and flirtatious, like Hollis, were interesting to men.

My arm tingled at his touch and my skin stood at attention. The sensation traveled down my spine until I felt it between my legs. With his other hand, Colton touched my face and traced the contours of my collar bone. Then, his fingers went around to the nape of my neck and up into my hair. With his palm behind my head, he pulled my mouth to his. His kiss was strong and confident. He knew I did not want him to stop.

"Relax," he said softly, and I did as I was told. He moved his mouth to my neck and ears, then took my breast in his hand. I gripped his shoulders and felt his muscles. With one motion, he picked me up and carried me into his bedroom. He put me down on the bed and then rolled on top of me. I was excited by the weight of him, and by the way he slipped my clothes off as if with a magic wand. Then he covered my body with his own hot, naked skin. He slid a hand down my back and rested it under my hip. I had no idea how I wanted to be touched, but he knew it all. I felt lucky to be in the hands of an expert guide. It hurt a little, so I was sure we were doing it right.

* * *

On the Sunday drive back to Halstead, we were quiet. Hollis and I barely looked at each other, and several times I noticed Shelby checking on me in her rearview mirror. She didn't ask any questions, but she seemed concerned. Just as we arrived back at campus, she said, "I'm not driving you back there until you've gotten yourselves fitted for a diaphragm. But don't bother going to health services. They won't do anything for you. I'll get you the name of a doctor in town. He'll fix you up, no questions asked. Oh, and if he tries to offer you diet pills, say no. Those things will ruin your life. I've seen it happen."

7

WHEN I TOLD ELIZABETH ABOUT MY VISIT with Dr. Hauptman, she was as disappointed as I was. I expected her to have a whole new crop of ideas, but she too was defeated.

"Maybe when you least expect it, you'll hear from one of the registries," she said, but not with her usual optimism. "And . . ." I could hear some hesitation in her voice, "if you don't, maybe that's good news, of sorts. If your daughter isn't looking for you, it could mean that she really is happy, that her life feels complete. I know that's a hard thing to hear, but that's what you want, isn't it? For her not to need you?"

It was, indeed, a very hard thing to hear, even though it was a line I had recited, to myself and to others, many times. I wanted my daughter to need me. Not that I wished her to suffer. But I wanted her to feel that she couldn't be real or whole without knowing me. I didn't want to be the only one of us who felt off balance all the time, untethered and disoriented. I wanted her to be as anxious to find me as I was to find her.

Also, and this surprised me, I was sorry to be saying goodbye to Elizabeth. It was unlikely that I would have any reason to talk to her again. So far, she had been my only ally in my search. I had entrusted her with my most guarded secret, and she had willingly become my advocate. She was the first person with whom I had been honest, and she had not judged me harshly. And this was the irony of which I was becoming aware: I had only just met her, and yet I felt more authentic with her than I did with my dearest friends. I felt close to Elizabeth because there was no barrier, no artifice, between us. What's more, I had discovered that being genuine with Elizabeth had made me feel more connected not just to her but to myself, my true self. This feeling of "real-ness" was a byproduct of my search that I had not anticipated. It made it all the more painful for me to look at Joyce a few minutes later when she leaned into my doorframe. We had been in this office together for many years now, and she did not know where my mind was half the time.

"The Hatchers are here for their ten o'clock," she said quietly.

"Thanks," I said, "I'll head to the conference room."

"Do you want a preview?" she asked, stepping into the room and closing the door. "They were very chatty while I was making their coffee."

"Sure," I said. "What am I in for?"

"Nothing complicated. They want to make a change to their will. Apparently one son makes good money at a pharmaceutical company in New Jersey, and the other son owns the Midas shop on Route Fifteen."

"Please tell me I don't have to disinherit the guy who fixes my brakes."

"Not to worry," Joyce assured me. "It's the other way around. They don't want to give a lot of money to the son who doesn't need it."

This I could handle. I had a pat speech, prepared just for this circumstance, about the importance of communication. So long as they explicitly conveyed their love and admiration for the child who was receiving less, they could do whatever they wanted with their money. I even had stock language we could add to the will attesting to the great pride they took in both their children's accomplishments. I would also recommend that they demonstrate their affection by leaving some beloved personal items to the more successful child.

"Got it. Thanks, Joyce," I said as I stood and gathered my legal pad.

Joyce walked back to the reception desk, and I thought about how many hundreds of these conversations she and I had had. When it came to the business of the office, we understood each other well. We could talk in shorthand, always with trust in the other's good faith. And yet she did not really know me. She thought she did, but the person she knew was constructed, a performance. And I was now coming to understand just how exhausting that performance was. And sad. Not for Joyce, of course, but for me. I wasn't sure that she would be any better off if she knew my deepest secret, but I was starting to think that I would. My life might be easier, I thought, if I didn't have to work so hard to be the person that I thought others wanted me to be.

When I entered the conference room, my clients greeted me. I saw trust and respect in their faces. I put my mask back on.

8

As soon as we got back from Thanksgiving weekend, Hollis went to see Shelby's doctor and got herself a diaphragm.

"It was so easy, Bonnie," she told me. "You'll see."

"Mm hmm," I said. Unlike her, I had no plans to return to Yale.

"It's not technically legal, so Dr. Wormsbecher just wrote 'cramps' in my chart. He said, 'Not everyone needs to know everything,' which I thought was right on."

I did not go to see the doctor, despite Hollis's glowing recommendation, because I didn't see the need. I had enjoyed sex with Colton just fine, but I knew already I would enjoy sex more with someone I liked better. I was relieved to have gotten the awkwardness of my first sexual experience out of the way, and I was resolved to be a little choosier, a little more deliberate, with the next one. I would get to know my future partners better, and doing so would give me plenty of time to get a diaphragm. If this sounds like a defense I constructed when I didn't hear from Colton in the weeks after our trip to Connecticut, well, okay, perhaps it was.

We were plenty busy in the last few weeks of the semester. We had a lot of schoolwork to complete, and there was a lot happening in the world. I tried to convince Hollis to watch the draft lottery with me on the TV in the common room of Walton Hall, but she wasn't interested. There were eight of us there, sitting cross-legged on the carpet or sinking into the old chairs. I understood that one day this event would be History with a capital H, and I wanted to see it for myself. But others were there because their immediate futures would be affected by how a relative or fiancé fared in the drawing. We were quiet as we watched a gray-haired congressman in black-framed eyeglasses reach deep into a tall, clear canister. The cylinder held mostly air, but at the bottom were three hundred sixty-six blue plastic capsules, each one containing a piece of paper with a date on it. Each capsule foretold when the young men born on that date could expect to be called up to the armed forces. No wonder the capsules looked to me like cyanide pills, each one a personalized dose of doom. The congressman grasped a fistful of the blue pods, and a few slipped out of his fingers, granting reprieve for some lucky young men who would never know their good fortune. When one capsule remained in his palm, he handed it over to a man at a desk, who cracked it open like a fortune cookie and pulled out the tiny scroll.

"September fourteenth," he announced without emotion.

We looked around to see if anyone seemed affected by this most unlucky of birthdays. Did anyone have a brother or a boyfriend who would soon be a soldier? But instead we saw in each other's faces just the generalized heartbreak of watching our generation sacrificed for a war that seemed increasingly misguided and unwinnable. The scroll with the date was affixed to a large display board next to the number zero-zero-one. Then the pantomime was repeated. A capsule was selected; a date was read aloud; the paper was posted to the list. Eventually, the process became tedious. The birthdays were just dates; none had any particular meaning for us. Even the Congressman got bored after he repeated the exercise a few times, and he ceded the task to younger men. After about half an hour, the numbers got bigger and the chances of being called up got smaller. We began to put our coats on and drift back to the library, where we probably should have been all along.

★ ★ ★

Hollis seemed extra busy in those days, because she started getting regular phone calls from Marshall. Every Tuesday and Thursday at 4:30, we could expect to hear "Phone call for Hollis" wafting up from reception. Hollis would drop whatever she was doing and run down the steps in her socks. Sometimes I would be in the middle of a sentence, and she would run out like a kid jumping in a pool when the lifeguard blows the whistle. Usually her phone calls with Marshall made her happy, and she would delight in relaying news of his life that didn't interest me, like that he got into Columbia Law School or was planning a trip to Miami Beach over Christmas.

But occasionally the conversations would make her cranky. After one Thursday call, she burst into our room with only a minute to change into her skirt and head back downstairs to the dining hall.

"Honestly, this is getting ridiculous," she complained as she tried to wiggle her foot out of her jeans. "Who cares what we wear to dinner?"

She had a point. We didn't even look presentable. Our skirts were rumpled and stained by now. We no longer even bothered to put on a clean white shirt. We stayed in whatever top we were wearing that day, no matter how badly it clashed, in color or in mood, with our skirts. We wore snow boots instead of pumps.

"I just washed those jeans," she said. "They're a lot more sanitary than this filthy old dirndl."

I was sympathetic to her complaint that some of our Halstead traditions required energy that we were unlikely to have at the point in the term, when we were feeling the press of final papers and exams. But I liked our Thursday and Sunday dinners. I liked the linen tablecloths and china dishes. Sometimes there were even candelabras. All of this pomp and circumstance reminded me that I had taken a big step up in the world by coming to Halstead.

But we were met with scolding eyes when we entered the room, because we were a few minutes late. We had held up dinner for the other fifty-eight residents of Coffett House, and our faculty guests for the evening: Professor Chester Hollander, who taught history, and his wife Mariana, an adjunct in the music department. It happened that the two empty seats left were at their table. None of this improved Hollis's churlishness. She seemed impatient with the conversation that had begun before we arrived. Althea and her friend Evelyn had Professor Hollander's ear.

"Why shouldn't we be able to learn our own history?" Althea was asking, in a demanding, rhetorical sort of way.

"Of course," Professor Hollander responded, just a little defensively. "I'm not saying that African American history isn't valuable. All my students read Frederick Douglass."

"But there's more to African American history than just slavery," Althea insisted. "What about all the things we have to be proud of? Why can't there be courses on the Tuskegee Airmen and Jacob Lawrence?"

Professor Hollander smiled with just a hint of condescension.

"But, my dear, who would teach those courses? I don't imagine we could find a scholar of Halstead's caliber who is versed in African American history. It's not a real discipline." He thought that settled the matter.

"Well, it should be a real discipline," Evelyn said. "And African American literature, too. There should be courses in the English department on Richard Wright and Zora Neale Hurston."

"Oh my," said Mrs. Hollander. "A communist and a segregationist. That's who you think you should be reading?"

Professor Hollander put his hand gently on his wife's.

"Now, dear, I don't think we should dismiss artists because of their political leanings. Senator McCarthy taught us that lesson, didn't he? Perhaps we could tweak our syllabi a bit, but not at the expense of teaching the canon. An entire course devoted to Black history or Black writers just isn't feasible."

I was surprised to see Hollis jump into the conversation, because I had never heard her express an opinion on the topic of African American studies.

"I don't see why it would be so difficult," Hollis said. "Just make up your mind and do it."

Althea and Evelyn nodded, and Hollis continued.

"Aren't you worried that Halstead won't be relevant in five years? The world is changing, and we're not changing with it. It's not just the courses; it's everything. It's these sit-down dinners, and all these rules. Mrs. Hollander, can I ask you something?"

"Yes, of course," she said, but a little warily.

"At your house, don't you and Professor Hollander eat dinner whenever you feel like it?"

"I suppose," said Mrs. Hollander, not sure what she had admitted to.

"And you wear whatever you choose to your own table, don't you?"

"Yes, that's right."

Professor Hollander saw where Hollis was going with this.

"You don't enjoy these formal dinners?" he asked, not unsympathetically.

"I just don't see how any of this is preparing us for the real world. For one thing, the real world has men in it."

Ah, I thought. Now we have arrived at what is really on Hollis's mind.

"How can Halstead be preparing us for our futures if we aren't learning anything about how to interact with men? Not to mention that this diet of mashed potatoes and pot roast is probably cutting off the oxygen to our brains. Why can't we have a buffet, with healthy foods like fish and salad? Why can't we show up in the dining room when we feel like it? Any time between, say, six and eight?"

"Is that really what you think the big problem is?" Althea challenged Hollis. "The mashed potatoes? What about the war? I have a twenty-year-old brother who would like to finish college, not get shipped off to Vietnam."

"I'm sorry," said Professor Hollander. "That is a lot to carry." It seemed to me that he really meant it.

"Of course," Hollis said to Althea. "But it's all connected, don't you see? Supposedly Halstead is empowering us to change the world, but it's not even empowering us to choose our own clothes. It makes no sense."

Hollander turned to me.

"How do you feel about all these rituals?" He asked. "Do you agree with Miss Locke?"

"She has a point," I said. "And Althea and Evelyn too. Some changes would be good. But I don't mind all the rituals. They make me feel like I'm a part of something."

That weekend Hollis and her diaphragm went back to New Haven, and, for the first time, I realized how quiet Halstead was on the weekends. Throughout the fall, our lives had become progressively more constrained. There was no more sitting on the lawns or smoking on the roof now that the weather was cold, and the days were short. And then on Friday afternoons, the place really emptied out. Hollis had to wait in line to sign out downstairs at the reception desk, and I waited with her just to have something to do. Then I went to afternoon tea in the dining room, but the only people there were Diane Hendel, Crutch, and two seniors. I had never spoken to either of the seniors, but I knew the rumor that they were a couple. Diane and Crutch were sitting at a table set with china teacups and a platter of cookies. Crutch waved me over and passed me the platter.

"The Linzer tortes come from a bakery in town," she said, "but the oatmeal raisin I made myself. *Bon Appetit.*"

"Thank you," I said, and poured myself some tea.

"How are your studies going, dear?" she asked. The motherly concern was evident in her voice, as if she knew what the answer would be.

I told her that I was working harder than I ever had. In the next three weeks, I had to write two papers and take two exams.

"And your job in the dining room keeps you busy too, I'm sure," she said.

"Yeah, but I don't mind," I said. "It's just a few hours a week, with a start time and an end time. It forces me to be organized."

"I think that might be my problem," Diane said. "My job has no boundaries. I waste so much time talking."

I knew this to be true. Diane's assigned task was to go room to room every Wednesday and collect the sheets for laundering on Thursday. She never got out of our room in less than six minutes.

"It's a fun way to get to know everyone, but then I wonder where the time has gone. I guess that explains how I ended up here all weekend. I'm so behind in my European History reading."

"The biggest problem with my job," I said, "is that I'm still coming up short every month. I guess that's how I ended up here all weekend."

"Well," said Crutch, "good for you two. There's nothing wrong with a weekend spent applying yourself to your studies. One doesn't have to stir the pot all the time, you know."

Crutch wished us a productive weekend and departed. Almost as soon as she was gone, the two seniors joined me and Diane at the table.

"Hey," they said, "you're Diane, right? The sheet girl?"

Diane knew their names too, and made introductions all around. They were Robin and Meg.

"We thought she'd never leave," Meg said, reaching for the cookies.

"Who, Crutch?" I asked.

"Obviously."

"She's not so bad, is she?" I half-said, half-asked. I didn't want to offend Meg and Robin, but I also didn't want to trash poor Crutch, who, after all, had just baked us cookies.

"Not to you, I'm sure," said Meg.

"You're her type," Robin added.

"What do you mean?" I asked. I didn't mind Crutch—honestly, she reminded me of Mrs. Piggle Wiggle—but I was pretty sure it was not a compliment to be labeled her type.

"You're good girls, you know. Polite, studious," said Meg.

"White. Straight," Robin added.

We were quiet for a few seconds while that sank in. I had always known Crutch was old-fashioned, and it had never bothered me. Being old-fashioned was her job. But making students feel unwelcome if they didn't fit her image of a Halstead woman was most certainly not her job.

"She does make a mean oatmeal raisin," Robin said, as she reached for another. "I'll give her that."

"So." Meg was looking at me now. "Did I hear you say you were looking to make more money?"

"I probably should be looking harder, but I've been pretty busy."

"I have a great job," she said, "and we're going to need another person next semester."

"You have my full attention," I said.

"I work in the art supply store on campus. Have you seen it? It's in the basement of MacKesson, where all the studios are. Most of the time it's really quiet, and it's just you and stacks of supplies. But there's a big rush at the beginning of the year. We assemble kits based on the supply lists that the professors give us for all the art courses. We put the right paints with the right brushes and the right tools with the right clay."

Like Santa's elves, I thought, but had the presence of mind not to say.

"Then, when classes start, women come in to buy the kit for whatever art course they're in. That's fun too, because you get to meet all the pretentious Halstead drama queens, without actually having to talk to them. Then it gets quiet for a few weeks, and you don't see them again until they lose their loop tools or run out of blue."

"And you think there's an opening?" I asked.

"Yeah. Iris Hubbard—she's in Phipps House—is going to take classes at Harvard next semester, 'cause that's where her boyfriend is. I doubt we'll ever see her again. We'll need someone to take over her shifts on Tuesdays and Thursdays."

"Thanks so much," I said. "That sounds great."

"And if you're looking for something to do this weekend, we're playing basketball tomorrow at four, and we could always use more players. We're trying to get a league going, and this weekend we're playing a team from Mt. Holyoke. They're pretty good, so it should be a fun game."

"I've never played basketball except in PE," I said.

"Me neither," admitted Diane.

"It doesn't matter," Robin said. "At this point we just need people. Once the league takes off, we'll start recruiting girls who know how to play."

★　★　★

When Hollis came back just in time for curfew Sunday night, I was so happy to see her. The weekend had been productive, for sure, but also terribly lonely. The library felt deserted, which was good when I was writing my Religion paper, but lousy when I wanted to break for a Coke. Hollis was shocked when I told her I had been bored enough to show up for Meg and Robin's basketball game on Saturday afternoon.

"It was a lot of fun," I admitted, surprising the both of us. "I was only on the court for a few minutes, but I had a good time."

"If you say so," said Hollis, though she clearly found it hard to believe.

I told her about my potential new job in the art supply store, and she told me all about her weekend with Marshall.

"Of course I'm not looking for anything serious," she said. "We're just having fun. But I honestly think he's the most interesting person I've ever met." She was dying to share with me all the details she found intriguing about Marshall.

"Marshall went to a very progressive high school," I heard. And "Marshall's family belongs to a country club just for Jews." Hollis worked very hard to inject Marshall's name into every sentence for no other reason that she enjoyed saying it. I, in turn, enjoyed seeing her so animated, even though I didn't find her boyfriend's biography at all interesting. I was content to let her rattle on until she tired herself out before I asked, as casually as I could, if she had seen Colton over the weekend.

"Just in passing," she said, not entirely convincingly. "I didn't get a chance to interact with him."

"That's okay."

"I have an idea, Bonnie," she said, consolingly. "When we come back from vacation, let's find you some dates. Not with stuck-up jerks like Colton, but with guys like Marshall. Handsome, fun. Maybe we can even find one who's rich."

"Okay," I said. "That sounds good to me."

"No more spending your weekends with lesbians, okay?"

"Okay."

I don't recall much fun those last two weeks of the semester. Hollis was busy finishing that paper on *Tristram Shandy* and making a plan to see Marshall in Florida over the Christmas vacation. I had papers and tests of my own, so I spent my evenings in the library, away from the distraction of the dorm. I really wanted to do well in my first semester of college. I wanted my parents to be proud of me, and I wanted to prove to myself that I belonged at Halstead. Unlike Hollis, I would not be travelling over the break. I would be spending the two weeks on the farm, with my parents, where we would milk the cows and host relatives for Christmas dinner, and then milk the cows again.

Hollis hugged me goodbye before she left for Florida.

"I'm going to miss you." she said.

"No, you're not. You're going to be sipping mint juleps in Palm Beach and having secret rendezvous with your new boyfriend."

"True. But I'll still miss you."

"I'll miss you too," I said.

9

"This just came for you," Joyce said.

She handed me a manila envelope wrapped in clear packing tape. According to the return address, the package was from Theo. Two weeks had passed since our dinner, and this was the first I had heard from him. Inside the package, wrapped in a plastic bag, was an old school notebook with a black and white marbled cover. There was a handwritten note attached with a paper clip to the front cover. "My uncle kept journals," it said. "I hope you find what you're looking for."

I opened the notebook and saw that Dr. Hauptman was a meticulous diarist. The cover was labeled July 19 - September 20, 1970. His entries were short, but it seemed he rarely missed a day. He had florid, feminine handwriting, so different from the tight scribbles I usually have to decipher when I deal with doctors in insurance and malpractice claims. His charts probably looked like wedding invitations. My heart pounded, and I could feel my fingers sticking to the paper as I looked for August 31. Could I hope there would be something about me in its pages? Even though the day I gave birth loomed large in my own narrative, it might have been unremarkable to the author of this diary. But as soon as I found the entry for August 31, 1970, I recognized myself. Not by name—had he even known it? —but by description. Dr. Hauptman had written:

In the afternoon, there were three deliveries. Two were run-of-the-mill, but one was noteworthy—an unwed girl who got herself pregnant while at college. So much for the civilizing influence of education on the fairer sex. She had no intention of raising her little girl, so it was her good fortune that I knew just the right family through TE.

So, I realized, I had not been wrong when I perceived him as contemptuous. When he was my doctor, he didn't think I deserved to be a mother or a student, or even his patient, for that matter. I tried to focus on my search for clues. What was TE? I wondered. That was the important question. I read on, hoping for more information.

I do hope the new arrival will bring cheer to Maureen, as she has been trying for so long. She needs some joy to ease the recent loss of her father. Every ending is also a beginning. Today I did God's work on earth by bringing together a child who needs a mother and a mother who needs a child.

There it was. After all these fruitless weeks of looking, all this work and all the disappointments, I finally had one item of so-called identifying information that the gatekeepers hoped I would never get. I had a name. Maureen.

At home that night, I had more time to look for more clues in other entries. I hoped that I might learn something about Maureen and her family. I desperately wanted to find a surname, a town, an age. Anything that would help me figure out who and where she was. In page after page, I saw signs of the cold and imperious doctor I remembered from my first encounter with him. The genial octogenarian I had visited at Sunrise Gardens was nowhere to be seen. As unsettling and unpleasant as it was to visit Dr. Hauptman's interior life, it was at least validating to know that I had been right about him all along. And, I reminded myself, after all the humiliation

I had endured in losing my daughter, I could suffer a little more to find her. That's what I told myself as I read.

August 15, 1970

Alice scolded me this morning for working too hard. She is cross that we have yet to visit Ogunquit this summer. She doubts my devotion to her, just because my patients must always come first. She is a broken woman, since we lost E.

Then August 16:

Before eight a.m. I delivered twins to JeanAnn. A Cain and an Abel. What a surprise for us all. The poor dear tried to argue with me. 'My eldest is barely walking,' she said. 'How can I manage three under the age of two?' As if I were responsible for her plenitude. I assured her that the Lord would not have sent her more than she could bear.

And here is August 23:

Martha continues to dominate the younger nurses, to a degree that impedes their training. She is so eager to demonstrate her expertise and her devotion that she does not let them do their jobs. If she continues to behave this way, I will have to speak with her. She must not allow her ardor for me to affect the division of labor—Labor! —in the delivery room.

By the time I finished reading the notebook, I was miserable. I had spent hours steeped in my most painful memories. I had obtained one piece of useful information, but it too brought me nothing but pain. I knew my daughter's mother's name, but now I did not want to know it. For twenty years, I thought of myself and my daughter as two partners in a dyad, strangers who were incomplete without the other. But the truth was that she had a mother all along. I had a hole in my life, but she did not.

When I thought about this Maureen, I had to acknowledge that she knew my daughter in a way that I only imagined I did. It was unlikely, I realized, that my daughter felt lonely or pined for me, because she had been raised and loved by a doting mother. It was Maureen who had done the nurturing that I had been unable or unwilling to do. On those nights when I studied for exams, Maureen soothed my baby with lullabies. As the years passed and I wondered what my little girl looked like, Maureen picked out dresses that matched her eyes. On the birthdays when I kept a lonely vigil in my house, Maureen baked my daughter's favorite cake. She had been there to kiss the boo boos and mark the milestones. She was the woman my daughter had turned to when she fell off her bike or got her first period. I had imagined those moments a million times, but I had not been there. I had missed it all.

10

WHEN WE GOT BACK TO HALSTEAD for our second semester in January 1970, life was noticeably altered in Coffett Hall. The smallest difference was that Hollis's parents, frustrated by their inability to reach her whenever they wanted, had bought her a princess phone, which we plugged into the jack in our living room. But there were far bigger changes. The complaints against convention we voiced in casual conversations had finally been actualized on the Halstead campus. For one thing, Crutch was gone. Disappeared without a trace. No goodbye, no explanation. We were left entirely to our own devices in the dorms. Another change was that there were no more formal sit-down dinners. Most importantly, all the old parietal rules had been retired. There was no more sitting bells, no more signing out, no more counting the number of feet on the floor.

"Please tell me your parents let you catch up on sleep instead of tending to the cows," Hollis said our first night back.

"They did at first, but after a few days I had no excuse. My father is so overworked. All he talked about were the bulk tanks and vacuum powered pumps they're using in Iowa. He's ready to give up and turn our whole property into a pick-your-own raspberry farm. The least I could do was give him another set of hands."

★ ★ ★

This new, more relaxed Halstead was even better than the staid, traditional Halstead I had loved in the fall. Everyone felt it. It wasn't just that we were excited about the prospect of inviting men into our rooms—though certainly there were a few women for whom that was the most appealing result of the rule changes. I think what lifted our spirits was the idea that we were in control. We were being treated like adults—grownups with agency and good judgment—not like ingénues whose greatest assets were purity and malleability. We were hopeful about the future, or, at least, about our own futures.

Hollis and I didn't have any classes together that semester. I had scoured the bulletin for courses that would look good on a law school application. I registered for History of Western Thought because it was a prerequisite for American Constitutional Development, which was a 300-level course. I couldn't convince Hollis to take it with me. She was taking introductory courses in studio art and sociology. She also insisted she was going to sign up for a botany course, just so she could spend her winter days in the steamy greenhouse.

It was very cold that January. You felt it on the wind sweeping down from the Berkshires, on the brass doorknobs that stung your skin, and on your own frozen eyelashes. We moved from building to building as quickly as possible, with our heads tucked into our coats like turtles. Some days I found the cold invigorating, merely another challenge against which to prove myself.

The second Friday of the new semester, I awoke and saw out the window that Halstead was covered in a deep and pristine blanket of snow. Out in the hall I heard girls squealing and doors popping open like Champagne corks. The groundskeepers were already shoveling the walks, but I wasn't sure anyone would be going to class this morning. I myself was considering treating the day like a holiday. I was still in my flannel nightgown when I heard a knock on our door. I recognized the woman standing there in a wool pea coat, a fisherman's hat and mittens. Her name was Carol Fraser, and she was Althea's roommate. I had met her at the barbecue on the first day of school but spoken to her only a few times in the first semester. Now she was in my Modern Poetry class, and I was sure we would get to know each other better.

"Didn't you tell me you're from New Hampshire?" she asked.

"Uh huh," I said. I did not know I had made any impression at all on Carol, and I was flattered that she knew at least one thing about me.

"That's what I thought." She was very pleased with my answer. "So, you're probably the right person to ask. Do you have a sled?"

"Of course," I said, "but it's at home."

"You didn't bring it?"

I looked around my room trying to imagine where I would have stored a Radio Flyer among the books and record albums that occupied every corner.

"No, I'm afraid not."

"That's too bad," Carol said, clearly disappointed. "I was really excited to learn to sled."

The very phrase made me smile. You didn't "learn to sled" any more than you learned to eat. You just did it.

"You've never been sledding?" My incredulity was obvious.

"I'm from Corpus Christi," she explained. "No snow. No hills. No sledding."

"You don't need a real sled," I explained. "Any smooth, flat surface will do."

"How about a chemistry textbook?"

"You'll want something a little more durable, and preferably waterproof," I explained. "You know what would be perfect? Those new enamel trays in the dining room."

"I knew there was a good reason to go cafeteria style."

She was practically hopping with impatience as her eyes went up and down the length of my nightgown.

"Take off that Laura Ingalls Wilder get-up," she ordered, "and let's grab some trays. I need you to show me how it's done."

"Okay," I said. "Give me a few minutes. Do you mind if I ask Hollis to join us?"

"You mean Gidget?" she laughed. "No, I don't mind."

I had never heard Hollis referred to that way, but I could see why.

"That's what you call her?" I asked.

"That's what everyone calls her. Didn't you know?"

I rapped on Hollis's bedroom door, and considered teasing her with, "Good morning, Gidget." There was no answer, and I took this as a sign that she was still sleeping. I didn't know if she would want to be awakened for the sake of sledding.

"Hollis? Can I come in?" I called softly.

There was still no answer, so I pushed the door open slowly. Hollis was lying in bed, but she was clearly awake. She was still and did not acknowledge me. Her eyes were open but unfocused. She looked like a woman exhausted from a night of keeping vigil against vampires.

"Hollis," I said tentatively. "Do you want to play in the snow?"

She didn't answer.

"Hollis?" I asked again, "are you okay?"

She didn't even turn her head to look at me.

"No, I don't think so," she said, barely audible. "I don't feel great."

I wasn't surprised to hear this. Now that Crutch was gone, there had been a near constant smell of weed on the second floor. I knew Hollis had been hanging out with the girls who lived there.

"Maybe you need a little break from socializing with Mary and Jane," I suggested. "A short one."

"No, that isn't it," she said. She sounded more upset than ill.

"Hollis?" I couldn't decide how worried I should be. "Please tell me what's going on."

She shook her head and started to cry.

"I'm so scared, Bonnie," she said, and finally looked at me. Her eyes were red with crying. "I was supposed to have my period by now. I wasn't paying close attention, but I realized it had been awhile. So I checked the calendar and now I realize I've missed two, not just one."

Hollis was always so blithe and unflappable. I had never seen her, or even imagined her, so distraught. I called out an excuse to Carol—something fearsome and contagious like a stomach bug or lice—and then sat on the edge of Hollis's bed.

"What am I going to do?" she said softly. "I can't go home. I can't tell my parents."

I did not answer her, because I was no longer thinking about her. I was thinking about myself, and about a fact that I had not yet shared with her. I too had expected my period while I was home in December, and it had not come. Until this moment I had been trying to convince myself it was a mere irregularity. College was a big transition, I told myself. We were under a lot of stress. Besides, I thought, I could not possibly be pregnant just when my life was brimming with possibilities. Not me, the cautious one. And not with him—aloof, conceited Colton. I had already determined that our trip to New Haven seven weeks earlier would be filed away in my mind as one of those life experiences that would be fodder for future reflection. It would be formative, sure, but only in the sense that it would shape the way I thought about sex and love and partnership. It would not in itself be consequential. It would have no meaning other than what I chose to assign it. That's what I had decided, and, by sheer will, I would make it so. But now I was realizing that if an unwanted pregnancy could happen to Hollis, a girl whom the angels had anointed with a charmed life, then certainly it could happen to me.

Reluctantly, I told Hollis the truth, and we agreed that we would go to health services together for a test. We were able to get appointments later that afternoon, despite the snow.

When I met Dr. Edelbaum, I wasn't sure why Shelby had warned us away from him. He was calm and businesslike as he instructed me in the unladylike art of providing a urine sample. He asked me some questions about when my last period began and how I was feeling. When I answered that it had been eight weeks and that I was feeling fine, he nodded and wrote this down on my chart. I waited, hoping he would assure me that my answers suggested pregnancy was unlikely. But he did not. I began to explain that, according to my mother, she had tried to get pregnant for two years before I came along, and for three years after. I said this as if Dr. Edelbaum were the arbiter of my fate and I had merely to sway him to my favor. If only I could convince him that we Kollers were not fertile women, then he would agree that I was not pregnant.

"Everyone is different," he said, almost apologizing that he could not be more helpful.

I sensed that there was more he wanted to say, that he was resisting the urge to ask more questions or offer more observations. I did not know if I wanted to hear his thoughts, so I was grateful that he kept them to himself.

"How long until the results come back?" I asked.

"A few days," he said. "We'll send this off to the hospital, and they'll let us know when they have an answer."

"A few days?" I was sure he could hear the panic in my voice. He let me stew in my own distress for a minute before he finally said what he had probably wanted to say all along.

"It isn't worth it, is it?"

For a second, I thought he expected me to answer, but he didn't.

"Why don't you girls understand? All this fun has consequences."

I didn't know what to say. I had never in my life been marked as irresponsible. I had never been seen as anything but mature and capable.

"I'm sorry," I said weakly, because I didn't know else to say. I didn't know how to redeem myself in Dr. Edelbaum's eyes.

"You don't need to apologize," he said. "It's not my life you're toying with. It's yours. That's what I want you to see."

He put down his chart and looked at me.

"Now," he said, "Let's assume you got away with it this time. Do you want to talk about how to protect yourself in the future?"

I told him I didn't think that would be necessary, because I was too ashamed to say anything else.

"Okay," he said, resigned and perhaps disappointed. "In a pinch you can always try a grape."

"A grape?" I asked. Was he testing me to see how stupid I was?

"Yes," he said. "When held firmly between the knees, it prevents pregnancy every time."

When Hollis and I walked back to Coffett, she asked if I had gotten a lecture too.

"Not a lecture, exactly," I said, "but some high-handed advice, for sure."

"Dr. Fuddy Duddy told me I should keep my head in my books and my feet on the floor."

I was quiet. I admired Hollis for not letting Edelbaum get under her skin. But I didn't see the point in ridiculing him. Yes, he was smug. But he could afford to be smug because he wasn't the one whose future was in jeopardy. He wasn't the one who would pay the price for the sexual revolution. It wouldn't be Colton or Marshall, either. They could continue to focus on their classes, their weekends, and how great their lives were going to be when they graduated. They were not thinking about how a cup of pee on its way to a hospital lab would upend their plans to be New York bankers or tax attorneys. The people paying the price would be Hollis and me. We were the ones trapped on the Titanic, begging in futility to be taken back to shore.

11

Toward the end of May, I decided to check in with Joyce.

"How is your workload?" I asked. "Do you need more? Less?"

"I wouldn't mind a little more," she said. "I'm subscribing to the 'keep yourself busy' approach."

"Tried and true," I said. I had been utilizing that method myself for twenty years, though I had never admitted it to Joyce.

"Actually," she said, "I made a plan for this weekend, and I was hoping you could do it with me."

"Anything," I said. We were back on comfortable ground, where I showed my devotion to her through actions, if not honesty.

"I'm going with my sewing group to see the AIDS quilt. Some of the panels will be at Dartmouth for a weekend. We thought it would be a good activity to do together, but I'd feel better if you were there too."

I understood Joyce's impulse to wrap herself in the world's largest blanket, itself a testament to absence and loss. Of course I agreed to go.

The exhibit took place in the Dartmouth hockey arena at the end of May. There were a lot of people inside, probably almost a hundred. But the building was as large as an airplane hangar, so the cavern felt empty. We may as well have been the only ones there. There were sections of quilt hung on the walls, panels draped over the seats, and squares spread out on the basin floor.

There was color everywhere, a vibrant collage of fabric, photos and words. Each square was a work of art, commemorating a single life, a person, as remembered by his loved ones. We walked the perimeter of the rink, reading names and dates, usually a lifespan of a mere twenty or thirty years. And there were images too, tributes to the tastes and talents of every lost son: flowers, paintbrushes, rainbows, crosses, tuxedos, guitars, handprints, ice cream cones, photos, red hearts, pink triangles, military medals, maps, flags, pets, butterflies. Celebrations of lives destroyed.

Joyce took my arm.

"How are you holding up?" I asked softly.

"I can't explain it, Bonnie," Joyce said. "But I feel like I belong here, like I'm finally with my people."

I gave Joyce's arm a squeeze, because I understood. I knew how people talked about Amber, in the last few years of her life—like she was too much trouble, not worth her mother's love. It was the same way some people talked about the men commemorated in this quilt. People said they were a blight, that they had brought this plague on themselves and deserved their own deaths. And I too had been told, by everyone at St. Gabriel's, that I shouldn't think about or care about my daughter once I gave her up. They said I should "get on with my life." Said I shouldn't "throw good money after bad." But that's not how motherhood works. Your attachment to your children can't be turned off with a switch. When they're gone, you love them even more.

When we got back to Hopkins, I knew it was time to tell Joyce that I too knew something of the pain and emptiness of having— but not having—a child. I told Joyce about the daughter I gave up and about my recent efforts to locate her. I told her that I knew the first name of the woman who adopted her.

"But then I stopped looking, because what would she want with me? She already has a mother."

I was just a vestigial organ, useless as a spleen.

Joyce took it all in without expression.

"I don't know about that, Bonnie," she said. "Didn't you have two grandmothers? Didn't you love them both? My father has two sisters, and I love both my aunts. Why shouldn't a person be able to love two mothers?"

I don't know which I found more beneficial: the compassion in Joyce's response or the sheer logic.

"I want to help you find your daughter," she said. "It's important to me. I don't have any chance of seeing my daughter ever again,"— her voice cracked— "but you do. We have to make the most of that chance."

This was the message from the quilt we had just seen, wasn't it? No one should ever bear the pain of losing a child forever unless they absolutely have to, unless there is no other option.

Joyce made me lay out what I knew so far so that we could devise a plan. We scanned our memories for any Maureens we might have met. The branch manager at the bank in downtown Hopkins was named Maureen, she offered. And the woman who ran the historical society in Canaan. Or was she Maura? I had asked Theo if he recognized the name Maureen, but he claimed not to know his uncle's social circle.

Joyce and I considered looking at old wedding announcements. Maybe we could find a Maureen who got married a few years before I gave birth. But we didn't know how many years. Dr. Hauptman said they had been trying for "so long." Was that a year, five years? We knew that the Maureen I sought had lost her father not long before August, 1970. We might have better luck looking for an obituary of Maureen's father. Yes, we decided, that would be the way to tackle this. We would look at each and every day's death announcements in the Monitor and the Union Leader, starting in August 1970 and going backwards, until I found a man whose survivors included a daughter named Maureen.

"I'm almost there," I told my daughter silently that night. "I haven't given up after all, and I'm going to find you. No matter what it takes."

★ ★ ★

We did all our searching in the state-of-the-art university library in Durham. Starting that weekend, we drove there every Saturday and scoured every newspaper, determined to find what we wanted. The library had two microfiche machines, side by side, in a large, airy room that overlooked the campus. The building was cool and deserted in summer, and there was no one to shush us when Joyce would call out her discoveries.

"Look at this. Sally and Bevins McCraw were married for seventy-seven years. They died the same week. Isn't that amazing?" or "Have you ever heard of Edna Jones? She was Miss New Hampshire in 1936." Sometimes she would go quiet and teary, and I assumed she was reading about a young person lost to accident or illness. But her energy never flagged, and she never lost interest.

We were able to get through about a month's worth of obituaries on each visit. Our third Saturday of searching we found a notice for a Maureen, described as a "devoted homemaker," who died in July 1969. The next week we found an obituary that listed a Maureen as the surviving mother of a beloved high school track coach.

"I feel like we're getting closer," Joyce said. "Isn't this exciting?"

I agreed that it was exciting, but added that it was also, at the same time, dull.

"I don't think it's dull," Joyce objected. "Especially now that we're homing in."

I didn't know how seriously Joyce meant this comment.

"You know," I said tentatively, "finding one Maureen, or even two Maureens, doesn't mean we're any closer to finding the Maureen we're looking for, right? They're not connected."

"Oh, Bonnie," Joyce said with an exaggerated sigh, "sometimes I think you don't understand the world at all."

12

I am not sure how Hollis and I got through those four long days waiting to hear back from health services. We mostly kept to ourselves, as I recall. The new changes in the dorms made it easier to come and go without a lot of interaction. We did not have to endure prolonged sit-down dinners with our classmates. Instead, we could show up in the dining room as soon as it opened, fill our plates from the buffet, and be done in fifteen minutes. I told myself that going to classes would be a good distraction and would make the time pass more quickly. But I couldn't concentrate on anything my professors were saying. It took all my effort just to contain my own fear and hysteria. There was nothing left over for learning.

During that time, Hollis and I spoke of little else when we were alone. Sometimes we recited optimistic platitudes, reminding each other that it's always darkest just before dawn and that what doesn't kill us makes us stronger. We told ourselves that this was just a scare so we would be more careful next time. Sometimes we spoke in self-punishing reprimands, lamenting our doom. I was grateful, at least, that in all our conversations, Hollis and I were allies, facing the same relief or the same dread. We always assumed we would face the same fate. That is why we were neither shocked nor surprised when both our tests came back positive. We had, by that time, convinced ourselves that this synchronicity was the only possible outcome.

"Does this mean I'm going to marry Marshall?" Hollis asked me. She said it as if marriage might be something that happened automatically, without human agency.

"Is that what you want?" I asked. But it was a rhetorical question. If she really wanted to marry Marshall, she wouldn't be speaking with the affect of a person stunned into paralysis by a blow to the head. "I'm certainly not going to marry Colton."

I shuddered at the picture of myself tethered to him for a lifetime of domestic tedium. I could practically hear the screams of a bellowing infant pinching on my hip and clawing at my neck. I could not do it, I thought. I couldn't bear to watch my classmates go out into a world blossoming with opportunity, while I stayed behind like Persephone trapped in the underworld.

"No, of course not," Hollis agreed.

We were silent for a moment, each of us waiting for the other to say what we both knew.

"I want an abortion," I finally said. "I'm not having a baby."

Once the word had been uttered, there was no going back to pretending there was any other option.

"I know," she said. "You're right. I'll talk to Marshall and see if he knows what to do. And you'll find out if Colton has any ideas."

"I wasn't planning to tell him," I said.

"Oh, Bonnie, you have to." I was surprised that she was so insistent. "Marshall and I can't keep a secret like that. It's too much."

★ ★ ★

I knew she was right that I should call Colton. He was older and better connected than I was, and he might have good ideas of what to do. How lucky, I thought drily, that Hollis's parents had given us that princess phone for this purpose.

When I reached Colton, he sounded wary, but not unfriendly. He was trying to gauge if the purpose of this call was to reprimand him for his disappearance or to schedule more sex. He wanted to foreclose the former while remaining open to the latter.

"How are things, Bonnie?"

I wasn't going to draw this out with small talk.

"Things aren't great, Colton," I said seriously. "There's something I need to tell you."

He didn't respond, though he must have had some idea by now, if only from the palpable fear in my voice, where this call was going.

"I went to health services a few days ago," I continued. I was ready for him to jump in with an expression of concern, an apology, a solution. The phrase "health services" could have meant only one thing, and he knew it.

"If you have the clap, you didn't get it from me," he said glibly.

I was silent, and he seemed to understand that his joke was not going to make the problem go away.

"Colton," I said eventually, and gave him one last chance to say something helpful. But he was going to make me spell it out for him.

"I'm pregnant," I finally said.

Now it was his chance to be silent. I heard him inhale.

"And you think it's mine?" he asked.

That caught me off guard. I had assumed Colton would at least acknowledge some responsibility, though I was under no illusion that he would respond kindly or generously. I did not expect his first response to be an attempt to deny the origin of this pregnancy. Did he believe I had slept with so many men that I couldn't keep track of them all? And to think that I had once been attracted to him because he had seemed to understand me. In our one evening together, he had not suggested that I needed to be what the Crutches of the world considered a "good girl" in order to be a good person. But it was clear now that he didn't know me at all.

"I'm absolutely sure it's yours," I said, getting angry.

I waited for him to process this.

"Bonnie," he said, sounding testy, "you can't do this to me now. You just can't."

The very idea that *I* was doing something to *him*, and not the other way around, made me reel, first with anger at him, then with fury at myself. Why had I ever thought this phone call—this expensive phone call—would have any other outcome?

"Sorry to inconvenience you," I said, confident that my sarcasm would jolt him into reality.

"Do you have any idea what kind of stress I'm under?" he asked. "Do you even watch the news?"

"What are you are talking about?" I asked impatiently. Was he trying to tell me that he had been in the news? Was there something I was supposed to know?

"I'm talking about my draft number," he said. "Don't you know about the lottery?" He was getting even more worked up. "*Seven,*" he said accusatorily, as if this low draw could only be the result of witchcraft. "My draft number is *seven.*"

I wasn't unsympathetic, and for a moment I was even hopeful. Perhaps he would see the parallel in our situations. We both had plans for our lives. We were both afraid that our plans would be snuffed out, his by an unpopular war, mine by an unwanted pregnancy.

"I'm sorry," I said. "You must be very worried."

"That's right," he said, and I thought we were making progress. "So you see?" he continued. "Your problems are pretty small potatoes."

That was when I made up my mind not to waste any more time on Colton Bingham.

I wished him luck, and I actually meant it. I did not want to see him punished with a tour in Vietnam. I had no illusion that I would be better off if Colton were killed in action. Besides, I didn't really think the army wanted a guy his age. The guys in real danger were younger, guys like my classmate Roger Tanzi.

"Thank you," he said, more gently than I expected. "You're a bright girl, Bonnie. You'll figure out how to take care of yourself. Right now the most important thing is to get this asshole Nixon out of office."

★ ★ ★

Hollis suggested that perhaps Dr. Wormsbecher, the doctor in town who prescribed her diaphragm, would be able to help us.

"He wasn't self-righteous or condescending like the Halstead doctor who did our tests," she said. "He's more with-it."

Hollis was able to get an appointment quickly, because she was already considered a patient of his. I tagged along, hoping I could avail myself of his services too. When he called her name off his clipboard in the waiting room, he sounded like he was hearing it for the first time. But when she stood up and said, "That's me," he smiled with recognition.

"So nice to see you again, Miss Locke," he said, as he gestured toward the exam room.

"Is it okay if my friend Bonnie comes in with me?" she asked him.

"Of course," he said. "You can invite whomever you want."

I was grateful to hear those words, because I had not liked being alone with Dr. Edelbaum back on campus. I had wished that Hollis and I could have faced him together, because I was sure she would have shut down his snide advice.

Hollis sat on the exam table, and I stood.

"How can I help you?" he asked. "I understand you told my receptionist it was urgent."

"Well," Hollis said, "I know you prescribed a diaphragm, and I used it. But, I guess, either I didn't use it right, or it was too late, or something."

He nodded without looking either of us in the eye, which led us to believe he understood. "So, you're concerned you might be pregnant?"

Hollis was right about him. He sounded professional, not judgmental, like he was describing a medical condition, not a divine punishment. He even seemed sympathetic. We explained that we both already had the results of the tests. He gestured for me to sit down next to Hollis.

"The thing is," she continued, "we can't be pregnant. We just can't. We're in school, and we need to finish."

"You must be very frightened," he said gently, "but you don't need to be. I am here to help."

"Thank you," said Hollis, and I heard her voice crack.

"Let me get some more information," he said, "and I'll determine what the best procedure is." Then he asked her some questions that were familiar to us by now. When did your last menstrual period begin? Do you have any family history of anemia?

He marked Hollis's answers in her chart, and then he turned to me.

"I can help you too," he said kindly. "Let's figure out how far along you are."

"I know exactly when it happened," I said, and I probably sounded strangely eager. I was so grateful to him that I wanted to be the best, most cooperative patient he had ever tended. "There's only one day it could be. November twenty-first."

Dr. Wormsbecher smiled ever so slightly.

"That's very helpful," he said. "And was that your first time?"

He hadn't asked Hollis that, I noted. But I answered his question.

"Sometimes a young man tells a girl she can't get pregnant her first time. It's a terrible trick." He looked almost ashamed on Colton's behalf. "We calculate the weeks from your last period, though, not from the date of sexual intercourse. Can you tell me when you last menstruated?"

That I couldn't remember. Freshman fall was a busy time, and by now it had all blurred together. It felt so far away that it was hard to believe it had just happened. He stepped behind the exam table to reach a stethoscope. I was relieved that I didn't have to look at him when I gave my failing answer.

"I'm afraid I don't know," I said, "but I am sure about the twenty-first."

"There is a way a doctor can tell," he said, and suddenly he reached from behind me and slid his arm inside my blouse, inside my bra. He moved his hand around my breast for a second in a way that felt more sexual than clinical. I was too shocked to breathe, to move, or to speak. I looked over at Hollis. Had she seen it? It had happened in her periphery, and I couldn't be sure. I turned my head around to look at Dr. Wormsbecher. I expected to see a guilty leer on his face, but he looked placid as he made more notes on his clipboard. Perhaps it hadn't happened at all. But it had, I was sure.

"You're about seven weeks," he said, as if he had not just violated me. "A little farther along than Miss Locke. We'd better get you in quickly."

Now my heart was racing, and my hands were sticking to the exam table.

"Come back tonight at eight o'clock, and bring three hundred dollars with you. And you'll have to come alone. I can't take the risk of having you both here. The reception area will be dark, but I will let you in the back door. Don't eat or drink anything between now and then. Assuming everything goes smoothly, Miss Locke can come at the same time tomorrow night."

★ ★ ★

Back in our room that afternoon, Hollis tried to give me 300 dollars.

"I'm not going back there," I said.

"Why not?"

So she hadn't seen it. Would she believe me when I told her? I hesitated, because I realized that Wormsbecher's actions had been a test, of sorts, and that I had failed. He wanted to know if I would stand up for myself—cry out, bite his arm, run from the room. Or would I just sit there, frozen into compliance? He wanted to know what kind of mark I would be, and I had made it clear I was the easiest kind. I braced myself for Hollis's reaction to my weakness. But instead she put her arms around me.

"Oh, Bonnie, I'm so sorry," she said. "I should never have brought you there. It's my fault. I'm the idiot who thought he could be trusted. I won't let you go first ever again," she promised.

We did not call the doctor to tell him I wouldn't be coming, and I don't know how long he waited. For all I know, he is still in his office, waiting.

13

JOYCE AND I GOT MORE EFFICIENT AS the summer went on. Loading the microfiche into the machines was belabored, but scanning the page for names took almost no time at all. By July, we could get through two months at a sitting. It felt like progress, but it was hard to know. I often thought of that famous math problem where you cross the street by repeatedly walking half the remaining distance. You are always getting closer, but you never actually arrive. By the end of July, we began to worry that we had wasted all our summer weekends. I had not expected to be walking into this building yet again on the first Saturday in August. Even Joyce had none of her usual optimism. The library's air conditioning was its sole consolation. We sat down at the monitors and I tried to focus. I was practically drifting off to sleep when I heard Joyce exclaiming, almost screeching, "Oh my God! I think this is it!" I swiveled in my chair and rolled over to her side, then leaned in to read in the April 10, 1969, edition of the Manchester Union Leader:

John Edwards Longstreet, 72, of Concord died Sunday after a brief illness. John served in WWI, then matriculated at Bowdoin College. Upon his graduation in 1923, he became an executive in the Boston and Maine Railroad. John served as Lieutenant Governor from 1953 to 1957 before resuming his career at B&M. He is survived by his loving wife of thirty-nine years, Ginny, a son Paul (Jane) of

Durham, and a daughter Maureen (Carter) of Essex, VT, as well
as two grandchildren. The funeral will be Saturday at 1:00pm at
Trinity Episcopal Church.

Joyce and I leaned back in our chairs and were quiet for a moment. After months of learning nothing, had we finally found what we were looking for? I went through it in my head one more time. Here was a married woman named Maureen, who had lost her father less than two years before my daughter was born. Perhaps, I thought, the "TE" in Hauptman's diary that I couldn't identify was Trinity Episcopal. Theo had told me that his uncle probably placed babies through his church. It made perfect sense that this Maureen and Carter could have adopted my daughter in August of the next year. This finally had to be it.

I'm almost there, sweet girl, I said silently, with a mixture of anticipation and relief. I even allowed myself some internal crowing over the reward for our persistence. How's that for *identifying infor-mation?* I thought.

And then, over the next two days, I felt more and more unsettled. For five months, my search had gone slowly, with false starts and dead ends. But now, random clues had come together and it was going too quickly. Joyce and I agreed that she would go to the Bureau of Vital Records first thing Monday morning—I couldn't face that place again—where she would, hopefully, get a copy of Maureen Longstreet's marriage certificate. If she could accomplish this, then we would know my daughter's family name. But I was consumed with doubt about whether the joyful reunion I longed for was a realistic possibility. Maybe, I now worried, the girl I wanted to meet didn't even know she was adopted. I had had no sign from the registries that she wanted contact with me. Worse, what if she knew she was adopted but refused to see me? Or wanted to meet me only to tell me that I meant nothing to her? Not knowing her had allowed me the freedom to imagine that our reunion would be perfect. But now that I was getting closer to her, I was terrified that she would be angry with me. I imagined her punishing me for finding and disturbing her, or maybe for having waited so long to look. And perhaps she would never forgive me for the original sin of giving her up.

These were the fears that caused my hand to shake on Monday afternoon when Joyce handed me a photocopy of the marriage certificate of Maureen Longstreet and one Carter Farnsworth, who had wed in June 1967. What were the chances, I wondered, that they still lived in Essex all these years later? Would I find them ninety miles up the interstate, or was this document merely another ticket to enter another rabbit hole? I called the operator in Essex, who found a Carter and Maureen Farnsworth nearby in Williston. In less than a minute, I knew their address and phone number. Joyce had the idea, since I had no meetings that afternoon, that we should drive up there, just to see the house.

But I was suddenly paralyzed. I was even hesitant, after all these months of hungering for information, to learn my daughter's given name. Once I knew it, I realized I could no longer think of her as mine. She belonged to the couple in the photo. They had named her and formed her. She might be exactly like them, and nothing like me. In addition to those fears, there was one last worry on my mind. My daughter might be happy to meet me, only to decide, once she got a good look at my life, that I had made the wrong choice. All the things I was proud of—my loyal clients, my cozy house—might seem paltry to her, poor compensation for the sacrifice of relinquishing her. *This?* she would say to me with scorn, *You gave me up for this?*

I was trying to figure out how to explain these fears to Joyce, when she handed me a piece of scratch paper with one word written on it: Stephanie.

"How did you get this?" I asked, baffled.

"It was easy," she said. "I called their number and got the answering machine. You know, 'You have reached . . .' and it says all their names."

★ ★ ★

Stephanie Farnsworth. My daughter was Stephanie Farnsworth, and she lived ninety minutes northwest of me. Yet for over a week, believe it or not, I sat in my paralysis. I was terrified that I would ruin everything in our very first interaction. I didn't want to ambush her. I wanted to approach her cautiously, sensitively. And I wanted to give her an out, a way to say you've got the wrong girl, if that's what she wanted to say. Also, I perseverated over whether I should go around her family or through them. Would they treat me like a poacher or like a long-lost friend?

Eventually, I crafted a letter that was intended to be lawyerly but not intimidating. At Joyce's suggestion, I wrote it as if it were from Lars, not from me. The letter claimed that he was writing "on behalf of a woman who gave birth to, and subsequently relinquished, an infant girl in 1970." Nowhere did it say my name, only that the "aforementioned woman" desired to make contact with the relinquished girl. I didn't even want Stephanie to know that my search had homed in on her, so the letter implied that many girls born in New Hampshire in her birth month were receiving the same letter. Finally, it asked Stephanie to contact its author if she "had any information" that would help him identify the girl in question. Most importantly, the letter promised that this would be the only correspondence she would receive, and that if she had no pertinent information, she could rest assured that Lars "would respect her privacy and never contact her again."

I mailed the letter and waited.

14

Once I accepted that Dr. Wormsbecher wasn't an option, I was consumed with fear about what would happen to me. In my classes, I heard the voices of my professor and my classmates, but every discussion sounded like a medieval trial. No matter the topic of the course, I imagined that I stood accused of apostasy and that they were the jurists who would soon find me guilty. I would be excommunicated from Halstead.

I contemplated confessing my pregnancy to my parents. They had always given me unconditional love. But, in fact, I had never tested its limits. I had been an ideal daughter, or so they told me. I had worked hard in school and helped out on the farm. I had never rebelled or acted out, so I didn't know if they could love a daughter who failed at college, the scorned unwed mother of a child with no future. I saw myself a year from now, back home with my parents, slave to a baby, no different from the Holsteins we valued for their milk. The friends I'd made here wouldn't even remember me.

Occasionally I would get called on in class, and I would crumple.

"Bonnie," I heard one day in Western Thought, "what do you think about our question of the day?"

All the women in the class were looking at me, and I saw sympathy in their faces. Everyone feels for the person being singled out by the professor. But the pity of my classmates only served to confirm my predicament. "Poor Bonnie," they would all be thinking soon enough. "She was one of us for a while, but then she couldn't cut it. I wonder what happened to her."

"I'm sorry," I stammered. "Can you call on someone else?"

The professor looked at me for a moment, trying to assess whether I was demurring because I was unprepared, or because I was truly in distress.

"Ladies," he said, addressing the class, "I know it's early in the semester, and I know you're very busy planning your next protest, but try not to fall behind in this class. We have a lot of reading to get through." And then, to my relief, he moved on and looked at someone else.

"How about you, Barbara. What do you think was Augustine's main purpose in writing his *Confessions*?"

When class ended, I couldn't get out of there fast enough. The heat in the lecture hall felt oppressive, and I naively believed that the cold outside air would relieve me. But it did not. When I walked against the wind to my new job in the art supply store, I was still pregnant. This is what I was just beginning to understand. This thing inside me, though smaller than a pea, was big enough to crush me. Though it sat deep inside me, it trapped me like a wall of prison bars.

One small blessing was that the store was quiet that day. Most of the work for the semester had to be done in the first week of classes. We assembled the kits according to the supply list for each art class, and we sold the kits as fast as we could make them. But now we were in a lull, when the only girls who came in were ones who made last minute changes to their schedules and ones who had discovered a mistake in their supplies.

I tried to get some reading done, but it was hard to concentrate. Why couldn't I make my period appear? I even held a tube of red paint and wondered if I could use a dab of it to fool the universe into believing I had miscarried. I was beginning to fear my own descent into irrationality when a customer walked in. Her name was Ingrid, and I recognized her only because she was a tall, striking presence on campus. When most of her friends had traded in their plaid Villager skirts for blue jeans, Ingrid had opted for black turtleneck sweaters and black slacks. Most of us had completely given up on makeup since we started Halstead, but Ingrid had doubled down on the lipstick, transitioning from a soft, natural pink to a shocking red. She was surprisingly chatty, given that she was a bit of a campus celebrity, and I was an anonymous freshman.

"Can you believe I talked my way into Painting 206?"

She slapped the change-of-course form, signed by the dean, onto the counter. This wasn't actually necessary, as students were allowed to buy whatever they wanted from the store. They didn't have to prove to me what courses they were in.

"I thought the cap was strict," I said.

"I thought so too," she said, "but it turns out that I am very persuasive."

"All the kits I assembled have been sold," I said. "I'm sorry, but it will take me a few minutes to put another one together."

"I'm not in a rush," she said, and waved her hand. "I can wait."

I turned to the shelves and began collecting paints and brushes. My back was to Ingrid, but I had the sense she was watching me. When I turned around and handed her the kit, she looked startled.

"Are you okay?" she asked.

"I'm fine," I said weakly.

"That's not what it looks like to me."

"Really. I'll be okay."

"If you say so."

She took out her checkbook. Without looking up at me, she said, "You're Hollis's roommate, aren't you?"

I wasn't surprised that Ingrid knew who Hollis was, but I was surprised that she recognized me.

"Yes," I said. "I'm Bonnie."

"Bonnie," she repeated. "I'm Ingrid. So, how is Hollis? I haven't seen her yet since we got back."

There was something purposeful in her voice.

"She's okay," I said, noncommittally.

"Really? I heard she had been AWOL for a few days, not coming to classes."

"She's just, you know, taking it easy." Perhaps Ingrid could hear a little defensiveness, a little obfuscation in my voice.

"It's okay with me," she said. "We all need a break from the man sometimes. But if she wants to talk, all the information is right there on my check." She ripped it out of the book and handed it to me.

I should not have been surprised when I returned to Coffett after my shift and found both Ingrid and Marcia in my room, talking to Hollis. The three of them stared at me when I walked in. Ingrid was the first to speak.

"I knew something was wrong. You went to that son-of-a-bitch Wormsbecher."

"You should have come to me first," said Marcia. "I could have warned you."

"Well, it's too late now," I said. "And it doesn't matter. I'm okay, I guess."

Their admonitions, in a funny way, made me feel better. They confirmed that I was right not to have gone back.

"Look," Ingrid said, "Now that I know what's going on, I want to help."

"Thank you," Hollis said. "Do you know someone?" She sounded more hopeful than I had heard her in days.

"Let's just say I have some experience in this department. It's a well-known secret that I had an abortion my senior year of high school. My doctor was wonderful, the most polite and professional man you could ask for. Definitely didn't try to feel me up. He even sent detailed notes of the abortion to my doctor in L.A., in case I needed any follow-up. His name was Dr. Nitta."

I did not feel relief just yet.

"That must have been very expensive," I said, hoping to be corrected.

"His fee isn't that high, actually," Ingrid said. "It's about 200 dollars. But the airfare is steep. And the travel is complicated."

"I don't know where I would find the money or the time to fly to L.A.," I said. "But maybe Hollis could." I wasn't sure about that either. I had noticed that people often overestimated Hollis's family wealth. She was comfortable around the girls with money, whose fortunes came from newspapers or department stores, but she wasn't really one of them. Hollis would always describe herself to me as "comfortable." When I looked over at her, she was quietly shaking her head.

"Dr. Nitta is not in L.A.," Ingrid corrected. "He works just outside Osaka. It cost me 900 dollars to fly there, and, of course, a few hundred more to stay in a hotel. But it was worth it for an abortion that was one hundred percent legal. I didn't have to worry about getting arrested or raped. Good luck finding that anywhere in this country."

I was dumbfounded. Was there something I was missing?

"Isn't Osaka in Japan?" I asked.

"Of course," said Ingrid. "Unless they've moved it since I was there."

"So you flew all the way to Japan?" I had never met anyone who had traveled that far on purpose.

"Yup," she said cheerfully. "Pretty much anyone who wants an abortion can get one in Japan. You have to claim that having a baby would 'harm' you. They are still pretty poor over there, even all these years after the war. They get that misery and poverty can harm people."

The insanity of what I was hearing gave me my first smile of the day, and Ingrid misunderstood. She looked very proud of herself for having provided such helpful information.

"So you'll find a way to get to Dr. Nitta?" she asked.

It was Hollis who burst Ingrid's bubble.

"Neither one of us has that kind of money."

Ingrid looked disappointed.

"Well," she said, "If I hear of anything on this side of the ocean, I'll let you know. In the meantime, don't take matters into your own hands. I'm sure you're smart enough not to stick anything sharp up your insides, so I'll spare you the lecture on avoiding knitting needles and broken coke bottles."

Hollis squirmed visibly, and Ingrid nodded with approval at her discomfort. That was exactly the reaction she wanted. Then Marcia jumped in.

"Don't try turpentine or bleach, either. You'll destroy your insides, and you'll never have kids. And stay away from Leunbach's Paste, no matter what you've heard. There are doctors who use it, but if you're not a doctor, there's no way you'll get it right. It will get into your bloodstream and kill you. I'm sorry I don't have anything more helpful to offer."

We thanked Ingrid and Marcia. We knew their interest in us was genuine. It certainly wasn't their fault that they had no solution to our problem. When they left, Hollis and I did not feel any closer to a resolution than we had before.

"My head is killing me," Hollis said.

I fetched her some aspirin and a glass of water, and we said nothing more that night.

15

As soon as I mailed the letter to Stephanie, I called Theo. I had to thank him again and tell him that the diaries had been the key to finding my daughter. Even if I didn't hear back from Stephanie, I owed Theo my gratitude.

"I am so happy to hear your voice," he said. "I've wanted to call, but I was afraid that I had set you up for disappointment when I sent you those journals. Now we should celebrate," he said.

I was touched, and I agreed.

"Can I lure you to Boston again?" he asked. "I want to hear all about how Nancy Drew solved the case of the missing daughter."

I almost suggested that he come to Hopkins, and then thought better of it. I didn't know Theo well, and I wasn't sure I wanted him on my home turf.

"I can come this weekend," I said.

"Great. I'll take you to a real restaurant this time."

"I'm in."

"There's a sweet little bistro that opened near Sunrise Gardens. Why don't we meet there? My uncle will be so happy to see you again."

How could I say no? The whole point of this phone call had been to tell Theo how grateful I was.

★ ★ ★

Knowing what to expect didn't make it any easier to entertain Dr. Hauptman. He and Theo talked about patients and research, with the occasional inside joke about hospital administrators, while I sat quietly. Theo was rigidly cheerful as he feigned interest in his uncle's medical advice. Occasionally Hauptman asked me if I were a doctor or a nurse.

"Neither," I said three or four times. "I'm a lawyer."

"Tell us about some of your cases," Theo suggested. His eyes were begging me to introduce something new—anything—into the conversation.

"Well," I said, "let's see. I have a client who just leased a space for a new restaurant. But right before he opened, he found out that the ground underneath his space was full of chemicals from an old dry cleaner. So now there's a big fight over who has to clean it up."

"A restaurant?" Hauptman asked. I figured that was the only word he had understood.

"Yes," I said. "He wants to serve California cuisine, which, as far as I can tell, means a lot of angel hair pasta and sundried tomatoes. Served with a dollop of tetrachloroethylene."

For the first time in our visit, Theo's smile seemed genuine and relaxed. I was happy to have added a bit of humor to an otherwise tedious task.

At dinner, Theo nearly gushed with appreciation.

"I'm not ready to become a regular," I confessed.

"I understand," he said. "But you're so good at engaging him."

I was a little unnerved by Theo's compliments. Why was he so impressed with me? He was eager to hear every detail of my search. "Tell me how you put the pieces of the puzzle together," he said, with a wide-eyed excitement I didn't recognize.

I knew I would be recounting this dinner to Carol later that night, and I could already hear her asking, "If he was so gung-ho to see you again, why didn't he call you weeks ago?" And I didn't know what I would answer.

"The puzzle pieces were microfiche strips," I said. I described how Joyce and I had spent our summer poring over obituaries and wedding announcements.

"You are a very determined woman. I admire that."

"I couldn't have done it without that diary you sent me, so thank you again."

"I'm glad there was a purpose to saving those old journals. My wife always threatened to dump them in the bay."

"It was more than just the journals. I felt like you were rooting for me, and that meant a lot."

"You are very welcome, Bonnie. As you probably know, I have kind of a professional interest in finding adoptees," he said.

I sensed our conversation had just taken an unexpected turn, and I didn't know where it was going. "I didn't know that," I said. "I don't even know what you mean."

"You know I study leukemia?" he said. "That's my field."

At first, he seemed to think that was a sufficient answer, but then he continued. "We have all these great therapies involving bone marrow transplants, but it's hard to find a match if the patient is adopted. Impossible, almost. Your best bet is a close relative, so if your patient doesn't know their biological family . . ."

"I see," I said, as I tried to take in what he was saying.

There had been so many times over the past twenty years when I had wondered if my daughter needed me, but it was always in the emotional sense. In my imagination she might need comfort or affirmation. I never thought she might have a life-or-death medical need. That had never crossed my mind.

"I can't believe any birth mother would choose protecting her identity over saving her child."

"You're probably right," Theo said, "but right now I'm hoping to find a child who wants to save a life."

"What do you mean?"

"I have a patient who really needs a bone marrow donor. He has a sister, but she can't help. Her health isn't that good. But somewhere out there the sister has a son, and there's a possibility that he could be a match. Problem is he was put up for adoption twenty-five years ago, and no one knows where, or who, he is. If we could find him, maybe he could save his uncle's life."

Did Theo really think that the young man he wanted to find could possibly have the same connection to an uncle he'd never met that I had to a child I gave birth to?

"Oh, Theo," I said, "that's so different. You can't assume that the boy will be willing to get involved. Honestly, that's more like helping a stranger than like helping your child."

Theo thought about that.

"Well," he finally said, "sometimes people help strangers."

"That's true," I agreed.

"So I was hoping you would help the sister. She really wants to find her son. I can tell it's not just about her brother's illness. She thinks the cancer is the sign from God that she and her son are supposed to be reunited. But she doesn't know how to begin. I was hoping you would meet with her. Just tell her about your experience."

It was strange to think of myself as having transitioned from the seeker to the guide. I certainly did not feel that I had become wise, or even knowledgeable, as a result of my search. I had been persistent, and I had been lucky. But I still didn't know whether the effort had been worthwhile, because I had yet to look in my daughter's eyes.

"I'll tell you what," I said. "If this woman really wants to meet with me, I'd be happy to help. But only if that's what she really wants."

"Bonnie, you're the best," he said before taking a sip of wine. "How are you enjoying your duck?"

Was that a non-sequitur? I wondered. Or were those two sentences related? Had I just accepted a bribe, with payment in the form of roasted fowl in an apricot-cranberry glaze?

"It's delicious," I said.

"Who says you need toxic stain removers to make food taste good?"

Theo was as sharp and cultured as I remembered, and the evening passed pleasantly. I was sure that Carol would approve when I told her about how sophisticated he was.

"He's very well-read," I reported. "And he was very sweet. I recommended a novel I thought he would like, and he actually wrote down the title."

"I can see how you would find that romantic," she said, bemused.

"Oh, and he recommended some exhibit at the Museum of Fine Arts. Do you want to go tomorrow?"

"Okay," she said, a little more doubt creeping into her tone. "But tell me this. Do you like him because he's informative? Do you want to date a human guidebook? Or did you really connect with him?"

I thought about that for a moment, and remembered what I hadn't shared with Carol. The truth was that, while Theo was a capable conversationalist on many subjects, no topic had animated him as much as the patient who wanted his nephew's bone marrow.

"Are you telling me you don't like him?" I asked.

"I'm not telling you anything," she said. She said it kindly, without any of the sarcasm for which I loved her. "I'm asking you. Is this what you want?"

★ ★ ★

A few days later Theo called me in my office to set up a time for me to meet his patient's sister. "I'd like to do it soon," he said. "There's a short window when he'll be healthy enough to do a transplant."

"Are you sure she wants to do this?" I asked one more time. But I already knew I would meet her. Clearly, this woman needed some-one on her side, and that someone would be me. I wasn't sure that even her own brother had her interests at heart.

Before Theo answered, Joyce came rushing into my office.

"It's Stephanie," she said breathlessly. "She's on the other line."

It seemed impossible.

"How do you know?" I stammered.

"It's her voice, Bonnie. She sounds just like you. I can't explain it."

"What did she say?" My heart was pounding.

"She said, 'Can I please speak to Mr. Lars Krutka?' And I just knew it was her."

"What do I do?"

Joyce had never seen me so flustered, so she kept talking.

"I told her Lars wasn't available, and she sounded quite disappointed."

"I don't want to frighten her," I said.

"Bonnie, she's on hold right now. We don't want to lose her. Let me talk to her for a few more minutes while you collect yourself."

Joyce disappeared and left me to sort out my terror and my excitement while I said goodbye to Theo. I had no right to be this happy, I thought. I had looked for my daughter out of concern, I told myself. It was for her sake, not mine. But now I was practically giddy at the thought of speaking to her. I was embarrassed for Joyce to see me so frazzled. My role, I had always felt, was to take care of other people's needs. I had no right to be the one feeling needy.

And then Joyce was back.

"It's definitely her, and she really wants to talk to you. Pick up the phone."

I saw my hand pick up the receiver and I heard myself say hello.

"Hi," said the girl on the other end. "Remember me?"

No recrimination. No accusation. Just a little joke between old friends. I gushed with relief.

"It's been too long," I said. And I understood why Joyce had been so sure of her identity after hearing her voice. I can name that tune in three notes, I thought.

"I've been looking for you," I told her.

"I've been looking for you too," she said. These were the words I most wanted to hear.

"They don't make it easy," I said.

"Not at all," she agreed. "There's a troll under every bridge."

What a perfect metaphor, I thought. My daughter is brilliant.

I told her all about my visit to senile old Dr. Hauptman, and about his diaries. I told her about my weekends in the microfiche room with Joyce. I wanted Stephanie to know that I had truly worked to find her. I told her about finally learning her mother's name from her grandfather's obituary.

"So Grandpa Longstreet brought us together from the grave," she said. "Cool."

Already, I loved the way her mind worked. She was an observer, with a sense of humor that wasn't afraid of the dark.

"Turns out we weren't very far apart."

I told her that I was a lawyer with a small practice in Hopkins, New Hampshire.

"I have about a million questions for you," she said, "but maybe I should ask your hourly rate first."

I wished she could see how much her joke made me smile.

"Don't worry," I assured her. "I'll give you the family discount."

"Speaking of family," she said, "that's what my first question is about. It's only sort-of about you. Do I have any brothers or sisters I've never met?"

I could tell by her inflection that she hoped the answer would be affirmative.

"No," I said. "I'm sorry. I don't have any children."

"Any *other* children," she corrected.

"Right," I said, "of course." It was all so new to me, and I had no idea what language to use with her.

"Are you married?" she asked. She sounded restrained, as if she were fishing for the explanation for my childlessness but did not want to be rude.

"Actually, no," I said. "I'm not. How about you?"

"What do you mean 'how about me?'"

"Are *you* married?"

"What? No. I'm twenty." Now she sounded really flummoxed, and I worried that I had completely derailed our conversation. "Wait," she said. "Was that a joke?"

"It was meant to be an ice breaker," I said. "I'm just trying to get a sense of who you are, of what you do," I said, hoping to get back onto her wavelength.

"What I do?" She laughed. "I go to college. Right here. At the University of Vermont."

I am almost ashamed of how glad I was to hear that Stephanie was in school. I should have been able to say that I just wanted to know she was happy, that I didn't care about her status or her education. But I had fought so hard to be in college when I was her age. We had something important in common, it seemed.

"Do they still call it Groovy UV?" I asked.

"Sure," she said. "A rhyme that good will never go out of style."

We talked for over an hour, though it felt like ten minutes. Our conversation was comfortable and natural, like catching up with an old friend who has been out of town for a long trip. The only reason our talk finally ended was that Stephanie asked if I would like to come meet her over the weekend.

"Don't you want to know what I look like?" she asked. It was like she was reading my mind. I was dying to see her in person, to know if her face would feel as familiar as her voice.

By the time we fixed a time and place to meet on the upcoming Saturday, I was completely besotted.

★ ★ ★

In the days leading up to that first visit, I barely recognized myself. Instead of the controlled professional I was used to being, I was anxious and sentimental, hardly eating or sleeping, worrying that it would all go horribly wrong. I was afraid that Stephanie would cancel, or that she would hate me. I even dreamt that I forgot to show up. You would have thought I was preparing for an important job interview, a date with the most popular boy in school, and a rush party at the most selective sorority, all at once. I planned my outfit—a jean skirt and cotton blouse—so that I would look good but not like I fussed. I perseverated over what gift I could bring Stephanie that would make me seem thoughtful but not presumptuous or overly ingratiating. (I settled on a blooming gardenia plant.)

And yet somehow I managed to get myself out of the house Saturday morning, to drive ninety miles without hitting anything, and to pull into Stephanie's cul-de-sac at the appointed hour. If I'm being truthful, though, I'll admit that the part about the "appointed hour" is not quite accurate. In my nervousness, I had arrived over a half hour early. Everyone knows that that is not "conscientious, punctual" early, but "neurotic, desperate" early. I sat in my car, trying to decide how much longer to wait before ringing their doorbell, and wishing that Stephanie had not chosen her family home as our meeting place. I was curious about the people who had raised her, of course, but I would have much preferred to watch a short documentary about them than to interact with them in real time. I had prepared various speeches in my head to assuage their fears. Some of my prepared remarks were more defensive than others, depending on what level of suspicion the Farnsworths displayed toward me. And then Stephanie's father came out of the house. He was a handsome man in his late forties with thick, almost shoulder-length black hair, wearing a sky-blue polo shirt and khaki shorts with too many pockets. He smiled warmly, and beckoned me to follow him up the stone walk to the house.

"You must be Bonnie," he said as he held out his hand. "I'm Carter. Stephanie is so excited to meet you."

He seemed relaxed, welcoming, secure. If he felt threatened by my sudden intrusion in their lives, he did not show it.

When I walked in the house, I could hear that Stephanie was in the middle of some kind of row upstairs.

"Mom, he doesn't need any of this crap," I heard.

But then Carter told her that I had arrived, and suddenly she was at the top of the stairs, looking a hundred times lovelier than I had even imagined. And then she was smiling, and then she was sailing down the stairs, and then she was in my arms. The girl I had thought of as lost in the ether was now pressing on my body, resting her cheek against mine. We stood like that briefly and then pulled apart just far enough to look at each other. There was a resemblance, for sure, but I was never that pretty. Never.

Maureen appeared at the top of the stairs and greeted me. She said something polite, as I recall, but she was stiff, and she kept her distance.

I'm not sure I can recount that day as a chronological series of events. I experienced it as a flood of impressions and emotions, dotted with a few particularly memorable moments. Stephanie was anxious to get out of the house, to be alone with me, so she proposed a walk to Lake Champlain. Just before we left, Carter put his hand on Stephanie's shoulder and looked her in the eye.

"Go easy on her." He nodded slightly in my direction. "She's our guest."

I was grateful for that. I was still afraid that her warmth during our first phone conversation was part of her strategy to disarm me for the hostile interrogation that was yet to come. And, honestly, if she had lured me up here just to berate me for abandoning her, I wouldn't have blamed her.

But that is not at all how it went. We sat by the lake and talked for hours. We talked about our favorite books and movies and pets and foods. Mostly I remember that we agreed on everything—that nuts are not dessert, that cocker spaniels are cute but dumb, that there was nothing redemptive about watching Thelma and Louise drive off a cliff, that pizza should be eaten with a knife and fork, that Joan Armatrading is an underappreciated artist, and that Charles and Diana's wedding was too boring to watch.

I learned that Stephanie was closer to her father than to her mother.

"My brother Drew is so obviously her favorite," she told me. "He was her miracle baby, and eighteen years later he still is. You want to know what we were arguing about when you showed up? She bought so much stuff for Drew to take to college. She walks in with these bags full of pens and notebooks and sheets and towels and blankets. She bought him a fan in case it's hot and a space heater in case it's cold. She even bought him a thesaurus and an atlas. It's such a waste. I'm pretty sure there's a library at Northwestern, and a JC Penney somewhere in Chicago. They didn't buy me any of that stuff. They didn't even let me go away to college. I had to stay in-state, where my dad is on the faculty."

"You don't like UVM?" I asked, sympathetic. I wanted her to know I was on her side.

"No, I love it. I love school. But I don't admit that to my folks. It would give them too much satisfaction."

I was happy to be her confidant, a coconspirator in her ongoing conflict with her parents.

"So why does Drew get to go away?"

"It depends who you ask," she said. "According to my parents, it's because after years of listening to my arguments, they finally came around to realizing I was right. But if you ask me, they just give Drew everything he wants."

"Maybe they wanted to keep you close because they love you more."

"Nice try, but no. That's definitely not it."

Even though I had told myself over and over that I hoped my search would lead me to the world's happiest adoptee, I found that I liked hearing about the friction in her family. Perhaps there was a place for me in her life. Or—and this thought occurred to me as well—perhaps I was a terrible person for wanting my daughter to be unhappy. Probably because of this guilt, I tried to deflect the conversation away from the topic of her less favored status.

"So you grew up as a faculty kid?"

"Yeah, my dad's in the engineering school. But now he's the provost. Don't ask me what that means."

"Okay," I said. "But the main reason I searched for you was so you could tell me what a provost is."

For some of that day, Stephanie told me more about school. She was a women's studies major, and she was looking forward to her senior year of college. She would be moving into an off-campus apartment with two new roommates at the beginning of September. She confided that, though there were plenty of people at UVM she considered friends, she still wasn't sure if any of them would end up being her true, lifelong friends.

Then she announced it was her turn to ask me more questions about what I do. I warned her that she would probably find most of my work dull.

"Who was that lawyer who wrote me that letter?" she wanted to know.

I explained that I had used Lars's name as a decoy when I wrote to her, so as not to overwhelm her.

"If you go back and look at the stationery," I said, "you'll see my name at the top."

"So he works for you, not the other way around?"

"Right."

"That's so cool."

She looked like she was trying to think of another question about the practice of law, but it wasn't coming to her. And then after a few beats she asked, "Have you ever met David Souter?"

I can safely say that that was the last thing in the world I expected to be asked. I would have been thrilled if my daughter had merely known the name of the recently appointed Supreme Court Justice from New Hampshire. But here she was expressing actual interest in him. I may even have laughed out loud before I responded, from surprise, but also from relief. I had been so worried that Stephanie's main objective in meeting me face to face was to excoriate me for giving her up. But it seemed that all she wanted was to know me. So here I was, talking about just the kinds of things I like to talk about. When I answered, I probably sounded like a teacher lecturing her smartest pupil.

"I faced him in court once," I told her, "very soon after I graduated law school. He was a tough Attorney General, for sure. I was representing a girl—I didn't know her, but I had done some work for her father—who had been arrested for protesting at a nuclear power plant. Souter really wanted the protesters in jail."

Stephanie jumped in.

"So he's an asshole?"

I had often heard my peers complain about the way young people tend to sort all humans into simplistic categories of good and bad. Now that I was seeing the tendency up close, I was totally charmed by it. I even envied Stephanie's uninhibited sense of conviction.

"I would never use that word to describe Souter," I said. "He was always a gentleman. He was doing exactly what I would expect any prosecutor to do. He got her sentenced to fifteen days, I think. Don't get me wrong. I didn't want this girl going to jail at all. And I was terrified of David at the time. But that says more about how insecure I was at the beginning of my career than it says about what kind of adversary he was."

"What happened to the girl?"

"She served about three days and then went home to take a hot shower. I think she got out of the protesting business."

And then I told Stephanie about the second time I had met Souter, at a bar association function, after he became a judge.

"I could see why lawyers liked practicing in front of him. He was very knowledgeable, very respectful in court, even to criminal defendants. And he was the center of attention at this bar association dinner." I smiled at the memory of what a polymath and raconteur he was. "He was quite charming, in a Cole Porter sort of way," I told her.

"Wait. Is that your way of saying he's gay?"

Again, I smiled. Her cultural knowledge was broad, but her tolerance for uncertainty was shallow.

"I wouldn't know anything about that," I said.

"I kind of hope he is," she said. "Maybe he won't be so bad."

Besides her interest in David Souter, one other question from our conversation that afternoon stands out.

"Is Hopkins near Dartmouth?" Stephanie wanted to know.

"Quite close, actually. Why do you ask?"

"Just wondering. I was there at the beginning of the summer. One Saturday afternoon, just out of curiosity, I went to see the AIDS quilt."

I was frozen. I looked at her with fear and awe at the way our lives had intersected just months earlier without our having known it. I explained to her, slowly, hoarsely, because I could barely believe my own words, that I had been there too. We discovered that we had missed each other by only an hour.

* * *

For days after that first meeting, I was animated by all the similarities and coincidences we had established. Stephanie had treated me kindly, more generously than I deserved, I thought. Even her father had thanked me for coming, told me that my presence meant a lot to Stephanie. I knew there was more she wanted to ask me, but she had been respectful and restrained. She asked me about her father, but she didn't pursue it once I told her that I barely knew him. She hadn't demanded an apology for relinquishing her, any more than I had demanded assurance that I had done the right thing.

The one thing that nagged at me when I looked back on our first visit was her dismay that she had no younger siblings to meet. She wasn't just disappointed, I could tell. She was also confused. She, like a lot of other people, assumed that one gave up a baby conceived at the wrong time so that one would be free to construct a family when the time was right. Hadn't relinquishing her liberated me to find the right partner and have the children I truly wanted? She wouldn't put me on the spot by asking me to explain why I hadn't done so, but she wanted to understand. Eventually I began asking myself this very same question.

I could have given her the answer about how my employees were my children and my practice was my legacy. I had used that one on occasion when I needed to deflect this particular invasion of my privacy. Or I could say something closer to the truth, which was that my education and my work took up most of my time, and all of my mental energy. But neither of those answers was the real truth. Over the course of my search for Stephanie, I had learned a few things about myself. I had come to realize that ever since I gave Stephanie up, I had two selves. One was that young woman, scared, weak, unable to control her own destiny. The woman I presented to the world today was an entirely different self, a carefully constructed version of an educated, capable woman. I assumed that if any man fell in love with my constructed self, I would have to spend my life hiding my earlier self. Should he ever discover it, he would no doubt walk away.

I had also learned that giving up Stephanie had changed me. What had begun as a matter of circumstance had morphed in my mind into a matter of character. I had chosen twenty years ago not to be a mother, and that choice had ossified over time, had become permanent. I could even name a moment when I believed I had proof that marriage and motherhood were incompatible with who I was at the core. It was at my fifteenth Halstead reunion. I was catching up with Diane Hendel, who, poor thing, was reeling from a recent family tragedy. Her brother had married an Israeli, a woman he had loved since they were teenagers together at summer camp. They lived in a town near Tel Aviv, and had twin sons. But six months earlier, Diane's sister-in-law had been killed by an explosive planted on a commuter bus. One of the boys had been with her, and she had died shielding him from the shrapnel. That's what a mother does, I thought. A mother instinctively throws herself on top of her child. If I had been unwilling even to curtail my education for the sake of my daughter, how could I be trusted to run into the path of a bomb?

16

THE DAY AFTER OUR VISIT FROM INGRID AND MARCIA, I again went to class unable to focus on anything but the embryo inside me, probably an inch long by now, which I dreamed of extracting, like a painful splinter. Hollis and I were dealing with our dread differently. I was trying, as much as possible, to go through the motions of carrying on with my life, while she lay in bed, inert. As buoyant as she had once been, she was now moody and unmoored. We barely spoke to each other when I left our room that morning. There was no rancor between us, though. We didn't speak because we didn't have to. We were so in tune with each other's thoughts that there was nothing we needed to say.

When I got back to our room after my morning of pretending to be an accredited Halstead student, I was surprised to find, yet again, a visitor in our room. This time it was Marshall. Even more surprising, he looked relaxed, and Hollis looked almost giddy. She was a different person from the listless waif I had left that morning.

"Bonnie," she said, excitedly, "it's all going to be okay."

I was too confused to respond, so she kept going.

"Marshall has a plan." She looked lovingly at her boyfriend, who said,

"We're not calling it the Marshall Plan, though, because that name is taken."

I couldn't believe that they were making cute jokes with each other.

"He has an aunt in New York," Hollis explained. "And they do abortions at her hospital."

"What do you mean they do abortions at her hospital?" I asked in disbelief. "How is that legal?"

Marshall explained.

"They have this committee that decides when an abortion is really necessary. My aunt told me about it a few years ago. During the German Measles epidemic, if a pregnant woman got exposed, the committee would okay an abortion. You know, because the baby might be retarded. Aunt Fern says these days they have better ways of dealing with medical complications. So now the committee mostly approves abortions for women who have what they call 'affective disorders.'"

"Basically, women who aren't right in the head," Hollis translated. "So we told her about how I cry all the time, and I can't get out of bed, and I have this awful headache. Dr. Pasternak—"

"That's my aunt," Marshall interrupted.

"—wasn't very optimistic. She said that probably wouldn't be enough, because one of her colleagues on the committee is a real stickler. This guy—"

"His name is Dr. Lauden," Marshall interjected.

"Right, Dr. Lauden. One time Marshall's aunt asked the committee to approve an abortion for a woman whose husband punched her. *Punched her.* Can you believe that? But this Lauden guy said no."

"He said the abortion wasn't medically necessary. My aunt was really angry. But they're kind of afraid of the Catholic Church."

"So that's why we didn't think they would approve me. But Marshall's aunt called him an hour ago and said the committee met this morning and gave us the okay. We're so relieved and grateful. We're going down to the city this afternoon, and they're going to do it first thing in the morning. Colton lent us his Pontiac, because we promised we would park in a garage overnight, not on the street."

"That's his biggest concern," Marshall said in disbelief. "That the car might get stolen or towed."

It was his way of telling me that Colton was hopelessly selfish, and that I shouldn't think his disregard for me was unique or personal.

"My aunt wants you to call her," Marshall added. "She doesn't think she can get two identical cases through her committee, but she has an idea how to help you. Oh, and she mentioned that her idea might cost about seventy-five dollars, so . . ."

Marshall cocked his head and reached behind him for his wallet. He took out a bill and handed it to me.

"Here," he said. "This is from Colton."

I didn't take it.

"Thank you," I said, "but I can see that it's not."

"It will be," he assured me. "At the end of every month I tell him what he owes me for the heat and the phone. I can make up any number I want. He never bothers to check. In fact . . ." Without finishing the sentence, Marshall took a second bill from his wallet and shook it at me.

"Just take it."

I did, and I thanked him.

"Call my aunt as soon as you can," he said. Then he picked up Hollis's suitcase in one hand, cupped the small of her back in the other, and led her out the door.

★ ★ ★

I called Dr. Pasternak, as instructed, and I soon understood why Marshall had turned to her for help. She talked to me with a matter-of-fact intimacy that was disarming but also refreshing.

"Frankly, I'm surprised that the committee approved your friend. I almost didn't bother bringing the case, but Hollis seems so *young*. I had to help her. To tell you the truth, I suspect everyone on the committee figured out I was trying to get my nephew out of a jam. They were just doing me a favor because I'm their colleague. That's why I don't think I could get your case through. But there's a hospital in Boston that has a Therapeutic Abortion Committee, just like ours. I asked around a little, and, well,"

She was hesitating.

"Yes?" I nudged.

"I don't like to cast aspersions on my profession, but the fact of the matter is that some committees are more ethical than others. You might not believe this after what I just told you about Hollis, but my hospital is known for having a lot of integrity. When they denied the woman with the abusive husband, the decision was at least technically correct, even if it seems inhumane. I heard that a committee in North Carolina said no to a young mother who was dying of breast cancer. They couldn't give her a little more time with her family because they didn't want to 'waste' an abortion on a woman who didn't have long to live."

"That's awful," I said. I was trying to muster up empathy, because the story really did sound awful. But I was too consumed with my own problems at the moment to register the full extent of the tragedy she described.

"Anyway, I asked around, and I learned that the committee in Boston is pretty lenient about granting abortions if you can get a letter from a doctor saying that your pregnancy is causing you 'profound mental distress.' I imagine you can do that, yes?"

The term "profound mental distress" was the perfect description of my state of mind.

"It's not just the pregnancy," I said, feeling myself cracking. "It's everything."

Suddenly, all the things I hadn't said to Hollis because I hadn't needed to came flooding out.

"It's the secrecy, and the fear that I'm going to lose everything. I won't be able to finish school. I won't be able to face my parents. They will be so ashamed, and it will all be my fault."

She listened quietly, occasionally saying, "I know," or "I understand" in a soothing voice. I blubbered about how I wanted desperately to bargain my way out of this pregnancy, and how I was all alone. I did not have an older, well-connected boyfriend like Hollis did. And once I started telling Dr. Pasternak how I felt, I couldn't stop. Now that I finally had someone listening to me, I told her about how I felt sore and bloated, and always on the verge of tears, how I couldn't concentrate, and that the worst part was that I had done this to myself.

"You didn't do this to yourself," she said. "Take it from a board-certified physician, that's not how conception happens." That little bit of sympathetic humor brought me back from the brink. She waited until I had collected myself enough to hear her before she spoke again.

"You know, Bonnie," she said kindly, "doctors take an oath to treat whoever walks in our door, no matter what they've done. We treat people who break their own necks jumping off of roofs into swimming pools. We treat people who set their houses on fire, or swallow things that don't belong in their mouths. But when they're pregnant, that's the one time we say, 'sorry, but you brought this on yourself.'"

"So you think I'll be able to convince a psychiatrist that I'm distressed enough?"

"I don't think you'll have any problem. The truth is that there are doctors who will write a letter for seventy-five dollars, without even seeing you. Oh, and it's very helpful if the letter says you are considering suicide."

That sentence jolted me awake.

As distraught as I was, the thought of suicide hadn't crossed my mind. In a panicky voice, I told Dr. Pasternak that I didn't want to kill myself and wouldn't even know how. The whole point was that I had a plan for my life; I didn't want to give it up.

Dr. Pasternak promised that she would closely guard the secret of my robust mental health.

Later that night, Hollis called from the doctor's apartment in New York.

"Bonnie," she said, "this building is so beautiful. There is a lobby with a black and white marble floor, and there is a man in a uniform who greets you and then takes you upstairs in an elevator that he has to operate himself by holding a crank."

I couldn't believe this was the same Hollis who had been sobbing on our couch all week.

"And Aunt Fern's apartment is so big. It's like a house, only it's in a building. I'm going to live just like this, Bonnie. I'll be really successful at something—I'm not sure what yet—and I'll live on West End Avenue and take taxis, and I'll always give big tips to the doormen who carry my packages. Just being here makes my aching head feel better. Have you talked to her yet?"

"Yes," I said.

"Isn't she amazing?"

"Yes."

"Is she going to help you?"

"Yes, I think we have a plan," I said.

"Good."

"Come back soon, okay?"

As soon as we woke up in the morning, I knew Hollis would get her abortion, and I would call the doctor in Boston who would write me the letter. It would be over soon for both of us.

17

BEFORE I MET STEPHANIE, I HAD IMAGINED that one visit, to quiet my curiosity, would be enough. But during the week after my trip to see her in Essex, while I was at the office, I spoke to her several times a day. The conversations were all in my head, of course, but they felt very vivid. I imagined myself telling her things I thought she would want to hear—observations about clients, or current events, or whatever else crossed my mind. I thought of various pretenses to phone her. Maybe she wanted my advice on which courses to take this fall? We had made no arrangements, had not discussed a shared vision of what our relationship might look like in the future. I wanted so much to see her again, but maybe she had gotten what she wanted from me and was ready to resume her life as the daughter of Carter and Maureen Farnsworth. I mulled it over for several days while I tried to focus on work. And then I realized that the date was August twenty-eighth. In three days, I would have the perfect reason to contact her, without having to worry about appearing overly attached. Without embarrassment, I could call to wish her a happy birthday. The thirty-first of August had always been a melancholy day for me, a reminder of the crucible I had lived through, but this year, for the first time in two decades, I could experience happiness on this date.

"Bonnie. I was just going to call you," Stephanie said when I reached her.

I knew it would be best not to ask why I hadn't heard from her in almost a week, but Stephanie offered an explanation anyway.

"It's been so chaotic, with Drew leaving for school and everything. But he and my mom finally left at five o'clock this morning. My dad and I can breathe again."

I told her I was calling to wish her a happy birthday.

"So today really *is* my birthday," she said, half questioning, as if this information solved a long-standing mystery. "Did you know that my birth certificate says September first? But my dad has always sworn up and down that they got the call from their doctor friend on August thirty-first. He thinks Hauptman changed the date to make me harder to find."

If that had been the doctor's plan, it had worked. Stephanie and I would have found each other through the registries much earlier if she had known her real birthday. I tried to squelch my rage at Hauptman's manipulations and focus on the happy occasion at hand.

"Do you have plans for tonight?" I asked.

"Not really. I have a babysitting gig next door. But tomorrow night, my real-fake-real birthday, we'll go out to dinner. Do you want to join us?"

She asked so innocently, as if there were no possibility that her parents would be put out by my presence at their daughter's twenty-first birthday dinner. I knew that this particular constellation of celebrants was far more complicated than she let on, but I certainly didn't want to turn down the invitation. I couldn't imagine anything I would rather do than mark Stephanie's birthday with her. There could be no better way to reclaim the day.

"I would love to, but . . ."

Before I could get to the second half of the sentence, she said, "Great. It'll just be my dad and me. Maureen won't be home from Chicago yet. It will be much more festive with you there."

I told her to check with her dad first, and to let me know if he had any objection to my presence. But she clearly didn't listen to me, because when I showed up at their house the next night, he looked surprised and a little confused. I'll give him credit. He regrouped quickly. He shook off the awkwardness like the deftest of actors. He said all the right things—how nice it was to see me; how special it was for Stephanie to spend her birthday with me. Only a slight fumble with his car keys suggested that he was flustered by my appearance.

"I'm sorry," I said to him while Stephanie ran upstairs to find her clogs. "I guess she didn't clear it with you. You weren't expecting an outsider."

He shrugged.

"Who's the outsider?" He held the door open for me. "Of the three of us, the only one who wasn't there the day it happened is me."

Stephanie wanted to celebrate her birthday with a burger by the lake. She didn't actually want a beer, but Carter insisted she order one.

"I'll drink it," he said. "But you can't skip this rite of passage. And just to make sure it means something, I'm going to keep an eye on the bartender. I want you to be the absolute youngest person who gets served a drink today."

When her Heineken arrived, she dutifully took a sip.

"Mmm," she deadpanned. "My very first beer." She passed it to her father.

"So, Bonnie," Carter said, "Steph tells me you're a lawyer."

Stephanie turned to me.

"I told him about how you represented that woman who was protesting nuclear weapons."

I heard the admiration in her tone, and it pained me to have to correct her.

"She was protesting nuclear power, not nuclear weapons," I said.

"Still," Stephanie said, "it's pretty cool."

Carter raised his eyebrows.

"That does sound like something you would think was 'cool.'"

I explained that that had been just one case a long time ago.

"Most of the work I do is decidedly room temperature."

I asked about his work and learned more about his early career as an engineer.

"My childhood obsession was granite excavation," he said. "I grew up not that far from you, near the quarries at Rattlesnake Hill. You know how some boys like to watch trucks and airplanes? Well, I loved watching the wire saws slice off a section of rock. Like a hunk of parmesan cheese. There's nothing quite like liquid-oxygen torches melting through stone."

This had led to a lifelong interest in structural engineering, which had somehow led to a professorship, a deanship, and now the title of provost, whatever that was.

"Please don't put Bonnie to sleep with your boring granite facts," Stephanie said, without any hope that he could be stopped.

Carter insisted that there wasn't any such thing as a boring granite fact, and he proceeded to tell me that quarries from my home state had produced the stone for both the New Hampshire state capital and the Library of Congress. Stephanie was horrified to discover that I not only knew these facts, having learned them on a sixth-grade field trip, but considered them interesting indeed. She made a show of rolling her eyes and announcing,

"Old people have a weird definition of interesting."

"You have a weird definition of old," said Carter.

I enjoyed watching their relationship play out. I had seen this show before—the parent and child who disguise their mutual affection with performative exasperation—but this was one of the best renditions. I appreciated the front row seat to their rapport.

"Did I tell you that Bonnie went to Halstead?" Stephanie said to her father.

This seemed to surprise him, and maybe even throw him off a little.

"No," he said. "That's a funny coincidence."

If Maureen had gone to the same college, wouldn't Stephanie have mentioned it?

"My grandmother went to Halstead," he explained. "I think she was the class of 1916."

"That's amazing," I said, relieved that I would not have to vie with Maureen for ownership of the Halstead experience. I wondered what Carter's grandmother would have thought of the Halstead I had attended. Some older alumnae felt a kinship with any woman who had withstood the school's academic rigor; some were envious of the freedoms claimed by later classes; but some thought that my generation had ruined Halstead, poisoned it with our radical politics and our lax sexual mores.

"She loved it," he said. "Second-best years of her life, she always said."

"Okay," I said. "I'll bite. What were the best-best years?"

"I'm sorry she's not here to answer that herself, because she never got tired of talking about the years she worked in Washington during the Second World War. Her children were grown and out of the house, so she volunteered. She worked in personnel, training, that sort of thing. She never realized how bored she was until she finally went to work. That's what she used to say. The problem was that eventually the men came back from Europe and put her out of a job. She was angry about that for the rest of her life."

We sat with the image of Carter's resentful, underutilized grandmother, until Stephanie said, "I feel like ordering another beer. Who's going to help me drink it?"

"It's the least I can do," I said.

She waved the waiter over and asked for another. But he didn't bother asking to see her driver's license this time.

"Well, that stopped being fun pretty quickly," she said. "Sooo," she dragged the syllable out to let us know she was changing the subject. "Let's talk about the day I was born."

Carter looked nervous.

"It's a fair question, right? Aren't we here to celebrate my birthday?"

"Right," said Carter skeptically. He wiped his lips with a napkin.

"So? I want to talk about the day of my birth. What could be more relevant? Or should we go back to talking about granite?"

Carter looked at her pointedly, as if giving her a chance to reconsider. Then he looked at me.

"You don't have to face the inquisition, you know."

He had read my ambivalence quite well, I thought. On the one hand I agreed that Stephanie deserved to hear about how she came into the world. Everyone does. The narrative of our own birth is an item of human patrimony to which we are all entitled. But, at the same time, I didn't care to recount any of that awful day. I was enjoying our dinner too much to revisit my miserable stay in St. Gabriel's.

"It was hot," I said. "I remember that much."

"I would have known that just from looking at a calendar," Stephanie said. "What else can you tell me? What did I look like?" she asked. "Did I have hair? Or was I one of those bald-old-man babies?"

"You've seen pictures of yourself," Carter chided gently. "You know you were a beautiful baby."

"But I want to know what Bonnie remembers." She turned to me. "You did see me, didn't you?"

"Yes," I said. "I got to hold you for a few minutes before they took you away." I didn't tell Stephanie that they were the most bittersweet minutes of my life.

"And what did you think?" she asked.

"I thought you were adorable," I said. The light mood from earlier in the evening was gone. "And that you would make your parents very happy." I felt a wave of loss and self-pity, as well as the maddening contradiction that, at the time, I had not wanted to keep her any more than I had wanted to give her away.

Carter looked at me appreciatively. I don't know whether he was thanking me for bestowing Stephanie on him many years ago or for managing her curiosity so deftly this evening.

"I can tell you what I remember," he offered.

"No," Stephanie said bluntly. "There are only so many times I want to hear 'It was the happiest day of my blah blah blah.' Your version is old news. I want the real story."

He took his credit card from his wallet and then looked up at Stephanie. "Alright, I'll make a deal with you," he said as he waved away the cash I offered. "If you leave Bonnie in peace, I'll tell you the real story."

"What does that mean?" Stephanie scrunched her face with distrust.

"Oh," he said in mock surprise. "So now you want to hear my version?" He had both rescued me from Stephanie's questioning and also returned to the easy banter at which he and Stephanie were so practiced.

"Now I do," she said.

"Okay," he said, as he slid his wallet back in his pocket. "You already know this part. Your mom and I had been married three years. We had been trying that whole time to have a kid and weren't having any luck. Your mom was very discouraged, and also crushed at losing her father. We hadn't considered adopting, but I knew we would have to do something drastic soon. And then, out of the blue, we got a call from your grandfather's friend. He knew of a little girl, born just that day, who needed a home."

Stephanie turned to me.

"Now he's going to say, 'It was like winning the lottery without even buying a ticket.'"

"Okay, I know you've heard that line," he said. "But this is what I'm trying to tell you, Steph. That's not how I felt at the beginning. I didn't feel that way until you were at least two."

Stephanie squinted. She didn't know what to make of this new claim.

"So that 'happiest day of my life' stuff was just bullshit?"

Carter tried to look innocent.

"That's the kind of thing a good father should say, isn't it? And you like hearing it. But, now that you're older, and have become annoyingly nosy, I'm going to admit that I didn't really love you, *really* love you, until I got to know you better."

Nothing about this confession surprised me. I knew plenty of fathers who became more attached to their children over time. And I myself felt a bond with Stephanie that I had not felt when she was an infant. But Stephanie was troubled by her father's honesty.

"If you didn't want me, why did you agree to adopt me?"

"I didn't say I didn't want *you*," he insisted. "There is a difference between not being ready for a baby and not wanting you." He looked at me for help. It was an odd turn of events that it was he, not I, who was trying to explain the distinction. I too had hoped she would not conflate my inability to be a parent with a rejection of *her*.

"Adopting a baby is scary, and your mother was the who one had lost patience. I could have waited a little longer."

"So why did you say yes?"

Carter sighed. He clearly hadn't meant for the conversation to turn this serious. He had only wanted to deflect Stephanie's attention away from me. But there was no going back now.

"Your mother was starting to think she would never get pregnant. It was hard to see her so unhappy. I did it for her."

"Of course you did." Stephanie reached for the communal beer and took a swig. "I bet she did that thing that she does," she said.

"What thing?" he asked.

"You know, when she acts like everything is so horrible and she's the most victimized person in the world, and if you really loved her, you would do . . . whatever. I call it her 'black mood blackmail.'"

Carter tilted his head and considered. "I didn't realize there was a name for it, but, yes, that's a pretty good description."

"It's so manipulative," Stephanie said, with audible scorn.

"Try to understand," Carter said. I could see he meant it seriously. "She was a wreck at the time. She really *really* wanted a baby. And you were a delight. You won me over a little more every day with your impish charm."

Stephanie was smiling now, though maybe she was trying not to. She seemed to have concluded that this new version of events was acceptable after all.

"That's not really *so* different from the story you've always told me."

"No, not so different, really," he said, reassuringly. "So now I'll tell you one more thing that will surprise you."

"What?"

"You know that doctor who gave you to us, your grandfather's friend?"

"Sure. The one Mom calls her knight in shining armor, the Sir Lancelot of obstetricians?"

"Yeah. That one." Carter stood up from the table. "Don't tell your mom, but he was a pompous ass."

★ ★ ★

After dinner, we walked up from the lakefront toward campus and stopped at an ice cream shop. Stephanie stood at the counter a long time—she recognized the young man scooping—while Carter and I waited outside. I told him that Stephanie was wonderful, and that she clearly had wonderful parents. I wanted to talk about Stephanie, to hear more about her, but I also wanted to say the right things, to demonstrate that I knew they were her "real" parents, that I knew my place.

"I'd like to think I did a good job," he said. "I certainly gave it my all. But I think she had good genes too."

It sounded suspiciously like a compliment, and I got flustered. I hoped that Stephanie would reappear, but, through the glass window, I could see her getting more animated. Then Carter stepped closer to me and dropped his volume.

"Bonnie," he said, "there's something I need to ask you."

"Okay."

"So far, Steph hasn't mentioned anything about trying to find her birth father."

I understood the nomenclature of adoption, but it still seemed strange to associate any permutation of the word *father* with Colton.

"Has she asked you for information about him?" Carter asked. I didn't understand why he seemed so nervous.

"She's asked me a few questions," I said, "but I don't have a lot of answers. He and I have had no contact for a very long time. Once I told her that, she didn't push it."

Carter nodded, as if to say he understood that this answer would simply have to be good enough.

"I just want to be prepared," he said.

I could appreciate that. I spent most of my life trying to be prepared.

"For what?" I asked, sensing that he wanted to air his fears.

"For every possibility. That he'll be some cross between Superman and Willy Wonka, who'll make me look mediocre by comparison. Or that he'll be a horrible person who is unkind to Stephanie. Or that he'll be a normal nice guy with a normal nice life, but won't be open to letting her in."

How similar his fears were to the ones I had faced, I thought. I doubted, though, that Colton would fit perfectly into any of those paradigms. Each one seemed too extreme.

"I don't think you have to worry about Stephanie's birth father," I said. "Trust me, he's not worth looking for."

This was exactly the answer Carter wanted. It restored his good mood, and enabled him to smile approvingly at Stephanie when she finally emerged with her melting ice cream. For their final act of the evening, Stephanie and Carter engaged in a lively debate about whether or not I would enjoy the story of how the London Bridge was dismantled and rebuilt over the Colorado River, and how Carter had traveled to Arizona to watch the reconstruction. I pledged my neutrality, and simply admired the show.

18

As I waited for Hollis to come back from New York, I had only one question on my mind.

Did it hurt? That's all I wanted to know. How much physical pain would I have to endure to be back to my old self, to set the derailed train of my life back on its track, to be free like Hollis was? I was not prepared for the story she told when she returned to Halstead two days earlier than I expected.

In a voice that was half sob, half complaint, she told me what happened on her trip.

Marshall and Hollis, hungry and groggy, took a taxi to the hospital at six o'clock on Thursday morning. Dr. Pasternak, who had been at work for an hour already, met them in the lobby and brought them up to her office. They knew something was wrong because she looked angry and distracted. She worked hard to speak kindly to them, to keep her rage in check.

Dr. Pasternak closed the door of her office and said grimly,

"We've been overruled."

Marshall and Hollis were too stunned to speak.

"I'm sorry," she continued. "You came all this way, and it was a waste of time."

Marshall was the first to recover enough to respond, though all he could say was,

"What do you mean we've been overruled? By whom?"

"By the chief of the department. Dr. Gottlieb. He has to approve every case. I've never known him to second-guess the committee. Until today, that is."

"But why?"

"I wish I could tell you," Dr. Pasternak said. "But he doesn't have to give me an explanation."

She fell into her desk chair and motioned for Hollis and Marshall to sit as well. Hollis did, but Marshall continued to pace. Standing felt like resistance; sitting like acceptance.

"Did I do something wrong?" Hollis finally asked.

"No, of course not," Dr. Pasternak said, softening. Her anger came down a register.

"This committee is Gottlieb's brainchild. His whole reason for setting it up was so that we could make impartial decisions. He wants our committee to be above reproach, and he thought it looked bad."

"I don't understand," Marshall said. "What looked bad?"

Dr. Pasternak focused her eyes on the ceiling, as if looking directly at her nephew could turn her into a pillar of salt.

"There's something I didn't tell you, Marshall. It turns out that the reason Lauden approved you is that he wanted *quid pro quo* from me. He needed my vote for his granddaughter, apparently. She's being prepped for a D&C at this very moment." By the confusion on Marshall's and Hollis's faces, she was able to anticipate their next question.

"A D&C is what they call it when they don't want to use the word abortion," she explained. "Anyway, I guess Gottlieb wasn't comfortable approving two relatives of senior doctors, while clinic patients were being turned away. So he overruled your case."

Hollis reeled from the import of this decision. And then she saw another doctor, judging by the white coat, leaned his torso into Dr. Pasternak's office. He had knocked with one finger and then, rather than wait for a response, pushed the door open with his knuckle.

"Sorry to interrupt," he said, but he did not wait for entry to be granted or denied. Based on Dr. Pasternak's refusal to greet him, Hollis concluded that this must be Dr. Lauden.

"That's a tough break, Fern," he said. "I came to tell you how sorry I am. I want you" —he looked at Marshall and Hollis— "all of you, to understand that there are extenuating circumstances. I wouldn't have let Gottlieb bump you like that if there hadn't been a good reason."

Lauden waited for Dr. Pasternak to ask him about the extenuating circumstances, but she did not. She looked at him coldly and expressed no concern for his granddaughter.

"I see that you're angry," he said. "And I would be too if I didn't know the whole story. There's a reason I pressured Gottlieb to put my Audrey first, and it's not that I think my family is more important than yours."

He stepped farther into the room and closed the door behind him.

"We've worked together a long time, Fern. I'm going to level with you. Because I don't want you to hold this against me forever."

He was not looking at Marshall and Hollis, but he was speaking for their benefit as much as for his colleague's.

"This fellow that Audrey has been going with, the one who got her into this mess . . . You have to understand," Lauden looked beseechingly at Aunt Fern. "He's a Negro." He said it slowly, as if the information would be difficult to process. "Now do you understand? You see what I'm dealing with? How could she possibly have his baby? She tells me he's a West Point graduate, as if that makes a difference. I have to look out for her, since she clearly can't look out for herself. You understand now, don't you?"

★ ★ ★

When Hollis finished telling me the story of her wasted trip to New York, she looked at me with her big, tearful eyes and asked, "What will I do, Bonnie?"

It was all I could do not to scream at her, *What will you do?* I was tired of pretending that her wellbeing was a higher priority than mine. *What about me?* I wanted to say. Following Marshall's lead had gotten her nowhere, and had gotten me several paces behind nowhere. But I held back my anger and panic, because clearly, she had already learned the lesson my questions would have taught her. The hospital bureaucracy had rendered Hollis as irrelevant as I had felt for the past two weeks. She had been ahead of me in what was beginning to feel like an exhausting and humiliating challenge on *Beat the Clock*, but Lauden's granddaughter had bested us both.

★ ★ ★

The next day, I received the letter from the Boston psychiatrist. He must have sent it the day my check arrived. Our contact had consisted of a ten-minute phone call. He asked me a list of questions, prefaced with the instruction that I should answer "yes" to all of them. "Are you experiencing profound emotional distress as a result of your pregnancy? Have you considered harming yourself as a result of this distress?"

The letter talked about my depression and suicidality, just as I expected it would, but in the last paragraph it referred to me by someone else's name. Clearly, this was a form letter, and the doctor did not bother to fill it out correctly. Back in my room, I called the doctor's office and asked them to please correct it. They wanted to charge me another fifteen dollars for a new letter, but I insisted that the mistake had been theirs and should be fixed free of charge. I sometimes look back and think of that as the very first case I won.

19

I N THE DAYS AFTER OUR BIRTHDAY CELEBRATION, Stephanie and I spoke regularly, for real. She told me how tedious her summer job was.

"It sounded great when I interviewed. People donate broken blenders and coffeemakers. We train homeless people to fix the broken stuff, and then we sell them in a thrift store. But all I do is put the price tags on the repaired appliances. I'm not even the one who decides on the prices. Someone tells me a number and I write it on a sticker."

She called once to mull over the possibility that she had outgrown college.

"It's a party school, and when they're not having beer-drinking contests, they're having pie-eating contests. I can't wait to live off-campus."

Then she asked if she could come to Hopkins for her last free weekend before school started up.

"I want to see where you live. And where you work," she said.

As much as I loved the idea of hosting a visit from her, that was the moment that, for the first time since I had begun my search five months earlier, a thought I had been suppressing shot to the surface. The words *I don't have time for this* spoke themselves in my brain. The fact was that finding and getting to know Stephanie had taken a lot of time and focus, and I had fallen behind in my work. I had due dates looming, and I had clients calling for status reports.

I had been planning to go into the office over the weekend to catch up on drafting and billing, not to give tours. But I had never said no to Stephanie. I didn't know what the cost would be. She was sensitive to rejection, and I didn't want to risk it. I told her that I would love to see her, and then told myself that this was mostly true. I had expected meeting Stephanie to be either wonderful or awful. I had not anticipated that it would be messy.

Stephanie was polite and appreciative when I showed her around my office. We both knew there wasn't much to see, but she was a good sport about mustering up interest in my bar certificates and Audubon prints. I tried not to glance over at the files I should have been working on. As soon as I mentioned that I had prepared lunch back at my house, she was suddenly very hungry. Once inside my home, she was much more deliberate in her exploration. She stood on the threshold and took it in slowly, not sure what to look at first. She began by walking around the periphery, looking at the watercolors on the walls, the books on the shelves, the family photos on the mantle.

"Are these my grandparents?" she asked.

Grandparents. Just to hear that word nearly knocked me over. I was too choked up to answer. She thought of my mother and father, whom she had never met, as her kin, connected directly to her. I nodded.

"Did they ever know about me?"

"They did," I said, and I felt tears coming on.

"Did they ever meet me?"

"No, I'm afraid not. They would have liked that." I felt unsteady on my legs and sat down on my couch. "By the time they took me home from the hospital, you were gone."

Next Stephanie examined the lamps and knickknacks on the side tables. She particularly admired a pair of ceramic candlesticks, hand-painted like Easter eggs in pastel squiggles. It was a funny choice for a girl in a black t-shirt and green painter's pants, I thought. She leaned in to get a closer look at a photo of me and my parents at my college graduation.

"You look happy in this picture," she said.

"I was," I agreed. The day of my commencement had been a good one. That was one of the few days when I felt gratified by my accomplishments and certain I had made the right choices.

Over lunch of poached salmon and salad, I told Stephanie more about my parents. Speaking of them was the next best thing to being with them, and I was happy for the opportunity. I talked about how hard they had worked, how they had doted on me, how sad it had been to lose them.

Stephanie, in turn, told me more about the roommates with whom she would be sharing an apartment beginning in a week.

"Carina and I have been friends since freshman year, but she won't be around much. She's hoping to work a lot of shifts in the med school library, to save up for after college."

"And who's the other roommate?"

"His name's Jason. I don't know him well, but we heard he was looking for housemates. He seems like a good guy."

"It's funny to think about living with a boy in college." I shook my head at the prospect. "It's just so different."

"So, all of your friends from college are women?" The concept was as foreign to her as the idea of cohabitation with a man was to me.

"That's right," I said. "And I have no complaints."

"Hmm," she said, while she thought about it for a second.

"Tell me about some of your friends from college," she said.

"Well, let's see. My best friend from college is definitely Carol. She's the one who lent me her phonebook to find Dr. Hauptman."

Stephanie seemed to think this was an interesting enough answer.

"When did you know she was your best friend?"

"When she lent me her phonebook."

"No, I'm serious. Were you, like, best friends from the moment you met?"

This made me smile, because I actually did remember Carol from my very first day at Halstead.

"No, not at all. Our first interaction was memorable, but not because we were instant soulmates. We didn't become friends until we had a class together second semester."

"What happened the first time you met?"

I hadn't told this story in years, and I wasn't sure what Stephanie would think of it.

"Well," I began, tentatively, "on the first night of orientation, there was a barbecue for our whole class. I was standing in line, waiting for my hamburger, or whatever, with my roommate Hollis. Then Hollis turned around and said to the girl behind us, 'So, who are you?' It was Carol. We went through the usual stuff about where we're from and which dorm we're in. Carol told us she grew up on a navy base in Corpus Christi. She said her father, at that very moment, was commanding an aircraft carrier in the South China Sea. And then suddenly a woman ten feet away—I don't even know how she heard our conversation—wheeled around and said, really loudly, 'So your father transports the bombs that kill the babies, but he doesn't actually kill the babies himself. Do I have that right?'"

Stephanie stopped eating.

"Wow," she said. "That's intense."

"It was," I said. "It was awful."

"What did you say?"

"I didn't know what to say. I was so shocked. I had never met anyone who talked so openly against the war. Who was so hostile. Luckily, without missing a beat, Hollis jumped in to say there was an heiress to the Oscar Mayer fortune in our class, and, if anyone killed babies, it was probably her family, because how else could that baloney be so pink? I was impressed, and really grateful, that Hollis could think so fast. And here's the funny part. Before we went to bed that night, I asked her what she would do if her comment ever got back to the Oscar Mayer heiress. She said, 'I'm not worried about that, because I just made her up.'"

Stephanie looked at me and smiled.

"Bonnie, that was obvious, even to me. Did you really not get that?"

"Not at the time, no," I admitted. "I wasn't very sophisticated when I arrived at Halstead."

She was shaking her head slightly. I was glad that my youthful naiveté amused her.

"Is Hollis still one of your friends?" she asked.

I inhaled and hoped the oxygen would steady me.

"That's a story for another day," I said. "But it all comes back to the same point. You don't know right away who is going to be a friend for life. It takes a lifetime to figure that out. A lot depends on what happens later, and, believe it or not, a lot depends on who makes the effort. Some friends return your phone calls, and some don't."

"Yeah, that's good advice. I'll mention it to Drew. He's flipping out because freshman orientation ended five days ago, and he doesn't have a best friend yet."

"So you've talked to him since he went to school?"

Stephanie hadn't told me much about her relationship with her brother. I didn't know to what extent the friction between Maureen and Stephanie had infected the interactions between the siblings.

"Yeah, we're buddies. I don't hold it against him that he's the perfect child."

And then she asked me if I would like to meet Carina the following weekend.

"She's going to come up to school a few days early so we can shop for the apartment. You can help us pick out some stuff."

I wondered if what Stephanie was really thinking was that she and Carina would do all the picking out while I would do all the paying for. I also wondered if I would feel sufficiently caught up in my work by then.

"I would love to meet Carina," I said. "But I have to see how my work goes this week. I'm not sure I'll be able to take another day off next weekend."

Stephanie looked more hurt than I expected.

"You don't want to meet my housemates?" She stopped short of whining, but came problematically close.

"Of course I do." Hadn't I said just that, not a minute ago? "I just don't know if it will happen so soon. I have a few things at work I have to finish first." Of all the things I thought I would be taken to task for, all the actions I thought Stephanie would resent, keeping on top of my work wasn't on the list.

"Well, I'm asking you to do this for me. I don't understand what could be so important that you have to do it on a summer weekend."

That was as far as I was willing to push. There was no point in telling her, for the third time, that I really did want to get to know her friends. It would be a waste of effort to point out that the weekends of September weren't really considered "summer weekends." It made more sense to capitulate. Hadn't I, since I met her, been mindful that Stephanie's mother made her feel secondary to Drew? Didn't I, of all people, see how much Stephanie needed to feel loved and special?

"Of course I'll come up to Burlington next weekend," I said.

She perked up immediately.

"Great," she said. "Then I should get going. I'm supposed to be home to meet some guys for dinner. I'm stuffed. I can't believe I'm going to eat again. That was so good, Bonnie. Can I use your bathroom before I go?"

I sent her upstairs with instructions to turn left at the landing. I was glad she was leaving in time for me to squeeze in a few hours back at the office. While I cleared the table, I pondered this new complexity. I was so overjoyed to find a daughter who wanted me in her life. But now I had to think through the possibility that she wanted me too much. Stephanie was needy in a way I hadn't expected, in a way that was obscured by her frequent expressions of certainty and sarcasm. I would have to navigate this carefully, I thought. Stephanie took her time coming back downstairs, but I didn't find out why until much, much later.

* * *

I did manage to make progress on my legal matters that week, so I could spare a day to visit Stephanie the following Saturday. And I tried not to be resentful of the way she had twisted my arm. I was a bit on edge when I first arrived, worried that the petulance she had employed to induce me to visit might reappear. But she was as pleasant a hostess as could be that day. I actually enjoyed tagging along while she and her friend Carina chose a futon and some non-stick cookware. And they didn't even ask me to pay for anything. I ended up, entirely of my own volition, springing for a couple of things at an upscale kitchen store on Church Street, just because I got a kick out of watching Stephanie and Carina together. They had similar tastes, and got excited over things like popsicle molds in the shape of rocket ships (purchased), rainbow colored paper lanterns (purchased), and an expensive Italian corkscrew shaped like a woman in a dress (not purchased).

Stephanie talked much faster to Carina than she did to me. They sometimes broke out into little bits of song without any cue that I could observe. I would ask, "Are the police here strict about enforcing the meters?" and they would sing, in unison,

"If you want to *find* all the cops, they're hanging out *in* the donut shop," complete with synchronous hip movements.

If I was quiet and let them forget I was there, I got to hear their complaints about their love lives. I gathered that Stephanie had recently broken up with a guy who was too clingy, and Carina had recently broken up with a guy who claimed to be "morally opposed to monogamy" and had two other girlfriends.

"I told him, 'You can date other women instead of me, but you can't date other women in addition to me.'"

Stephanie approved.

"Saying you're against monogamy is really just another way of saying you're a douchebag," she assured her friend.

Half an hour later, as we emerged from a bookstore on Church Street, our visit took a strange turn. Suddenly, we were face to face with Maureen, who looked as surprised as we were. She took a moment to process what she was seeing. I expected her expression to reflect comprehension and then betrayal. But it was she who looked like she had been caught doing something she shouldn't. Then her face softened.

"Well, isn't this a surprise?" she said. She was gracious enough, but I wasn't sure she was genuine.

"Hi, Mom," said Stephanie, who appeared to be the most relaxed of us all. "I was just giving Bonnie a tour of downtown Burlington."

Maureen responded as if this explanation were amusing.

"And what will you do for the other fifty-two minutes of the hour?" she asked.

Stephanie smiled at her mother's sarcasm, but it was clear that this jab at their home city was one she had heard before.

"Maybe hit the mall," Stephanie said, not taking the bait.

"I just wanted to wish Stephanie well in the new school year," I said, as if I needed to justify my presence.

"That's very thoughtful of you," said Maureen, calmly tolerating my unwarranted nervousness. "And as long as you're here, you must try the chocolates."

She fished her wallet out of her purse and handed Stephanie some money.

"Go get Bonnie a small sampler," she said, and jutted her chin toward the end of the street.

"Sure," said Stephanie, surprisingly cooperative. It was clear to me that Maureen had something she wanted to say, but Stephanie did not seem to have picked up on this.

"Milk or dark?" she asked me.

"You figure it out," I said.

As soon as Stephanie was out of earshot, I said to Maureen,

"I hope she told you I was coming."

She was calm. "She didn't," she said, "but that's okay. I don't need to keep daily tabs on her."

"No, of course not," I said, "but no one likes to feel sidelined."

That wasn't the word I meant to use. I hadn't meant to suggest that I had preempted Maureen in Stephanie's affections. Now I worried I'd overstated my position, and Maureen was about to inform me that I couldn't displace her if I tried. This wasn't how I expected to have this conversation. Way back when I talked about the registries with the kind social worker Elizabeth, she had told me that it was important to defer to the adoptive parents. Your presence could throw them off balance, she had warned. You have to assure them that you come in peace. But I had never imagined that I would have to make these assurances during a surprise meeting on a public street, and that I would have only as much time as it takes to order a half dozen chocolate caramels. I was doing a terrible job of it.

"You're very thoughtful," she said. I don't think she meant it. She was just trying not to engage. "Admittedly, I didn't anticipate this encounter." I noticed then that, despite her words, Maureen looked as if she had, in fact, expected to be seen that day. She wore makeup and a stylish fall coat. "But I'm happy that you two are spending time together. That's what I wanted to say. She seems happier since she met you. More grounded. Less volatile."

I was surprised by Maureen's generosity, but even more surprised by her description of Stephanie. I had seen that Stephanie could be impulsive. She could be mature and insightful one moment, and thoughtless and cutting another. But I considered these foibles to be minor, even endearing. Maureen seemed to be suggesting that the Stephanie I knew was an improved version of the one she knew.

"I'm glad to hear it," I said.

"It's hard to move on from your past when you don't know your past," she continued. We could see Stephanie emerging from the sweet shop and walking down the block toward us. "She's been stuck for quite some time now."

Stephanie was almost in earshot when Maureen finished her point. "We all were. But now there are no more missing parts. She can move on with her life." Maureen dropped her voice and seemed to be talking more to herself than to me. "We all can."

Stephanie was back, and she handed me a small bag.

"I went with the dark chocolate truffles," she said.

"Those are my favorites," I assured her.

"I figured," she said.

★ ★ ★

"I hope my mom didn't say anything creepy," Stephanie said as she and Carina walked me back to my car.

"Not at all," I said. By now I had recovered from the strangeness of the interaction. "It's clear that she really loves you."

"Yeah, probably," Stephanie said, unwilling to concede. But before I could decide whether or not to press the point, we were walking past a scene of semi-chaos. As we approached, we could see that there were people, maybe twenty of them, protesting in front of a women's health clinic. They stood at the curb with crosses, rosaries and poster-sized pictures of babies. There were also a few people in Day-Glo orange vests flanking the door of the clinic and walking patients into the building. Thankfully, everyone seemed smart enough to keep their distance from their ideological enemies, and it looked like there would be sufficient room on the sidewalk for us to pass.

I'll admit that I was nervous, not about the conflict, but about the conversation that the conflict was likely to spark between me and Stephanie. She had asked me, the very first time we met, if I had considered an abortion, and I had deflected the question by answering, "I got pregnant in 1969," and hoping that her knowledge of history was such that she could fill in the rest. She had also asked me if I were troubled to learn that she had been raised Episcopalian. I answered with a simple, "No, of course not," and realized only later that the question was premised on the assumption that I was Catholic.

This is to say that Stephanie and I had not yet aired our views on this particular source of national division. I realized that I had no idea where she stood or how she would react to the scene in front of the clinic. The protesters were hardly an intimidating lot, mostly older women, maybe even nuns, with white hair, holding pictures of the Virgin Mary. And then one of them stepped out of the huddle to approach us. I don't know if she mistook us for patients or was simply trying to place her flyers in as many hands as possible that day, but she held out a leaflet to Stephanie.

Stephanie stopped, looked down at the paper, then up again.

"Oh, go suck Jesus's cock," she snapped.

The woman froze. Several people gasped, and I admit that I was one of them. I grabbed Stephanie's elbow and pulled her away. She was practically giggling.

"What were you thinking?" I demanded to know.

"Aw, c'mon. I was having some fun. I've done the training to be an escort, you know. But you can't talk like that when you're wearing the orange vest. In the training they tell us not to escalate the confrontation."

"You might need a little more training," I suggested. But I was unable to convince Stephanie that she had done anything wrong.

★ ★ ★

I told Theo about the incident the next time I saw him.

"She sounds positively unhinged," he said.

Though I had been similarly critical of Stephanie in the moment, his characterization made me want to defend her. But we were waiting for his patient's sister, the woman who hoped I could guide her through the process of finding her son. She walked into Theo's office before I had the chance. He had told me very little about the woman, and I wondered if he knew her at all, or if he thought of her merely as a conduit to a potential source of bone marrow. I imagined a woman just like me, or rather, like the me I had been just six months earlier.

But as soon as Theo introduced me to Constance Fallon, I was concerned that she was emotionally unprepared to undertake a search. She was too thin, I thought, as if she had spent time interned in some kind of penal colony. And she was nervous, hesitant to look me or Theo in the eye. She sat where Theo told her to sit, and she did not speak directly to me. It was Theo who spoke to her first.

"I can't thank you enough for agreeing to meet," he said. He spoke softly and gently. "I know this is very painful for you, but I truly believe that a lot of good is going to come from this. For both you and your brother."

Constance nodded, but she seemed unconvinced. Theo continued, "My friend Bonnie wanted to talk to you, because she knows what you've been through. And she knows a lot about the ins and outs of finding an adopted child. I don't want to speak for her, but I think I can say she has found it very rewarding to meet her daughter."

Theo's words had just the right calming effect on Constance. She looked at me. "Is that true?" she asked.

"Yes," I assured her. "It took time, and some of it was quite painstaking, but it was all worth it."

She didn't respond, so I offered, "Do you want to hear my story, or do you first want to tell me what you've done so far?"

She looked at me as if I were a teacher who had requested a progress report on a term paper.

"I haven't done anything so far, except for the letter I left for him when he was a baby. I put it in his file, in case he ever came looking for me. And I always keep my address up to date with the agency. I don't know what more I can do."

Constance looked like she was about to cry, and Theo jumped in. "It's sounds like you've done all the right things so far. Bonnie has a few more ideas she'd like to share."

I had underestimated Theo. He was as patient with Constance as he was with his uncle. I considered advising her that searching for a relinquished child required a steely disposition. But it would have been pointless, not to mention slightly disingenuous. I had hardly lived up to my own standards of self-control throughout the process. Instead, I told her about the registries, and about how to exploit the flimsiest of clues. I asked her what she knew about the family who had adopted her boy.

"I was told they were a good, Irish family who had already adopted a girl. The father was a doctor, and the mother was a house-wife. I remember they said the mum was very musical. They were quite grudging about telling me even that much. But I was making a big fuss about signing the papers. They were afraid I wasn't going to do it, so they answered some of my questions."

At that last sentence, I sensed a shift in Constance from sadness to anger. I was skeptical of the agency's description of the family, but I kept my cynicism to myself. The family sounded just a little too perfect. If I were trying to convince a reluctant birth mother to give up her baby, I would depict the expectant parents exactly as the agency had, whether it was true or not.

Theo asked her if she had been told where the couple lived. But instead of answering him, she looked at me. "You remember how it was," she said. "Don't you? They didn't tell you anything in those homes. We weren't even allowed to use our real names with the other girls. I was supposed to go by 'Anne.'"

She looked at me, thinking that I could help her educate Theo. But I didn't know very much about homes for unwed mothers. Perhaps I had been luckier than I realized at the time. My parents had welcomed me home and protected me from harsh gossip. Clearly, there were humiliations that I had been spared.

I could tell Theo was worried. Allowing Constance to revisit the misery of her pregnancy was not going to move us forward.

"One thing Bonnie learned," he said, trying to get back on track, "is that it's helpful to know if your adoption was public or private. What's the name of the agency?"

"I don't know the name, but it was public, I think," she said coldly. She was making an effort to tamp down her rage. "I'm not sure. I remember the social worker telling me that the State covered my stay at St. Mary's. That if I didn't give the baby up, I would have to pay the money back."

Theo and I winced at this. Constance's newborn had been treated like a commodity, one she would have to buy back from the adoption agency. And yet they expected her to be grateful to them. That I could relate to. I had been made to feel similarly at St. Gabriel's.

"I'm sorry," Theo said. "No woman should be treated like that."

Constance shook her head.

"Woman," she repeated, as if this were an interesting word to ponder. "I wasn't a woman. I was a sixteen-year-old girl."

Constance looked down into her own lap and went quiet. Theo raised his eyebrows at me in a silent request that I take over. "You have every right to be angry," I said to her. "No one can blame you for that."

"Thank you," she said. "But I don't think anyone can really understand, you know? There's no point in trying to explain."

I wish I could say that I bared my soul to Constance so that she would bare hers to me. I might have told her the story of my years of being too afraid to search, might have been honest about my own fears of being judged by strangers and scorned by friends. I could have reassured Constance that she would discover kindness in many corners even if she didn't discover the truth. I should have told her that finding my daughter had eased a loneliness I didn't even know was there.

But that is not who I am, and that is not what I did. I am neither comfortable nor practiced at forging emotional connections with strangers. But I have learned over years of doing client intakes that people want to tell their stories. In fact, sometimes this is their only reason for seeking legal counsel. They want to be listened to and taken seriously. They especially want to watch you nod your head in sympathy and write their words down on yellow lined paper.

"If you're going to search for your son," I said gently, "you're going to have to tell people what happened."

Constance nodded her understanding.

"I found that it's a good idea to practice with a sympathetic audience." I paused to let her consider my idea. "Why don't you try with me right now? Forget that anyone else is in the room. I'll just listen, and the next time you have to do it, it will be easier." I looked right at her so she would know that she had my full attention.

"Yes, I suspect you're right," she agreed. She took a deep breath and spoke softly.

"I grew up west of here. It wasn't far, but it was different. It was a small town. I was in high school when I got pregnant. I wasn't even sure I'd had sex." She exhaled an involuntary rueful snort. "Sure I felt *something* when it happened, but I had no idea what it was supposed to feel like. All my girlfriends were having sex, and they would ask me if I'd done it yet, and I didn't know how to answer. My boyfriend had no clue what he was doing, and there was no such thing as birth control, as far as I knew. I had no idea I was pregnant until one day my clothes didn't fit anymore.

"I told my mother first, because she and I had always been close. I thought she would make it all okay. But instead, she screamed at me. 'How could you do this to us? This will kill your father.' She acted like I'd shot the Pope. From then on, I was the black sheep of the family. My pregnancy was an affront to their good values. She told my brother not to date any of my friends. If they hung out with me, then they clearly weren't nice girls, she said.

"They sent me to St. Mary's when I began to show. The baby's father tried to visit me there, but the nuns chased him away. I'm not sure whether that's because boyfriends weren't allowed inside, or just because I couldn't take a break from my chores. He didn't come back after that. The other girls were nice enough. Of course, we called each other by our real names, even though we weren't supposed to. I kept hoping one of them could tell me what was going to happen to me, but they didn't know anything either. Each time a girl went into labor, she disappeared. We never saw her again.

"Even before my son was born, I knew that he loved me more than my own mother and father did. They didn't love me at all, as far as I could tell. They didn't contact me once when I was in St. Mary's. The only time I called them was when I went into labor. I was so scared, but my mother just said, 'Good. It's almost over, and you can put it behind you.'

"I was terrified of delivering, and they just made it worse. They acted like my body was in the way. They gave me an enema, and they even shaved me . . . down there. I didn't think it could get worse, but then they strapped me to the bed. I wondered if they did that to everyone, or if this punishment was just for me because I had done something particularly terrible."

I didn't know the answer. I just sat in silent gratitude that I had been spared.

"At least I got to spend a few days with my baby before they took him away. I named him Sean. I would unwrap his blanket and trace his soft skin with my finger. I would talk to him about how we were going to run away, and how I would never turn my back on him the way my parents had done to me. But I think I was also trying to memorize his perfect little body. Because I knew it wasn't true. I knew I couldn't take care of him. I couldn't bring him into my home; my parents had made that much clear.

"Still, when the social worker told me to sign the papers, I said I wasn't sure. I said I wanted to keep him. She said, 'Fine,' and for a split second I thought she was going to help me do it. And then she started telling me how much it had cost for me to live at St. Mary's, and how much the hospital bill was. She even added up the cost of the diapers we had used in a week. She told me if that I wanted to keep Sean, then I had to pay back all the money they had spent to take care of me for those months.

"When I got home, it was like I was in shock. My mother kept telling me that I would be able to get on with my life as soon as I apologized to my father for what I had done to him. We never talked about the baby. Never. I never forgave her, and I never stopped thinking about my son. He is with me all the time. I have never been able to love anyone like I loved Sean in that one week we spent together. And the way he looked up at me, I could tell he loved me too. More than anyone has ever loved me since."

I was afraid to react. I was so saddened—horrified, even—at what Constance had endured. I worried that if she saw my revulsion at the sheer cruelty of her ordeal she would think I was judging her. And I didn't want her to know that I hadn't actually shared her suffering. I tried not to reveal much emotion while I said, "I'm so sorry. I am so, so sorry."

She smiled weakly in gratitude.

"I'm sorry too," Theo said. We had forgotten he was there. "Thank you for sharing your experience. That was very brave of you."

"I feel a little light-headed now," she said. "Is there anything to eat?"

"Certainly," Theo said. "I'll get you something from the cafeteria."

As soon as he left the room, Constance turned to me. "If I tell you something else, will you promise not to tell Dr. Theo?"

"I keep secrets for a living," I assured her. "And, besides, I hardly know the man."

"There is a part of me that is grateful for my brother's illness. I know that sounds terrible, but I was finally able to say to my parents' gravestones what I could never say to them when they were alive. I went to the cemetery last week, and I told them that this was all their fault. They should never have made me give up my baby. If they had let me keep Sean, then they would have a grandson, and he might be able to save my brother. It felt good to finally get it out, even though it was too late."

★ ★ ★

Theo and I had a drink after the meeting, and he got right to his most pressing question.

"What do you think the odds are that we'll find the nephew?"

"I don't know," I said. "It doesn't sound like she has much to go on."

"That's too bad. Her brother's a real fighter. But she struck me as someone who just crumples when things get tough."

"That's not quite fair," I said, still thinking about all she had told us about her ordeal. "What happened to her was really traumatizing. Much worse than what I went through."

"Well, of course," Theo said cheerfully. "You had my uncle."

This was what I found so puzzling about Theo. When I watched him interact with people, he was deferential and decent. But when those people weren't around, he was judgmental and cutting. He treated his patients kindly and yet he blinded himself to his uncle's failures of kindness. I thought about Dr. Hauptman's description of me in his diary: an unwed college girl who got herself pregnant. But I chose not to tell Theo any of this—not how his uncle had made me feel when I gave birth, and not how, in the doctor's notes, he had accused me of the medically improbable feat of auto-impregnation.

* * *

As the fall went on, Stephanie got busier with school and I got busier with work, but we talked on the phone a few times a week. So this is what it feels like to be friends with your own daughter, I thought. Our initial reunion had been so intense and emotional, but now we were settling into more mundane interactions. Sometimes I questioned whether we were taking steps forward or steps back. I was never quite sure if I was calling too much or too little, being too intimate or too distant. The whole situation reminded me of what I've been told about learning to drive in England. At first it feels totally foreign to drive on the left side of the road; you know you're doing it right because it feels totally wrong. But when driving on the unfamiliar side starts to feel normal, that's when things get really dangerous.

Some of our conversations, I'll admit, would have been downright boring, if I had had them with anyone else.

"We put an old couch on our front porch," she might say. "We got it from Jason's grandmother's house."

"In Lyndonville?" I would ask.

I never admitted this to her, but I used to keep track of the details of her stories by jotting them down in a little notebook on my desk.

"Yeah. Jason and I drove there last Sunday to get it. On the way back, we picked some apples near Stowe, and then made a pie back at the apartment. Jason's grandmother gave us the recipe."

I was beginning to notice that Stephanie never missed an opportunity to slide Jason's name into the conversation.

"Did Carina help you make it, or just help you eat it?"

"Neither. She was at work."

According to my notes, Carina worked four shifts a week at her library job and was rarely home. I heard about how Jason taught Stephanie to rollerblade, and she reciprocated by teaching him to make macaroni and cheese. In one conversation, Stephanie told me that she had started to read *The Unbearable Lightness of Being*, but couldn't finish it because the male characters were all despicable. I was envious that she had, so early in life, realized that she was entitled to cut her literary losses and toss an offensive book in the trash. Hearing her talk about Kundera, though, also got me thinking about the possibility of taking a trip with Stephanie. Czechoslovakia had recently undergone its velvet revolution, and tourists were flocking to Prague. Maybe in the spring, when Stephanie finished school, we could see it for ourselves.

I did get to meet Jason once, when I drove up to Burlington on a late October Saturday. He was a mature looking young man, with a beard and the kind of broad shoulders one might get from chopping down trees. I was surprised that Stephanie had not mentioned this as one of his salient characteristics. She gave me a tour of the apartment and took special note of all the things we bought together over the summer. The tour did not include Jason's bedroom.

"From the smell, I think he might be running an underground petting zoo in there," she said, loudly enough for him to hear.

"Nah," he said. "The zoo is just a cover for my marijuana farm."

I took them to lunch at a Mexican restaurant around the corner. When Stephanie and I both ordered chicken enchiladas with red sauce, black beans, extra sour cream, and no cilantro, his eyes went wide, as if we had just performed an astounding parlor trick.

"No way."

Stephanie shrugged it off.

"That? We always do that," she said. "We like all the same stuff."

"What else?" Jason asked.

"Oh, you know," I said, "piña coladas, getting caught in the rain. That sort of thing."

Jason laughed. I remembered how, a few months earlier, I had been the audience for Stephanie and Carter's banter. I relished my new role as the insider.

"You guys are funny," he said. "Steph, I didn't see you chilling out like this last week when we went out with your other mom."

I felt a disorienting jolt, then instantly told myself to calm down. I shouldn't be jealous, I reminded myself, because no good could possibly come from that. And I shouldn't expect Stephanie to report to me about every time she socialized with her parents. Of course Carter and Maureen were going to continue to see her more often than I did. They lived nearby, and, as I kept reminding myself, they were her parents. But I didn't have to like it. I wanted to think of Stephanie's attachment to Jason, the secret crush I had detected, as a part of her life to which only I was privy. I simply didn't want to share it.

"Ugh," said Stephanie. "Wasn't my mom *so* annoying?"

"Not really," he said. "I can put up with a lot in exchange for free food."

I sensed that this was not the first time Stephanie had tried to enlist Jason to join in criticizing her mother and he had resisted.

"She kept asking you all those questions." Stephanie said it as if Maureen's interest in Jason were offensive. "And then she acted like your answers didn't pass her test. What's it to her if you want to paint houses for the summer after graduation?"

"It didn't bother me so much. Really, Steph. My own mother doesn't like the plan either."

"Do you have projects already lined up?" I asked, trying to shift the conversation away from Maureen and back to Jason.

"No, I'm going to get a house on Martha's Vineyard with seven or eight other guys. We'll all get jobs out there."

"Doesn't that sound fun?" Stephanie said to me. "Maybe I'll get a job out there too, in a store or a restaurant."

Jason chuckled. "Yeah, right," he said.

"What?" Stephanie asked. "You think I can't sell kitschy beach souvenirs?"

"I'm sure you can," he said, "but why would you want to?"

I couldn't believe Jason was this obtuse. Surely, he had to know what would motivate Stephanie to join him in Martha's Vineyard. Was it possible that he had not yet figured out what was so obvious to me?

"It's a compliment, Steph," Jason continued. "I don't see you ringing up starfish mobiles for a living. Wouldn't you rather move to New York and organize a nanny's union or something?"

"It's so weird that you would suggest that. Did you know that Carina wants to move to New York?"

"She does?"

"Yeah. She said she wants to get a master's at NYU. She said she wants me to come too."

"Well, I would definitely visit you if you were both there."

"I haven't been to New York in ages," I said. "I went to see the big Picasso show, and I think that was over ten years ago."

Stephanie looked at me as if she had forgotten I was there.

"Maybe we could go together," I offered. "A little sight-seeing trip over your Christmas break? We could look at some different neighborhoods, see if it's for you. What do you think?"

"Sure," Stephanie said, still not sure it was a good idea. "That sounds great."

So much for Prague, I thought.

20

After the hospital committee changed its mind about granting Hollis an abortion, we all gave up on any hope that we could get the procedure legally. The committee in Boston rejected my application too; the letter I purchased dearly had been worthless. A part of me was relieved. I didn't actually want a panel of doctors to believe that I was mentally ill. My whole life I had been the girl who was smart, grounded, and going places. That was my identity. I didn't want to trade it in for a damaged psyche.

Reluctantly, Dr. Pasternak said she knew a doctor who could help us. Though she insisted she would lose her job if her colleagues knew of her involvement, she gave us the name of Dr. Arthur Klein. She had trained under him during her residency, and now he was enjoying a placid retirement in the Berkshires. I happened to be the one home in our room when she called.

"He's a good man," she assured me. "He might not have all the latest equipment and training, but you can trust him. He's not in it for the money, and he'll look out for you."

Just hearing Dr. Pasternak express concern for my safety made me want to cry with gratitude. She was turning out to be my most loyal supporter in all this.

I thanked her, and my voice cracked with emergent sobs.

"Oh, Bonnie," she said, and she sounded like she wanted to cry too. "You shouldn't be thanking me. I feel like I've let you down."

"No," I insisted, "you've done so much."

"It's a crazy system," she said wistfully. "We thought we were making it better with our committee. We could at least help some women. But it doesn't really make sense to have panels of strangers making decisions for women they don't know. People think it would be chaos if we just let women figure out for themselves when an abortion is their best option. Okay, maybe it would be a little messy, but it's like what Winston Churchill said about democracy. The worst system in the world, except for all the others."

★ ★ ★

Dr. Klein said we should come see him first thing Saturday morning. We should come together, and bring someone who could drive us home. Already I felt better, because I remembered how Dr. Wormsbecher had insisted I come to his office alone. Also, we knew stories about girls who had been directed to wait alone on a street corner and then shoved into a car, blindfolded, and driven in circles for hours. It was reassuring that Klein wanted us to be accompanied, even though our companion would be a witness, and therefore a liability for him. Klein's only request was that we not tell anyone where we were going.

Marshall slept over the night before so that we could leave at the crack of dawn. None of us spoke on the ride to Dr. Klein's house on a country road outside Lenox. The curtains of his home were drawn, as if the owners had gone south for the winter. The sun was barely up as we got out of the car, and we worried that the sound of three car doors closing would draw attention from the neighbors. We rang the doorbell. Almost instantly, the door opened a few inches, and we were told to hurry inside. The woman who beckoned us was brusque and anxious, and she looked us up and down. She did not introduce herself.

"I'll tell my husband you're here," she said with resignation.

She walked out of the room and left us standing in the parlor. We took what comfort we could from the fact that the room was clean and tidy, indicative of a respectable retired doctor, not a butcher.

The woman we assumed was Dr. Klein's wife reappeared and told us to follow her down a hallway.

"He's all set up in the back bedroom," she said. "Don't touch anything."

The lights were off in the house, but for a single lamp at the end of the hall. We found Dr. Klein sitting on a stool in a room with rose-colored walls, twin beds, and a dollhouse on the floor in between them. This man has young granddaughters, I thought, with relief. One bed had a floral blanket and a teddy bear on it. The other was covered in a white sheet. At its foot, by the stool where Dr. Klein sat, was a bright reading lamp. A tray of medical instruments, not unlike the clay carving tools I sold in the campus art store, was set on the top of a wood dresser. Dr. Klein stood up when we walked in. By his white hair and lined face, I would guess he was about eighty. I had not realized, though I should have, that the man who would be operating on us was so old. I instinctively looked down at his hands. When I saw no tremors and no dirt, my stomach relaxed.

"Tell me your names," he said.

We weren't sure who should speak first, so we were quiet.

"Just your first names, of course."

Dr. Klein nodded at each of us in turn as we introduced ourselves.

"Which one of you is related to Fern Pasternak?" he asked. But his wife, still standing in the doorway of the bedroom, interrupted before any of us could answer.

"Arthur." She sounded worried more than angry. "Why would you even want to know that? Just get on with it, please."

There was a little bit of desperation in the *please*.

"All right, then," the doctor said sheepishly. To us, "No need to answer. Fern is a gem. That's all I wanted to say."

But his wife was not quite ready to leave it.

"Is that why you're willing to risk spending your retirement in jail? So you can reminisce about old friends?"

Dr. Klein, probably tired of this conversation, looked at us with eyes that said, *Please forgive my wife.* "Bea, that isn't necessary. These are our guests, and they've come here for our help." He wasn't saying she was wrong, just that there was no point in talking about it. "Let's not dwell on unlikely outcomes."

"Unlikely outcomes? For all we know, the police are taking down the license plate of that car in our driveway. That's what they do, you know."

Though the prospect of discovery was unsettling, Hollis and I shared a tiny smile over what we knew that the Kleins didn't: the car belonged to Colton. And I, for one, though I couldn't speak for Hollis and Marshall, found comfort in Mrs. Klein's stern oversight. It meant that this doctor was accountable to someone, and, unlike Dr. Wormsbecher and the so-called butchers we had come to fear, would not take unnecessary risks or sexual liberties with us.

He held out a small paper cup of pills and asked, "Which of you is going first?"

We had not discussed this, but I can't say I was surprised when Hollis took the cup from his fingers and said, "I am."

She had, after all, promised that she would never again put me in the position of being the first to face a dangerous situation.

"All right," said the compliant doctor, who clearly had no preference. "Take these, and I'll return in a few minutes. When I come back, you should be unclothed and lying on this bed here with the white sheet."

Hollis began to take the pills out of the cup, but Marshall gently put his hand on her arm.

"What's in here?" he wanted to know.

"It's some Seconal, some Demerol, and a little scopolamine for nausea."

"Is this going to hurt?" Hollis asked.

"I hope not," said Dr. Klein. "I will do everything I can so that it doesn't." He watched her take the pills and said to me, "In about twenty minutes, my wife will bring you yours. Any other questions before I leave you to get undressed?"

"Can I get some water?" Hollis asked.

"Of course," he said. "Bea, would you be kind enough to get these young ladies some water? Just a little."

He turned and left the room, and his wife followed him. She returned moments later carrying a small tray with three small glasses, each filled halfway with water. As she set the tray down, she looked each of us in the eye and said, "Pain is mostly fear. You have nothing to be afraid of. My husband won't hurt you, and he'll get the job done. You will repay his kindness by never telling anyone what he did for you."

When Dr. Klein came back into the room, Hollis was lying down on the bed as she had been instructed. It was just a normal bed, without the stirrups that doctors need to do their jobs. Mrs. Klein brought in two kitchen chairs and set them at the end of the bed. She gently lifted Hollis's legs and placed a heel on each stool. Marshall sat on the floor in the narrow space between the beds and held Hollis's hand in both of his. I sat on the other bed and tried to pay attention to Dr. Klein as he rotated between his instrument tray and Hollis's splayed legs.

"I'm going to dilate your cervix now," he said, "which might feel uncomfortable."

I winced when I saw the metal rods of increasing thickness going inside Hollis, and Dr. Klein instructed me to take my pills. Hollis remained focused on Marshall's face. He soothed her by stroking her hand and speaking softly to her. I hoped he would do the same for me when my turn came.

After about a half an hour, when it seemed like Hollis could not bear the discomfort of another rod, Dr. Klein finally picked up from the tray a sharp curette.

"I'm going to begin scraping now, and this could hurt a bit. Feel free to squeeze that boy's hand as hard as you need to. He's a strapping young man and he can take it."

Dr. Klein leaned in and furrowed his brow in concentration. His wife watched anxiously over his shoulder, and I began to feel a swirling sensation, like I was on a teacup ride that was just getting started. My body seemed to drift around the room and hover over Hollis. I felt like I was watching from far away.

But then Hollis yelped and her legs convulsed. Dr. Klein pulled his hand away. He and his wife exchanged worried glances.

"Are you okay?" he asked Hollis. He put a hand gently on her knee to settle her.

"I think so." She sounded far away. "It hurt for a second."

"I have to make sure I get it all, and that may mean you feel a scrape. Try not to move suddenly." Then, moving his eyes to Marshall, he said, "Imagine trying to shave the inside of a wet paper bag."

Soon, though, I could see blood on Dr. Klein's hands, and I could see Marshall getting agitated. He stood up and demanded to know what was going on.

"I'm okay," Hollis said to Marshall, but she was too out of it to know what she was.

"It's just blood," said Mrs. Klein. Her tone was not reassuring, however. She sounded like she was trying to convince herself. "That's what a D&C is. You're trying to stimulate bleeding. Eventually the embryo will come out."

"She'll be fine," said Dr. Klein, but he too had a tinge of worry in his voice. "This will all be over soon, and the bleeding will stop. You'll rest, and you'll be fine. The most important thing to remember is not to drink any alcohol. There could be a terrible reaction with the Demerol."

"Alcohol!" said Hollis, drunk on sedatives. She found the thought very amusing. "It's not even noon." Then, as if that outburst had drained all her energy, she added, "Besides, I prefer aspirin."

She probably thought this would bring some levity to the tense room, but the sentence had the opposite effect. Dr. Klein looked even more worried than before.

"How much aspirin?" he asked.

"Oh, no more than a bottle a day," she said, still thinking she could save the moment with her breezy humor.

Dr. and Mrs. Klein looked at each other again, and she pulled her husband out into the hall. We could hear them as if they were in the same room as us.

"I told you this was a bad idea," she was saying.

"I couldn't let her go to a stranger," he answered.

"This isn't what you promised." She was practically pleading. "You promised me peace and quiet in the sunset of our lives. Those were your exact words."

"She'll be fine," he insisted. "I think I got it all."

"No good deed goes unpunished. Aren't you the one who is always saying that? I mean, my god, *aspirin*? Such stupidity. What on earth made you think we could trust these kids?"

Dr. Klein hushed his wife, and they came back into the room, visibly worried. Dr. Klein's hands, which had been reassuringly steady an hour ago, were shaking now. He opened his mouth to speak, but before any words came out, his wife said to us,

"You have to go." She pointed to Marshall. "You. Carry her to the car. Quick." She looked at me. "You. Help your friend."

I stood up but was so overwrought I could barely maintain my balance. In my head, I was screaming,

"What about me?" and I couldn't understand why no one could hear me.

"Keep an eye on her," Mrs. Klein said to me and Marshall. "If the bleeding doesn't stop by tonight, you'll have to get her to a hospital for a coagulant. Tell them it was a miscarriage. A spontaneous miscarriage."

"Please," my brain was crying out. "Please don't make me leave." But everyone was focused on Hollis. No one was looking at me.

We weren't moving fast enough for Mrs. Klein, so she looked directly at Marshall and said, "Let me hear you say it. 'Spontaneous miscarriage.'"

She waited until Marshall repeated the words, like a schoolboy required under duress to apologize to a teacher.

Mrs. Klein stood outside the front door to be sure that no one saw us carry Hollis to the car. I looked pleadingly at Dr. Klein. Couldn't he do the abortion before he kicked me out? But his wife was adamant that we had to go.

I sat in the back seat with Hollis, her head in my lap. Marshall drove us in silence, and I stroked Hollis's head.

"Am I going to be okay?" she asked me.

"Yes," I said, and hoped that I sounded convincing.

"Did I do something wrong?" She started to cry.

"No," I said, trying to sound soothing. "Nothing."

"Why did they seem so mad at me?" she asked, sounding more and more like a little girl.

"They're not," I assured her.

"This is my fault," Marshall said from the front. "I should have remembered that you can't take aspirin before surgery. I wasn't thinking. I'm the one who messed up, not you." He sounded genuinely angry at himself.

"No one messed up," I said. "Hollis is going to be fine."

I have sometimes wondered if things would have turned out better if Crutch had still been there to look after us. She might have known what to do. All I knew was that we were going back to school, and nothing was better. Everything was worse.

21

As Thanksgiving approached, I daydreamed that Stephanie came to my home to spend the holiday with me. In my mind, my parents were there too. They welcomed her with familial grace, and she charmed them with youth and spunk. I imagined the reciprocal love across the generations, perfectly balanced on a scale for which I was the fulcrum. In addition to this fantasy, I also harbored some hope of being invited to spend the holiday with Stephanie in Burlington. In truth, I wanted to be invited more than I actually wanted to go. How ironic, I thought, that I had been wary of Stephanie's neediness over the summer. Who was the needy one now?

I tried not to be disappointed when no invitation to the Farnsworth home came. I knew I was welcome at Carol's, but I was not yet ready to tell her about the secret relationship that occupied most of the space in my head these days. At the last minute, I accepted an offer to celebrate the holiday with Lars and his family.

Before I left for Lars's on Thursday, I got a call from Stephanie.

"Are you going to be around tomorrow?" she asked.

"Well, yes," I said, "but I was planning to go to work." I can get a lot done while the rest of the world is shopping Black Friday sales. "Why? Are you going to be driving through?"

"I was hoping I could come see you. Just for a little bit. I could drop by your office. That would be perfect, actually."

While I enjoyed Lars's hospitality, I wondered what Stephanie's call was all about. I tried to resist the feeling that she had summoned me to appear at her convenience, even though she hadn't included me the day before. I tried instead to be pleased that I would be seeing her over the holiday weekend after all. I wondered if perhaps this is the lot of all parents of semi-adult children, adopted or not. What they want from you might not quite match what you can give. And what you want from them might not be exactly what they're offering.

★ ★ ★

Stephanie arrived in the early afternoon, and, to my surprise, wasn't alone. She hadn't told me she would be accompanied, but when I opened the door, she was standing next to a young man I didn't recognize.

"Hi, Bonnie," Stephanie said. She put her arm around my shoulders, almost like a hug, but not quite. "This is my brother Drew."

"Yes, of course," I said, and reached out my hand.

He shook it as Stephanie said, "This is Bonnie, my, well, you know."

"Hey," he said, cocking his head and looking mostly, but not entirely, in my direction. I sensed that this visit had not been disclosed to Maureen and Carter, and that Drew was not entirely comfortable with the subterfuge.

"Can I offer you anything?" I asked. "I have drinks in the fridge and some snacks too, I think."

"I'll take a ginger ale," said Drew, at the exact moment that Stephanie said, "No, thanks."

I invited them to sit at the small conference table and asked them genially about their family's Thanksgiving.

"It was fine," Stephanie said, and shrugged. "My mom's a pretty good cook, and she only picked one fight. It was the one about how Drew is spending too much time with his friends while he's home on break."

Drew laughed.

"Right," he said fondly, "and you didn't contribute to the tension at all with your rant about white settlers giving smallpox to the Indians."

As Stephanie recalled the conversation, she looked quite proud of herself.

"Native Americans," she corrected, with a guilty-as-charged grin.

They asked about my day, and I briefly recounted my afternoon watching Lars's son paint his arms with mashed sweet potato. When I finished, there was the briefest lull, and I saw Stephanie nudge Drew.

"What?" he said to her. "Are you sure?"

"Drew, it's fine," she insisted. "Bonnie's the right person to ask. We've been over this, like, five times already." She seemed a little exasperated with him, and he seemed equally so with her.

"Can I help you with something?" I finally asked.

Stephanie raised her eyebrows insistently at Drew, until he started talking.

"It's just . . . I have a question. I'm confused about something that happened a couple of weeks ago. Steph thought maybe you could help me," he looked at her "—help us—figure it out."

I nodded, put my forearms down on the table and clasped my hands.

"I'm certainly happy to try," I said.

Drew fidgeted with the tab on his can of ginger ale. Without looking up at me, he started to talk.

"Last month, my mom—our mom—came out to school to visit me. Without dad. She did all the usual things, you know, met my roommate, took me out for brunch. But she also went into the city by herself. No big deal. I mean, I had work to do, and Chicago has a cool downtown. I thought she was just walking the Miracle Mile and going to museums. But a week later she tells me that she actually looked at apartments, with, like, a broker. And she saw one she wants to buy."

It was clear why Stephanie and Drew might have felt confused, but not yet clear why they wanted to consult me.

"Here's the part I think is weird," Drew continued. "She wants to put it in my name. She put a huge chunk of money in my bank account, and she wants me to apply for a loan and sign a bunch of papers." His volume trailed off. "And I just don't know."

Stephanie took over.

"Does that sound illegal to you?" she sort-of asked and sort-of demanded. "Could Drew get into trouble? That's what we really want to know."

I sat back in my chair and took in the situation. I was being asked only for legal advice, I understood, but I assumed their real questions were about what was happening to their family. And in that department I was as much in the dark as they were.

"Well," I started, and I drew it out just a bit to give myself a few more nanoseconds to come up with my answer, "you're probably not doing anything illegal, but without knowing why Maureen is structuring the transaction this way, I can't say for sure. If she were trying to hide assets from a creditor, then yes, it could be fraud. And I would tell you not to do it. But we don't have a reason to think that's what she's doing. Do we?"

They assured me that they didn't.

"What if she's doing it to keep the apartment a secret from our dad?" Stephanie asked. "Like she wants it to be just hers. Then is it illegal?" She sounded as if she had just stumbled upon evidence of Al Capone's tax evasion.

"It wouldn't be illegal," I said, "but it would be pointless. In the unlikely event of a divorce,"—I saw them shoot each other looks when I said that— "the apartment would be treated as marital property, meaning that both partners own it, no matter whose name it's in. Does that make sense?"

They both nodded, but neither said anything. I sensed that my answer was more mundane than they hoped. I think they wanted my response to be a call to action of sorts, but I couldn't tell what they wanted that action to be. Did they want to prevent or hasten the rift they saw looming between their parents?

"And there's also the matter of your credit," I continued. "Assuming Maureen makes all the payments for the mortgage and condo fees, it will help you establish good credit. But if she misses any payments, it will ruin your ability to buy a home of your own some day. You might not want to be in that position."

They sat with that advice for a minute, not quite sure that they knew any more now than they did a few hours ago. Clearly, I had not addressed the real questions on their minds.

I offered to take them for a late lunch or an early dinner, but they insisted that Drew had been AWOL long enough and should head home.

"She'll send a homing pigeon to pick us up if we're not back soon," Stephanie said, apologetically.

I kissed Stephanie on the forehead before they left.

"Hey," I said, "We're still going to New York next month, right?"

"Yeah, sure," she said, though she was thinking about something else.

* * *

Three weeks later, at the beginning of her December break, I was packing for our weekend in New York. For a while now, Stephanie had resisted constantly probing the past and had forged a relationship with me that was rooted in our present lives. But I knew she still had questions. She had never specifically asked to see her original birth certificate, but it would be a gesture of goodwill to show it to her. That had always been the key, hadn't it? All the time we had been looking for each other, we each had had the wrong map. She had the page I wanted, and I had the page she wanted. I planned to take the document with me to New York, and to share it when we were alone together. If nothing else, it would prove that, for her entire life, she had been wrong about her own birthdate.

I looked for it on the Saturday morning of our departure while I waited for her to arrive at my house. But strangely, it was not in the drawer. Had I not put it back in its folder the last time I looked at it? Had I brought it to the office? I was still trying to remember the last time I had it, when I looked out my office window and saw, down below, the Farnsworth car pulling into my driveway. Our plan was to leave together in my car as soon as she arrived and get to the city in the late afternoon. By early evening, I hoped, we would be in line in Times Square to buy discount tickets to an eight o'clock show. I had taken Monday off from work so that we could have a full two days in the city.

When I went downstairs to greet her, I was surprised to hear voices outside and the sound of more than one car door closing. For reasons that were unclear to me, Stephanie's entire family was in the sedan. I watched as Carter got out of the driver's seat and walked around back to the trunk. He reappeared with a suitcase in his hand and accompanied Stephanie to my door. My travel partner did not look as excited about our trip as I was. She looked glum and resistant, and Carter was practically nudging her up my walk.

By the time I opened the door, Carter had manufactured a smile.

"Special delivery," he said with all the enthusiasm he could muster.

"Come in, come in," I insisted, as the cold air invaded my foyer. They walked past me, and stood stiffly just inside my door.

"My parents are afraid to leave me alone with you," Stephanie said.

Carter forced a laugh.

"Not true." Carter said. "To the contrary, you inspired us. The more we thought about it, the more we realized that a trip to New York was a great idea. Why should you have all the fun? Besides, imitation is the highest form of flattery, right?"

"If you're going to spy on me," Stephanie complained, "the least you could do is put on a trench coat and a mustache."

Carter turned to me.

"I promise you, we're not going to get in your way. We don't expect you to spend any time with us—unless you want to. We're open to meeting up. Maybe tea at the Plaza? A sundae at Serendipity? Our treat, of course."

"It's not gonna happen, Dad," Stephanie said, and she picked up her suitcase. I have a picture in my mind of her tapping her foot impatiently, but I may be imagining that detail because it so perfectly captures her demeanor that morning.

"Ready?" she asked me.

I didn't want to be in the middle of this. I wasn't interested in sharing Stephanie, but it wouldn't be right to dismiss Carter. He had always made me feel welcome in Stephanie's life. Whether his invitation was prompted by generosity, as I suspected, or possessiveness, as Stephanie clearly believed, I didn't judge him for it. In fact, I could relate to both impulses.

"Thank you," I said. "It's kind of you to offer. I doubt we'll take you up on it, though. We have a lot of plans, and will be hard to pin down." This was not true. I had a lot of suggestions of places to see in the city—Theo had been particularly helpful in this department—but Stephanie and I hadn't talked about our itinerary.

Carter nodded.

"I understand," he said. Then he turned to Stephanie. "You see?" he said to her. "That's all you had to say. Clear. Direct. Polite. It's not so hard."

He took out of his coat pocket a custom embossed matchbook and handed it to me.

"This is the hotel where we're staying, just in case you change your mind or need to get in touch with us."

While he was opening the door to leave, he turned back and said to Stephanie,

"Let us know if you join the Rockettes."

★ ★ ★

"I'm sorry about that," Stephanie said as soon as were on the road.

"It's okay," I said. "It's a big city. We won't even know they're there."

"I'll know."

"I think he'll give us our space. Your dad is very tuned in to you." I glanced over to see if this observation was improving her mood. "I find it endearing."

"Yeah." She continued to look out the window. "He has a soft spot for you too."

"What does that mean?"

"I don't know. Just that he's always telling me to go easy on you."

"Easy on me? In what way?"

"You know. To just enjoy getting to know you. Not to ask too many questions."

I focused hard on maneuvering around a Volkswagen in the slow lane, while I considered the news that it was Carter's influence that had induced Stephanie to curb her interrogations.

"He probably wants to protect you," I said. "Or maybe your mother."

Stephanie thought about this.

"Maybe," she said eventually. "But that's not what he said. He said that when you gave me up, it was probably a terrible time in your life, and I shouldn't ask you to revisit it. I think he feels bad."

"What would he feel bad about?"

I turned the heat down. The day was warming up, and the air in the car felt stuffy.

"That you had to give me up in order for him to get me. He says now that he's a dad he totally gets how hard it must be for a parent to give up a child and never see that child again. He doesn't like the idea that he profited from your pain."

I felt my chest knot. *My pain*, I thought. I had come to think of my pain as the tree falling silently, imperceptibly in the forest. No one had ever acknowledged it, and therefore it might not exist. But if Carter knew that the pain was there, even though he had never seen it, never heard me talk about it, and never touched it, then surely it was real.

By this time in our drive we were approaching the hills of the Pioneer Valley. I knew that Halstead was just beyond them to the east. It was kind of Carter to try to protect me, I thought. And considerate of Stephanie to stifle her curiosity. But she was entitled to know about how she came into the world. It was foolish, and not at all fair, for me to think that she and I could spend a weekend together and talk superficially about books or roommates or the Christmas displays in the department store windows.

"That's where I went to school." I pointed to my left with my chin. "About ten miles that way."

Stephanie must have realized this was an opening, but she waited. She would leave the topic suspended in the air between us just long enough to sense I wouldn't change the subject. When she felt sure she had understood my invitation, she said, "What was it like, Bonnie?"

"Halstead? It was a wonderful place."

"No, I mean what was it like being pregnant in college? I can't even imagine." She shook her head slightly, as if to ward off the prospect.

"It was hard," I said. I had not admitted it for twenty years. "It was really hard."

It was such an obvious statement, yet it felt liberating to say it out loud.

"Can I ask you a question?"

I sighed and braced myself.

"Yes, of course. You can ask me anything you want."

"The thing I've always wondered," she dragged it out, "is, didn't people *notice*? I mean, didn't you get, you know, fat?"

I was relieved that she had started with a softball.

"I was only at school for the early months," I reminded her. "Then I went home for summer. And I certainly wasn't the only girl who gained twenty pounds our freshman year. The scalloped potatoes at Halstead were legendary."

"But how did you get through those early months?"

There was a lot I had to explain to Stephanie about the spring of 1970. She was right that I hadn't been able to focus on schoolwork, but neither had anyone else. It wasn't just my world that was spinning out of control that spring; it was everyone else's world too. The United States invaded Cambodia, I told her, and the Black Panthers were on trial in Connecticut. Students all over the country were walking out of their classes and protesting the Vietnam War.

There were student strikes at so many schools, including Halstead. And then the police and National Guard started shooting college kids dead, first four at Kent State and then two more in Jackson, Mississippi. Everyone I knew was in mourning for one reason or another. My distress had simply blended in with Halstead's and with the nation's. Nothing seemed to matter any more that spring. Most of my exams were cancelled because of the protests, and the school year just petered out. We drifted home one by one, each of us shell-shocked in her own way.

Stephanie took it all in quietly. I was very grateful to her at that moment. She could be brash, but she could also be sensitive.

"Was college ruined for you?" she asked.

I had to think about that for a couple of miles. College had been the most valuable experience of my life. It had brought me to where I was.

"No, not ruined," I said. "It took a while, but it got better. Sophomore year was a blur, but by junior year, I had my bearings back. I had good friends, and I loved my classes. I read a lot of Victorian novels, and it turns out that all those subordinate clauses prepare you well for a life of reading contracts."

"Did you regret giving me up?"

And there it was. The question that I had been dodging all these months. How could I possibly explain to Stephanie that my primary emotion toward her, toward my own motherhood, was neither regret nor relief, but rather the combination of emotions known as ambivalence? I wished I had never gotten pregnant, and yet I loved her. I loved her, and yet I did not wish I had raised her. How could it make sense to her, when even I knew it defied logic?

"You have to understand," I said. "I didn't want a baby. I never thought of that baby as *you*. I'm not sorry I gave up the baby I didn't want. But I am overjoyed"—I know I didn't sound it— "to be in this car with *you* at this moment."

I kept looking at her for a sign of understanding.

"Does that make sense?" I asked.

"Sure," she said, though I could tell she hadn't decided. She was pensive for a while after that, and I turned my attention to driving. We had reached the northern border of Connecticut, and the traffic was far denser than it had been before. And then, a silent half hour later, I looked off to my right and saw Harkness Tower, that architectural reminder of how it all began, looking just as it had from Colton's roof. It is visible from the highway, and, on those rare occasions when I had driven past it, I had felt it following me, watching and judging me.

"Your father went to Yale," I said to Stephanie and waited for a reaction.

"Oh," she said and went quiet. She leaned to the right and searched, as if the landmarks of the campus, if she could find them, would tell her something about herself.

"How did you meet him?" she asked.

That was when I first told Stephanie about the night I spent in New Haven.

"Your father was sharp, a little full of himself. I was taken in, even though I could see he had a mean streak. Also, I was bored that night and there wasn't much else for me to do."

"What's my father's name?" She sounded like she was testing me to see if I remembered.

"Does it matter?" I asked. "Ultimately, he was awful. He wouldn't have anything to do with me when he learned I was pregnant. I never heard from him again."

"You only met my dad that one time?" she asked in disbelief.

"Just once," I told her.

"Sheesh. No wonder you didn't want me."

I opened my mouth to challenge her, but it wasn't necessary.

"I know, I know," she said. "Not *me*. You didn't want *a baby*."

"You're getting it," I said.

"So, this roommate of yours . . . did she know you were pregnant? She must have noticed *something*."

That is when I began telling Stephanie the truth about Hollis. As we followed the Merritt Parkway, I told her that Hollis had also gotten pregnant, either that night, or some time soon after. I related the story of how we sought help from the lecherous Wormsbecher and from Hollis's boyfriend's aunt. I told her about the hospital committees that decided who got an abortion, but she did not believe that such a thing could possibly have existed.

"So it was like a lottery?" she asked, unable to fathom.

"Far too much like a lottery, as it happened. And you needed a man's permission to buy a ticket."

Our conversation petered out as I needed all my concentration to navigate the Bronx. Then, I needed Stephanie's help to find our hotel and check ourselves in. I had chosen a small hotel with a great midtown location, and I was gratified that Stephanie appeared more enthusiastic about our trip with each step. Our room was small and appointed in cheap, boxy wood furniture and thin bedspreads. But Stephanie pronounced it perfect. Then she sat down and said, "Bonnie, there's something I want you to understand. I wouldn't want any woman to have a baby she didn't want. Even if that baby was me."

So she did understand the distinction.

"I gathered that from your potty-mouthed performance in Burlington, but it's still nice to hear."

"Oh, that." She smiled at the memory of her own moxie. "Yeah, that was funny."

She picked at the pilling on her bedspread. "I mean, even if I didn't exist, it's not like I would *know* that I didn't exist. Does that make sense? You have to exist to think, 'Oh, it's such a bummer that I don't exist.' That's impossible," she said, "and also dumb." My young philosopher smiled at her own insight, and I loved her even more at that moment than I had before.

"Shall we go for a walk around the neighborhood?" I asked.

"No, not right now. I want to hear the rest of the story."

"You know how it ends. Here we are."

"Yeah, but I still have a lot of questions. Like, what happened to your roommate? And her boyfriend. What was his name?"

"Let's just call him Boyfriend. It's easier that way. Okay?"

"Call him whatever you want. Just tell me the truth."

By the time I told her about Hollis's and my visit to Dr. Klein, it was dinnertime, and I was hungry. I had read about a restaurant called Miracle Grill, and I wanted to try it. It was in the East Village, and I hoped Stephanie might envision herself following her friend Carina to the neighborhood. We took a break from my painful memories, and we had a wonderful meal. We briefly explored the gentrifying streets of Alphabet City, but Stephanie was eager to get back to the narrative. We bought a bottle of wine and went back to our hotel room, where we sat like teenagers in a suburban basement, and I told her what happened to Hollis after we left Dr. Klein's.

22

I HAD NO IDEA HOW WE GOT HOLLIS back into the dorm without anyone seeing. Perhaps all the students had the good sense to sleep late on this frigid Saturday morning.

Marshall and I took turns fetching cold water for her and holding her hair as she threw up in a bucket. But mostly we watched helplessly as she got worse and worse. The bleeding didn't stop. It was all over the car. It soaked through her clothes and her bedspread. By early afternoon she was clammy, and by the evening she was hot to the touch. She thrashed and she wept. Her eyes were glassy when she looked at us.

"Tell my parents I'm sorry," she said, over and over.

In the middle of the dinner hour, when most of the Coffett women would be in the dining room, we finally got Hollis out of the room and back into the car. We forgot to bring our coats, but having Hollis next to us was like sitting by a fire. It was a thirty-minute drive to the hospital in Springfield, and, by the time we got there, Hollis's blood had soaked through four towels. She was limp and barely conscious.

We drove right up to the entrance of the emergency room, and together Marshall and I hoisted her out of the car, her arms on our shoulders, our hands around her waist. We dragged her into the hospital entrance, where, I had assumed, someone would surely see our desperation. I imagined they would swoop in, take her off our hands and immediately begin to revive her.

But they looked at us skeptically. One doctor, barely older than we were, walked over to us slowly.

"You can't put her down in here. We'll clear an exam room for her."

He walked away briefly, and Marshall and I just stood there, trying to bear Hollis's weight. The young doctor did not appear to be hurrying, but he did eventually return.

"Follow me," he said sternly.

We continued to carry Hollis, whose feet were now dragging on the floor, through the double glass doors that led to the belly of the hospital. She was heavy, and she stuck to us with sweat. The doctor directed us down the hall and into a small exam room. He told us to deposit Hollis on an exam table that had been covered in several extra layers of white paper. Then he looked directly at me.

"Tell me what's going on here," he commanded.

"She's having a miscarriage," I said, my voice shaking. "The bleeding won't stop. She's been taking a lot of aspirin lately."

"Oh, a *spontaneous miscarriage?*" the doctor said, with a knowing smirk. He was not just skeptical; he was offended that we thought him so gullible. "That's not what it looks like to me." He waited for us to respond, but we had told him all we planned to tell him. It was obvious that Hollis needed help, and we figured he would give it to her. But he was not even looking at Hollis. He was letting her bleed while he interrogated us. Eventually, Marshall spoke, "Does it matter? She's lost a lot of blood, and she has a fever. Can't you treat her first and play detective later?"

"I'm not *playing* anything," the doctor sneered. Hollis moaned, but he ignored her. "I'm willing to bet that this so-called miscarriage was induced, not spontaneous." He scanned our faces for confirmation, but we had already made a silent pact with each other to reveal nothing. "That's a crime," he said, "and I have an obligation to get to the bottom of it."

I couldn't bear his accusatory demeanor any more than I could bear Hollis's cries. To make them both stop, I begged,

"Please. You can see she's in pain. Please help her."

"She'll get the help she needs when she tells me who did this to her."

Marshall and I were stone-faced.

"What do you mean?" I asked. I was sure I had misunderstood. He couldn't possibly care more about ferreting out Dr. Klein than he cared about saving Hollis.

"I mean, tell me the name of the butcher who did this." He picked up a pen, confident that we were about to obey his order. But once again, we said nothing. Answering his questions would merely prolong the conversation and defer Hollis's care. "From the looks of her," he said, "she won't survive the night."

This sentence shocked us. It had not occurred to me that Hollis couldn't be made better with some antibiotics and a blood transfusion. I looked at Marshall, who looked at me. We each saw panic on the face of the other. The doctor tried to use this crack in our stony affect by adding, "If you won't tell me, I'll ask her." Would he really do that? I wondered. "I need to gather evidence while I can."

He turned his attention to Hollis. She looked delirious to me, and I couldn't imagine that she had followed any of the conversation. She was slick with blood and sweat, and her eyes seemed unable to focus. But then she looked at me and said, more lucidly than I would have predicted, "Let's just tell him the truth." She licked her dry lips. "It's okay if he knows how stupid I am." Then she tried to lift her head to look at the doctor. "I did this to myself," she said weakly. "It's my fault."

I couldn't believe Hollis had the strength to say all that. I wasn't surprised that she was lying for Dr. Klein's sake, but I didn't think she could get all those words out. The doctor was unmoved. He looked at Hollis and said, "So you're lying to protect them, and they're lying to protect you. Fine. But the police are going to ask you the same questions when they get here, and I recommend you don't lie to them. Now, I have other patients, so I'll get someone to take you to the ward. You may as well get to know the other two ladies there, since you'll be going to jail together. I know how it works. You take your Friday paycheck straight to the abortionist, and then fill up my ward all weekend long."

He left the room without looking at us. We sat, immobile, until an orderly appeared and started to wheel Hollis away. As he exited with the gurney, he said to us, "You'll have to clear this room. We need it for patients."

Marshall and I staggered back into the waiting room and, as the name suggests, waited. We didn't know where to go or what to do. Over the course of an hour Marshall asked two orderlies if we could see Hollis, and was told we could not. I inquired about her at the nurses' station, but no one would give me any information. It was a Saturday night, and the hospital was thinly staffed. So we sat there, objects of interest to every doctor, nurse, orderly, or receptionist who passed through the waiting room. They nodded their heads in our direction and whispered into each other's ears. At first, we avoided eye contact with anyone, but eventually we stopped pretending we were invisible. We wanted those hospital workers to know we existed, that the patient they were treating had friends. We started following doctors and nurses with our eyes, keeping them in our gaze long enough for them to know they were being watched.

A couple of hours into our vigil, Marshall said to me, "I should have married her." He shook his head with regret. "Maybe we would have been happy. It would have been tough with a baby and law school all at once, but it might have worked. She was sure her parents would have helped us out, even though I doubted it."

"I don't know them well," I said. "But I think you're right. They never struck me as generous or kind."

Marshall didn't look at me.

"That's what I thought," he said. "I told her they would be furious and would never give us a dime."

"That's very possible," I said.

"Hollis said that they just needed a little time because I'm 'not what they expected.'" Marshall sounded rueful. "I didn't think a little time would help. Even if they came around when the baby was born, the truce would last no more than eight days. That's when you've got to decide if the kid is getting baptized or circumcised. That was going to be a big fight."

He wanted me to tell him he was right, but I had no idea. I said nothing.

"You know what Hollis said about that?" He chuckled slightly at the memory. "She said, 'Then we'll just have to make sure it's a girl.' That's what was so great—is so great—about Hollis. She's hopeful, and she's sweet. Really, really sweet."

His voice trailed off.

"Hollis is ga-ga for you too," I said, but immediately saw that this was the wrong thing to say. It made Marshall feel worse. I changed course. "But I think she would eventually resent being married before she was ready."

"She dreams big. That's one of my favorite things about her, and it's the thing I would be taking away. And you know what else? I think I can say this to you, because, well, you're also . . ." He didn't finish that sentence before starting another. "I don't want to get married just to prove a point. She wants to win this battle of wills against her parents. But I don't want to be a pawn in that game."

"Hollis deserves someone who really wants to marry her."

"Exactly," Marshall said. "And that's going to be one lucky guy. He won't be marrying her just for the thrill of sticking it to her parents. And you know what's funny? Where I come from, I'm considered a catch. You should see the looks on the faces of the women at my temple when they hear I go to Yale. They can't pitch their daughters at me fast enough. It's embarrassing, but it beats getting treated like I'm inferior, you know? Does that make me terribly selfish?"

I told him I didn't think so. He already knew we had this in common. I too was a golden child back home, and I understood how a place like Halstead or a person like Hollis could make you feel second class.

At around eleven o'clock that night, Marshall and I realized we were both hungry. In the windowless, fluorescent lit waiting room, we had barely registered that it was late at night. Marshall got the nurses to tell us about a deli a short drive away.

"What should I get you?" he asked me.

"It seems crazy to think about food now," I said.

"You don't have to think about it. I can make a decision when I get there."

It was while he was out that I saw two police officers enter the hospital doors and walk across the waiting room, then through the double doors at the other end. And for a moment, as crazy as this might sound, I felt hope. I figured that, if the police had come to interrogate Hollis, she must have been getting better. She had been so weak when they wheeled her out of the examining room. Perhaps, I told myself, they had been able to do something to restore her to strength. Maybe they had called the police because she was well enough to sit up and talk. At this point I didn't care what Hollis told them. I was just relieved to imagine her conscious.

Twenty minutes later the police officers came out into the waiting room, and walked straight over to me. I was terrified, and I wished I wasn't alone. I was eighteen years old, and I didn't have a Dr. Pasternak or a Dr. Klein, or even Crutch, to help me face off against two adult policemen in uniforms with guns. All I had wanted was to be a college student, and here I was practically a criminal defendant.

They casually pulled two chairs around to face me, as if we were going to have a friendly pow-wow. They didn't look angry the way the doctor had. If anything, they looked a little weary. The younger one even tried to look worried about me.

"Why don't you tell us what you know," said the older of the two. "You're in a bind, and we want to help you out."

I was too afraid to speak, and he continued.

"Your friend told us everything, and we know that you helped her come up with the money."

Now it was the other one's turn.

"We would hate to see you in hot water just for trying to cover for a friend, especially, you know," he tilted his head to demonstrate his sorrow at the fickleness of females, "a girl who was willing to spill the beans about you like that." He looked at his partner, who picked up where he left off.

"If we told the DA that you helped us out, he would probably go easy on you, maybe even overlook the fact that you got her into this mess in the first place."

By the time they finished talking, I understood that they were bluffing. It was ludicrous to imagine that I, who had had to work two jobs and accept a subsidy from Colton in order to accumulate seventy-five dollars, had helped Hollis financially. Moreover, if Hollis had in fact told them everything, they would have known that Dr. Klein hadn't asked us for money. He had been willing to risk his freedom just because a beloved protégé had asked him to. He did it so that Fern Pasternak could sleep well, knowing that her nephew and his girlfriend were safe from the type of unscrupulous or incompetent charlatan these cops thought they were about to uncover.

Perhaps it was my realization that the police were just guessing, or perhaps it was the sight of Marshall walking in the door that boosted my strength. Or maybe it wasn't strength at all that allowed me to lie to the police officers. Perhaps the only reason I was able to blubber falsehoods was that I had given up. If the cops had been unable to get the doctor's name from Hollis, it probably was because she had been unable to communicate. She might be unconscious, or in a coma, or worse. When we first brought her into the hospital, the doctor led us to believe that whether or not she recovered depended on whether we gave up Klein. A name in exchange for her survival. But now it was clear that it didn't matter. There was nothing I could say that would make this situation any better for Hollis or for me. I might as well say whatever I wanted.

"I found her in her room this afternoon," I said. I started to cry, as if I were unburdening myself. "I don't know where she went or who took her there."

I looked at the cops, hoping they would believe me.

"She's just my roommate," I added. "We aren't really friends."

That felt like the cruelest betrayal of all, and I cried harder. Though my words weren't true, my guilt and sorrow were as real as they could be. Marshall stood over us and spoke angrily, "She can't help you." He sounded stern. "She doesn't know anything. Leave her alone."

The cops probably thought he was more important than he was. He certainly looked well-educated and confident. It's also possible that they no longer cared who had performed the abortion on Hollis. They already had a good story about some stupid scared kids they could recount to their buddies over doughnuts and coffee, and maybe that was all they really wanted. They shook their heads.

"Just be glad it's not you in there," the younger one said. "You might have to live with what you did, but at least you'll live." And they walked away.

Any relief I felt at being released from their scrutiny was completely cancelled out by the terror that their parting shot had provoked in me.

And then Marshall handed me a turkey sandwich.

"Don't listen to them," he said. "They're just being cruel." He passed me a wad of napkins.

"I don't have tissues," he said, "but you can use these."

When I was wiping my eyes, we both noticed that the doctor we had seen when we first came in was walking out of the hospital, no longer in his white coat. Heading home in his street clothes, he had lost interest in us. We looked around to figure out who was now in charge. After observing for a few minutes, we noticed that the doctor who seemed to be the busiest, answering questions and telling people what to do, was a Black man even younger than the first doctor. The staff were more relaxed around this new doctor, and we decided I should approach him. I hovered as he finished a conversation with a nurse, and when she turned to walk away, I stepped up.

"Excuse me," I said, as I checked his name tag. "Dr. Haynes, are you the head doctor?"

He seemed amused by my inartful approach.

"If you mean am I the resident in charge, the answer is yes, for the next twenty-two hours and"—he checked his watch— "fourteen minutes."

I opened my mouth, but I wasn't sure what to say. To his credit, Dr. Haynes did not walk away.

"Can I help you?" he asked, with a lot more patience than was warranted.

I finally got the words out.

"Would it be possible for me to see my friend?"

His eyebrows came together in confusion. But he was not scolding me when he said,

"Visiting hours are long over. It's the middle of the night."

"I know," I said, afraid he would walk away, "but we brought her in a few hours ago, and we have no idea how she's doing. We wouldn't stay long."

The request was so outlandish that it piqued his curiosity, and he wanted to know more.

"Is she on the ward, or is she in a private room?" he asked. He wasn't saying no. I considered this progress.

"I'm not sure," I said. "We haven't been told anything."

"Well, what's her name?" With each question he asked, I became more encouraged that he might let me in.

"Hollis Locke," I said, hoping that these would be magic words. The name did have an effect, I could tell, and his face changed. It became both kinder and more troubled at the same time.

"I see," he said. He looked down at his shoes, and then he looked up. "You should know that the infection was very far gone." He sounded apologetic. "Too far for the antibiotics. We tried giving her blood, cortisone, and hydrocortisone." He must have been saying this for his own benefit, because it meant nothing to me. "Nothing is working. If you want to see her, you should follow me."

"Can her boyfriend come too?" I asked.

"No. Just one of you. That's already one more than is allowed."

I tried to keep pace with Dr. Haynes as he led me back through the double doors and down the hallway. Most of the rooms off of the hall were empty, but a few had patients I had seen in the waiting room earlier in the night. At the end of the hall was another set of double doors. He stopped before pushing through them and he turned to me.

"I want you to know what to expect," he said. "Patients with sepsis often remain lucid until the end."

Some of his words were unfamiliar to me, but the ones that stuck in my head were "the end." How did we get to the end? He held the door open for me, and I entered a large room with six beds, half of which were occupied. The room was dim, but not the enveloping, comfortable dark of a bedroom. It was a semi-dark that I would later associate with fitful overnight flights to Europe. Too light for the people who want to sleep, and not light enough for the people who have to do their jobs. Dr. Haynes pointed to a bed in the corner.

I walked through the room afraid of what I would encounter when I got to Hollis. As I sat down on the edge of her bed, I could see that her body had begun to shut down. She was pale and limp. Her breathing was rapid and shallow. I took her hand, and it felt like dead weight, though I could feel fever in her fingers. I had never specifically noticed the rhythmic beat of the human body, but I noticed its absence in Hollis. And yet she looked at me calmly.

"Bonnie, you've come," she said.

"Yes, I'm here."

"This wasn't supposed to happen," she said. "I wasn't supposed to die."

I stroked her hand, and I tried to think of something to say. I wanted to whisper words of hope, but I had none. We both knew that I would not have been allowed back here if there had been any hope.

"Shhh," was all I could say.

She shuddered in pain, and bit down on her lips, which were already raw.

"I was supposed to grow up," she said matter-of-factly, "and now I won't."

She was simply stating the truth, and I couldn't contradict her. This was a different Hollis from the one I knew. This one stared at her fate with clear eyes. For the first time since we met, I was the one falling apart, while she was controlled and practical.

"Tell my parents I'm sorry," she said.

Dr. Haynes approached and handed me a Styrofoam cup of ice chips.

"These might help," he said. "Let her suck on them one at a time."

"Thank you," I said, and he could hear both gratitude and desperation in my voice. "Thank you."

"It's good that you are here." His voice was soothing. "I wouldn't want her to be alone."

He hesitated for a moment, and I sensed that he had more to say.

"There is something I want you to do for me."

I could not bear it. Why did everyone want something from us? Why couldn't anyone help us without extracting payment? I hated being so weak.

"What?" I asked, inaudibly.

"I want you to look around this room and remember what you see."

I told him I did not understand what it was I was supposed to notice.

"This is the ward where we send the women who can't afford an expensive illegal abortion and can't afford a private hospital room. Who do you see here?"

I did not want to look around. I had made a point of not noticing the other patients. I wanted to give them at least the illusion of privacy and dignity. But at Dr. Haynes's insistence I surveyed the room, and I saw that there were two other women on the ward, one conscious, one not. Both of them were Black. When Dr. Haynes was sure I understood, he said, "I care about your friend." I didn't doubt that he meant it. "And I'm asking you to care about my friends, my sisters, and my cousins. Last month a girl from my church came in with a coiled-up catheter in her uterus and I was not able to save her either."

"Why are you telling me this?" My voice sounded hoarse to me.

I already knew that this night would haunt me. I did not need to hear about even more horror.

"Forgive me," he said gently. "It's just that I'm desperate. You see? No one pays any mind to Black folks, especially when they have no money. But maybe people will care about your friend."

"I don't see how that will help," I said.

"Maybe not. But we have to start by getting their attention. Would anyone have gone looking for brother Chaney if he hadn't been with those white boys, Goodman and Schwerner?"

For the next hour, I sat by Hollis's side and slipped ever-shrinking disks of ice into her mouth. She did not speak again, nor did I. There was nothing left to say. Eventually she was too weak even to part her lips. I dipped my fingers in the cold water and touched her face. She shuddered and then relaxed. But there came a point when she stopped reacting to me and instead thrashed against the prison of pain that trapped her. She turned her head from side to side and kicked her legs and moaned. I wish I could say I sat with her until the end, but the truth is that I recoiled in fear, and stood up from the bed. Dr. Haynes gently led me by the shoulders out of the room.

"You did what you could," he said. "We all did."

★ ★ ★

I found Marshall asleep in the waiting room. He was rumpled and ready for a shave. But what I noticed most was that he had been crying.

"You're still here," I said.

"Of course. Did you think I would leave you here? Either of you?"

"No, I guess not," and I sat down in the chair next to him. I faced him, and I was silent, because I couldn't bear to tell him. He spoke first.

"She's gone, isn't she?"

I nodded, and I began to sob. He took me in his arms and held me while I cried, while all the sadness gushed out of me like air escaping an untied balloon. And like that balloon, I felt myself careening around in space, but for the support of his shoulder. I could hear that he was crying too.

"I should never have . . ." he started to say, but I stopped him.

"Let's not," I said. I did not want to start apportioning blame, because, once we started, where would we stop? Was it his fault? His Aunt Fern's? Was it Lauden's or Klein's? Was it mine?

So instead I said to him what Dr. Haynes had said to me. "You did what you could. We all did."

"What are you going to do, Bonnie?" he asked when he dropped me off at Halstead just before dawn. His voice was cracking.

When we were thinking about keeping Hollis alive, I had briefly forgotten that I was still pregnant. But by the time he asked me that question, I had already accepted that I was going to have a baby, whether I wanted to or not. Abortions were too rare and too dangerous. Hollis and I had tried everything we could think of, and there were no options left. I told him I would wear sweaters for as long as possible. I would hope that school ended before it became too obvious. And then I would go home to the farm for the last few months.

"You're going to be okay, Bonnie," he said. "You're strong. You'll see."

I had heard this enough times now to believe it might be true.

★ ★ ★

I expected that we would see each other again soon, that we would travel together to Pennsylvania for Hollis's funeral. But her parents made it clear that we weren't welcome. They told their friends that Hollis had died of a sudden embolism, and they demanded that we never say otherwise. The only people at school who knew the truth were Marcia and Ingrid, and they both graduated that spring. There were rumors, of course, but none of them originated with me. I heard women whisper that she had gotten married back in Sewickley or that she had transferred to a co-ed school. I didn't challenge any of these explanations, but the one I liked best was that

Hollis had been expelled for plagiarizing her *Tristram Shandy* paper. That was the story that, I thought, best captured the truth—that Hollis had broken a rule and paid the ultimate price.

The chatter about Hollis at least kept my classmates from asking too many questions about me, and allowed me to keep my head down and my stomach covered for a few more months.

$$23$$

By the time I finished telling Stephanie about Hollis's death, it was almost two in the morning. The next morning, Stephanie seemed softer, more relaxed than before. She had her answer about why I had capitulated to my fate, and she also had a deeper understanding of why the shame of my pregnancy still pressed on me almost twenty-two years later. We both awoke ready to move on from our night of confession and absolution to a day of eating and sightseeing.

She indulged me with a few hours at the Met before we headed downtown for some shopping. Somehow, I ended up buying her a dress at Putumayo and a stack of CD's at Tower Records. If Stephanie was taking advantage of me, I didn't mind. In fact, I liked being treated like a regular parent—tolerable company, a little gullible, capable of being generous when manipulated in just the right way. A few times, when the crowds got thick near the Fifth Avenue windows, she looped her arm through mine. She recited a list of places and activities she wanted to avoid, lest we run into her parents and brother: Rockefeller Center, the Empire State Building, *Cats*.

"Admit it," I said. "You can see yourself living here."

Stephanie smiled.

"Yeah, it does seem cool," she conceded. We had found an inexpensive Indian restaurant, a new experience for both of us. "I'm glad we wandered into this place." She broke off a piece of papadum from the basket.

"So," I asked coyly, "are you reconsidering? Is Carina still planning to move here?"

I saw her stiffen. The easygoing, forgiving Stephanie was gone, and guarded, put-upon Stephanie was back.

"I will not be living with Carina," she announced, unequivocally.

I waited for her to explain her response, but she didn't.

Instead, she looked down at the menu and said, "I have no idea what any of this stuff is, so order whatever you want."

"Did something happen with you and Carina?" I probed.

"With *me* and Carina? Not exactly," she said, and she wouldn't look me in the eye.

Her efforts at avoidance were too obviously an act. She was going to make me work to extract what she clearly wanted to tell me. She wanted to maintain the illusion that it had been pried out of her, that she had not been looking for sympathy or support.

"What does 'not exactly' mean?"

Finally she looked up at me.

"It means that when I came home after my psych final last week, I saw some skank coming out of Jason's bedroom wearing nothing but his Nirvana t-shirt, and, upon closer inspection, the skank turned out to be Carina."

I recognized the anger in her voice as the kind that springs from pain. I felt protective of her, and I also remembered the sting I myself had felt the night I first met Reed Masters's fiancée. I knew exactly how Stephanie was feeling.

"I'm sorry," I said. She looked like she was about to cry. "That's lousy. Believe me, I know."

She was sad and indignant at the same time.

"It's bad enough I have to live with them for another five months. I can't look either one of them in the eye. For two days they couldn't stop apologizing. But then suddenly they decided that really everything was *my* fault. Like I shouldn't have walked in the door when I did, or I shouldn't have acted surprised. Now I just stay in my room and I'm afraid to come out. The whole thing is so humiliating."

"Oh, Steph." I reached across the table and touched her arm. "You can't live like that."

"I don't exactly have a choice. What am I supposed to do? Ask them to please break up so that I can sit in the living room?"

Our food arrived and she looked defeated, as if this unfamiliar cuisine was yet another insurmountable challenge.

"No, I was thinking of something else entirely. What does your lease say about subletting?"

Stephanie shrugged.

"I don't know. I've never seen it."

"You signed a lease without ever seeing it?"

She flashed me a look. It was a warning that I had come a step too close to condescending to her.

"No," she said. "Only Jason signed the lease. I just pay a third of the rent."

I was excited at the legal implications of this information, but Stephanie was getting annoyed with my questions.

"So all you have is an oral agreement with Jason?" I asked.

"Hardly." The bitterness was unmistakable. "I'd say Carina is the one who has an oral agreement with Jason."

"I was referring to the legal term, not the sex act, thank you very much. If you never signed anything then you're free to walk away."

We ate quietly for a few minutes after that.

"Thanks for the advice," she finally said, just grudgingly enough that I knew she didn't entirely mean it.

"I'm sorry," I said, as I poured some wine into her glass. "I know I turn everything into a legal problem."

"You could have asked me how I felt," she said, "instead of lecturing me about my rights."

This response was encouraging. She wasn't forgiving me just yet, but she was signaling that I had correctly identified what I had done wrong. That was worth a few points, I was sure.

"I know," I said. "I like to find solutions, even when I haven't been asked to. It's the only thing I'm really good at. I'm sorry."

"Oh my god, Bonnie." Her annoyance was escalating, not abating, as I had hoped. "Why are you always apologizing? I get it. You were trying to be helpful. Just own it. Stop acting like I'm going to kick you to the curb if you don't behave."

Stephanie seemed unaware of the contradiction in her expectations of me. Apparently, I was wrong to have offered advice but also wrong to have acknowledged my wrongness. But I chose not to point out the trap she had constructed. At least I was able to stop myself from apologizing.

"So what do you want to do tomorrow?" she asked. Apparently, she was done with her scolding, and with the topic of Jason and Carina altogether. I, too, was happy to move on. I suggested some museums I wanted to visit. She countered with a plea to visit Canal Street, which, she had heard, was both an open-air mall of counterfeit luxury goods and an inexpensive buffet of Chinese dumplings. I pretended to resist her suggestion, but we both knew I was going to give in eventually. After dinner, I tried to convince her to walk along Fifth Avenue, to see the Christmas windows. But she overruled me, and we instead went to a piano bar in the West Village. We couldn't believe there was a place in the world with this much life on a Sunday night. We stayed out until midnight and fell asleep as soon as we got back to the hotel.

★ ★ ★

I awoke in the morning expecting to have an hour or two to myself while Stephanie slept. It was early by the standards of a college student. I was very surprised to see that Stephanie was not in her bed. I called her name and checked the bathroom, but she was not in our room. I got dressed and went downstairs, but did not find her in the lobby. I walked down to the deli on the corner, which we had visited the day before. She wasn't there either. I went back to the hotel and asked at the front desk if they had seen Stephanie.

"What room are you in?" the receptionist asked with helpful efficiency.

"304."

"I thought so. Your daughter asked me to give this to you."

Inside was a handwritten note from Stephanie that said, "Gone to see my dad. Go to a museum without me." I was surprised, but not surprised. Yes, she had been adamant that she hoped to avoid her family while we were in New York. But she and I had had a lot of intimate conversations over the past two days. Being with me had probably sparked a lot of conflicting feelings, and maybe she needed a break. I knew her well enough to know that if she were angry with me—or disappointed, or confused—the person she would call would be Carter.

I wanted confirmation of my hunch, and I wanted reassurance that Stephanie wasn't angry with me. I went back up to the room and dug out of my handbag the matchbook with the name of the Farnsworths' hotel on it. I dialed the number, and when the operator picked up, I asked for Carter Farnsworth. I was connected with a brisk, "One moment, please."

Carter answered almost in a whisper. I remembered it was still early.

"Carter." I was trying to sound calm, but I was clearly nervous. "It's Bonnie."

"Oh, hi, Bonnie." He sounded pleasantly surprised. "How is your weekend going?"

Since he knew the answer to his own question, I did not respond directly.

"I'm calling to check on Stephanie. I just want to be sure she found you." I meant to sound untroubled by the fact that Stephanie had skipped out on our weekend together, but my voice gave away my concern. I was starting to worry that Stephanie had concluded, now that she had her questions answered, that she had no more need of me.

Carter's tone shifted down two registers of seriousness.

"What do you mean? Why isn't Stephanie with you?"

"Isn't she with you?" I asked.

"No." Now he was sounding worried. "What makes you think she's with me?"

"Her note said she was going to see you. Maybe she's still on her way."

"That's unlikely," he said. "She doesn't even know where we're staying. I gave that matchbook to you because she refused to take it."

And that's when I realized that "gone to see my dad" did not mean Carter.

"Oh no," I said, hoarse with fear.

"Bonnie?"

What had I unleashed? Where was she, and would she ever come back?

"Tell me where you are," Carter said. "I'll be right there."

★ ★ ★

Carter arrived fifteen minutes later, and I met him in the lobby. I had worked myself up while waiting for him, and I was agitated when we sat down in the back corner. I was sure Carter would be angry that I had driven Stephanie out into the streets of New York.

"I think I know what happened," I said. By then I had pieced a few things together. "I think Stephanie has her birth certificate. She's trying to track down her birth father."

I probably must have sounded like the records clerk I encountered when I first embarked on my search, the one who spoke as if the document itself were radioactive and belonged buried in the New Mexico desert. "I think she's had it for a while, actually. Since the summer. She must have taken it from my house when she was upstairs after lunch."

But Carter seemed unperturbed.

"I'm sorry," he said. "She shouldn't have gone through your stuff."

I was shocked that he thought that was the issue.

"I don't care about that," I said. "I should have given it to her earlier, really. The real issue is that she has disappeared, and we have no idea where she is. This is a big city, you know."

"Bonnie," he said reassuringly, "she's not Little Red Riding Hood on her way to grandmother's house."

"You're not worried?"

"About her? No. She's almost a college graduate."

"Then why did you come running over here?"

"Because I was worried about *you*." He was trying to get me to look at him. "You sounded really upset."

I didn't contradict him or object. I was indeed upset, and my fear was far out of proportion to the actual threat to Stephanie's safety.

"I know you're right," I said. "It's just that when I woke up this morning and she was gone . . ."

"What?" Carter interrupted, sympathetically, "you assumed that she was gone forever?"

When I heard him say it, I had to acknowledge how absurd it was.

"What are you so afraid of, Bonnie?" he asked.

"We talked on Friday," I admitted. "I told her some things about her birth that she hadn't known."

He waited for me to continue, but I didn't.

"Things you can tell me?" he asked.

"I admitted to her that I had tried very hard to get an abortion. I gave up when I realized how dangerous it was. Maybe that was hard for her to hear."

"I see," said Carter, but I wasn't sure what he saw. That I was a terrible person? That Stephanie had been right to run away from me?

"Bonnie," he said gently, "you have to stop thinking that being Stephanie's birth mother is a test you're failing."

Wasn't this exactly what Stephanie had been trying to tell me the night before?

"So you think she forgives me?" I finally had the courage to ask.

"For what? For telling her that you didn't want a baby when you were nineteen?" He was trying not to laugh at me. "She was nineteen herself a few years ago. I think she understands."

Maybe he was right. But I didn't feel absolved yet. I felt I had twenty-one years' worth of accumulated sins for which I wanted to be forgiven.

"I mean for all of it," I said. "For giving her up. For not finding her sooner. For wanting to be a student more than I wanted to be a mother. For building a career instead of raising a baby." As I recited my many infractions, I became even more convinced that I could not be absolved. Carter listened patiently for a minute, but then he put a hand gently on my knee, as if to still me.

"Bonnie, look at me," he said. He waited until I met his gaze. For a moment I took in the handsome asymmetry of his face, the creases at the corners of his eyes. In his expression, I could see his concern for me, but also a touch of patient amusement.

"Bonnie, I don't even know where to begin. First of all, you gave her a great life. With *me*. I mean, yeah, you probably would have been a good parent, but not as good as *me*." He found this observation funnier than I did. "And second of all, she's not going to forgive you, because there's nothing to forgive. You were young and you did what you thought was best for her. Not wanting to raise a baby when you're a nineteen-year-old college student is hardly a crime. And even if it were, it was a long time ago. Hasn't the clock run out? For Christ's sake, the statute of limitations on *armed robbery* is—what? —ten years?"

"Six, actually," I corrected.

He smiled even more, and I felt better, though not because I instantly agreed with his point. To be sure, he had given me good advice. But even the best advice, I knew from years of dispensing it, is not internalized instantaneously. I felt better because I knew that Stephanie, despite having a prickly mother, and an undeservingly preferred brother, had been raised by a kind, loving parent, who provided fatherly wisdom with humor and compassion. Perhaps, I thought, I had done well by her after all.

★ ★ ★

Carter thought the worst thing we could do was run after her, and he advised that we get some breakfast.

"The trick is," he said, "to get just involved enough in their lives to show that they're important to you, but also to give them some slack, to show that you trust them."

"How do you know you're doing it right?" I asked.

He laughed to himself.

"Know you're doing it right? That's a good one, Bonnie." He raised his coffee mug as if to toast my cleverness. "You don't ever think you're doing it right. You just get used to feeling like you're doing it wrong."

It was a little hard to square this self-deprecating maxim with his obviously close bond with Stephanie. But he looked genuinely rueful.

"How is your weekend in the Big Apple?" I asked in a neutral, conversational tone.

I did not want to let on what I knew about Maureen's forays into the Chicago real estate market. I certainly did not want to probe an open wound. But we had talked about me for quite long enough, and it would be rude to not even ask how they occupied themselves for two days in the city.

"Not great," he said. "It's a little lonely for me when Steph isn't around." I wasn't expecting such a revealing answer.

"She tells me that Maureen and Drew are very close," I said, because sometimes a person wants assurance that you already know what they mean, that whatever they are about to say won't shock you. Or they want to know that they have already said enough, that you understand.

"Well, they were," Carter said, looking down into his coffee. "But he's in college now. He doesn't want to be mama's little boy anymore. But the more he tries to break free, the more she clings."

"That sounds hard to watch."

"Yesterday," he went on, "she tried to follow him into the dressing room in a Banana Republic." Revisiting the memory triggered a new round of bafflement. "Drew told her to back off, loud enough for everyone in the store to hear. It was mortifying."

"And you're in the middle?"

"Hardly. I'm completely on the periphery. I don't factor in. I just stood there trying to figure out what the name of the store means. Is it supposed to be a joke? Is there some Latin American country whose only export is khaki shorts?"

But then he got more serious.

"I know this is going to sound crazy, but I think Maureen never really recovered from those years of not being able to get pregnant. She was miserable, and angry too. She felt like she had been cheated. I was so sure that everything would be better when we got Stephanie, but it wasn't. All that built-up resentment was still there. Then she got pregnant with Drew, and it went so smoothly. I thought, okay *now* everything will *really* be better. And I suppose it was better for her. She was so happy being Drew's mother. She nursed him for over a year. But there was no room for anyone else. Not for me, not for Steph. And now that Drew has moved out to start his life, it's like all the anger of the years of infertility has come back."

He sat back in his chair. He looked defeated.

"But she doesn't have any reason to be angry at *you*? Does she?" It felt good to reciprocate the support that Carter had shown me.

"It doesn't matter," he said. "I'm the only one around. The only one left to be angry at is me."

"That doesn't sound fair," I said.

"Sometimes that's how marriage works, Bonnie."

I thought about saying, "I wouldn't know," but I didn't want to sound self-pitying. Besides, he was still unburdening himself.

"Maureen told me last week that she wanted to move to Chicago. She admitted that she'd even looked at apartments on one of her many visits. I talked her out of it, I think, and suggested that we take a family weekend in New York. I thought it would help, but we're really just acting out the same tensions in a different locale."

I wanted to say wise, encouraging things to him, just as he always did to me. But his confession had depleted my limited reserve of optimism. And before I could muster even a disingenuous platitude, he suggested it was time to track down Stephanie.

"Based on what you've told me about her biological dad," he said, "I'm surprised he has entertained her even this long. Do you know how to find him?"

"I doubt it will be hard," I said. "But there's something I should tell you first."

"I'm all ears," he said.

24

I EXPLAINED TO CARTER THAT THE SUMMER I was pregnant with Stephanie, my parents were as kind as I could have hoped. They took care of me, though it was obvious that my mother was already severely compromised. She was exhausted and in pain from the multiple sclerosis that would soon incapacitate her and eventually claim her life. Yet despite her sadness, I saw nothing but compassion from her during the months I was home. I don't know whether she was sad for me because I had gone so far off course, or sad for herself that her body was failing her and she couldn't offer me another option. Or perhaps she was simply sad to think that she would never get to know this child I was producing.

I didn't see many people in those months, and my father drove me all the way to St. Gabriel's, which wasn't the closest hospital, whenever I needed to see a doctor. He didn't want me to endure the discomfort of being recognized, either by a neighbor who might see me at the doctor's office, or by a nurse who might see me at the grocery store.

On the August day when my contractions began, my father loaded me and a pre-packed suitcase into the truck. It was nothing like our ride to Halstead a year earlier, when we were confident and hopeful. On this trip, we didn't speak. When we arrived at the hospital, we were separated from each other, and I was told no one was allowed in the delivery room with me. My father tried, he told me later, to see me after the baby was born, but was rebuffed. He drove home, and I did not see him again until he came to pick me up five days later. I remember feeling very alone, and I kept looking for a Dr. Pasternak to advocate for me, or a Dr. Haynes to speak to me kindly. But the doctors and nurses were cold and peremptory. In the delivery room they barked orders at me, never once saying a soft word of encouragement or comfort. They spoke to each other but barely acknowledged my presence. After the birth, which was painful and terrifying to me but seemed unremarkable to the others in the room, no one said anything to me about the baby.

All I heard was the doctor's instruction to the nurses: "Put her with the other unmarrieds."

They brought me to recover in a room with a dozen other beds, not unlike a reformatory. It was gloomy, with no natural light and not a single decorative touch. There were four of us in that room; I was the oldest. Frightened teenagers, every one of us. We did not talk to each other. We probably imagined that our own misery was unique, in both kind and degree, and therefore could not be shared or explained. There was no point in even reaching out to each other.

The next morning, when I was still stiff and sore, the doctor came to see me. I would be lying if I said I remembered anything about Dr. Hauptman as a younger man. I only remember what it felt like when he approached my bed and asked if I had seen the baby yet. I said I hadn't.

"Would you like to?"

I thought he was offering.

"Yes, of course," I said, not realizing that this was a negotiation. I expected him to ask an orderly to walk me to the nursery. But instead he asked, "Why don't you first tell me what you plan to do with her? You don't think you can provide for her by yourself, do you?"

I told him that I planned to give her up and go back to school.

"Then you are one very lucky young woman," he said. I was skeptical of this conclusion, because I did not feel lucky. But Hauptman looked pleased, as if I had unexpectedly passed his test. "I can help you," he went on. "I know a family that can give this baby a much better life than she could have with you." He waited for me to respond, but I didn't. "Doesn't that sound like the right thing to do?"

Although I had known all along that I was going to give up the baby for adoption, I resented Dr. Hauptman's tone. It was true that I did not want to raise a baby alone. But was it really true that I would be so inadequate or inept a mother that the baby would be better off without me? Perhaps it was.

"Yes," I finally whispered. I stared at the ceiling, unable to look Dr. Hauptman in the eye. "That sounds fine."

"Good girl," he said. He gave my forearm a perfunctory pat, and on his way out of the room, he stopped to talk to a nurse by the door. He tilted his head toward me. "Let's move Miss Koller upstairs, and then bring the baby to her for a little visit, shall we?"

A half-hour later, that nurse collected my things into my small suitcase, and took me to a different ward on the third floor. Unlike the room down in the basement, this one had large windows, and the walls were painted with puppies and ducks. Here the women were older, and their faces were bright with lipstick, mascara, and smiles. They chatted with each other about their babies and their husbands. Almost every one of them had an infant in her arms.

"This will be your bed," the nurse said to me, "but you're ready to walk around. There's coffee and rolls on the first floor. Let me get some information from you, and then you can see the baby."

She grabbed a clipboard, sat down in a visitor's chair next to the bed—there had been no visitors in the room downstairs—and clicked her pen.

"We need to file a birth certificate, believe it or not. It's just a placeholder, but it has to be done. What is your full name?"

"Bonnie Koller."

"Your date of birth?"

"May tenth, 1951."

"Have you ever been known by any other name?"

"No."

"Address?"

I told her my address.

"Father's name?"

"Sigfried Koller."

"No, not your father," she said. "The baby's father."

Just thinking about my own father, just saying his name, lifted my spirits. For the first time in the three days that I had been in the hospital, I did not feel dirty or inferior. Just knowing that I had been blessed with a kind man for a father, a man who loved me and was proud of me, was a comfort. Every girl should have a kind man for a father, I thought. And so I responded the best way I could.

"Marshall Eckstein," I said.

I thought this lie was a gift my daughter deserved.

25

ONCE CARTER UNDERSTOOD THE PROBLEM, Marshall Eckstein was easy to find. It took one call from the hotel lobby to 411 to learn that he was a partner in a large law firm. His office was in midtown, in a steel and glass tower with an enormous atrium. As soon as we walked in, the noise of the taxis and Salvation Army bells yielded instantaneously to the quiet echo of heels on marble. We felt out of place among the people in suits and long camel coats who were walking purposefully in and out of the building.

A high reception desk staffed by two men in uniforms ran the length of the lobby. Carter, to my surprise, hung back and allowed me to approach the desk. The confident expertise Carter exhibited when it came to parenting was nowhere in sight when it came to navigating an office building.

"What floor for Frum, Fink and Schnabel?" I asked.

"Twenty-six," the guard said, and pointed us to a bank of elevators. I had to wave for Carter to follow me, as his attention was focused on the lobby's travertine marble walls and celestially high ceiling.

He was even less at ease when we rode up in the elevator. When we arrived at the law firm's offices, we faced another receptionist, a pretty woman whose turtleneck sweater matched her lipstick. Behind her, a wall of windows provided a view of other office towers, sprouting like weeds in a garden. Again, Carter let me do the talking.

"We are here to see Marshall Eckstein," I said, as if it were a request.

"Yes, he's expecting you," she said. This surprised me. "Let me just tell his secretary you're here." She motioned to a waiting area with a beige couch and a glass coffee table. "Please, have a seat."

I saw Carter touch the soft leather of the couch in disbelief and then look through the stack of periodicals offered on the table.

Another woman appeared, this one in pearls and heels, and said with the smile of a maître de, "Welcome. Right this way, please."

We followed her down a carpeted hallway, until we stopped at a door where we saw Marshall's name engraved on a brass plate.

His office was huge, with built-in oak bookshelves, an oversized desk, and a wall of windows. There was even room in one corner for a table and chairs. That's where we found Stephanie, eating a doughnut. To our great relief, she looked happy.

Marshall walked over to me and opened his arms. I'm not sure I would have recognized him. He had gained weight and lost hair in the decades since that night in Springfield.

"Bonnie," he said as he embraced me. "You look exactly the same."

"It's great to see you, Marshall," I said, and I realized it was true. After my long morning of worrying about Stephanie, I was suddenly grateful to her for bringing about a reunion that I should have effected a long time ago.

Stephanie turned to Carter.

"Dad," she said, "this is Mr. Eckstein."

Marshall waved his hand.

"No, no. Call me Marshall," he said.

He turned to us.

"I've been enjoying my chat with your daughter," he said, trying to be vague about which one of us to look at when he said "your daughter." "That is, once we straightened a few things out."

"It was a little awkward at first," Stephanie piped in, and she and Marshall laughed at their shared joke.

I was not sorry to have missed those initial exchanges in which Stephanie and Marshall unraveled the knot I had woven decades earlier with my wishful thinking.

"I'm glad you two have made friends," I said.

"Imagine my surprise when I learned that's *all* we are," Stephanie said, with only the slightest hint of accusation in her tone. Though she had already progressed from confusion to humor (or from anger to forgiveness?), she still planned to hold me somewhat accountable.

Marshall turned to me.

"Stephanie gave me the synopsis. You're in the practice too, I understand." He looked pleased. "I knew that's what you always wanted to do."

He said it as if we had something in common, as if this Manhattan skyscraper bore some resemblance to the converted house whose dining room I called my office, as if the mergers and acquisitions he negotiated were no different from the wills I drafted. But Marshall was kind enough to express admiration, not disdain, for my modest practice.

"I'm very happy that it worked out for you," he said sincerely. "It sounds like you built a great life for yourself after all."

I wasn't sure how much he meant the part about the great life. But I believed the part about being happy for me. In all the years since he returned me to my empty room at Halstead, I had wondered if Marshall blamed me for Hollis's death. But the way he looked at me now told me that, to him, my survival was the only beam of light in the darkness of that memory. It was tragic enough that one young woman had lost her life that night. He was thankful it hadn't been two.

I looked over at Carter and saw that he had begun to relax, and I understood that both his competing fears had been quelled. When I first met him, he confessed his concern that, if Stephanie went looking for her father, she might find him only to be rejected. But thus far in her search, she had been warmly welcomed. Nor had Carter's other worry been borne out today. Stephanie had not replaced him. Marshall would not be a rival for Stephanie's filial affection; he had extended no more than the fondness that a girl might find in an old family friend.

"Marshall has kids," Stephanie informed us brightly, before dropping her voice a register. "But, you know, just a reminder, I'm not related to them."

"Right," Marshall said. "I have two. Joel is a freshman in high school. And our daughter just turned thirteen." He looked directly at me. "Her name is Hilary."

He was trying to tell me something. Diane had long ago explained that every Jewish name was a tribute to a loved one who had died; she herself was named after her grandfather Daniel. Marshall wanted me to know that Hilary's name was chosen in order to keep Hollis's spirit alive. I was stunned by his generosity.

And what about me? How had I honored her memory in all these years? I had done nothing but punish myself with loneliness. Marshall had married and raised children, even enlisting his family to bear witness, to ensure that fragments of Hollis lived on. I, only I, had constructed my house around a shrine to my own shame. And what good had it done me?

"I wish you had shown up a few weeks earlier," Marshall continued. "You could have come to her bat mitzvah."

"My biological dad has kids too," Stephanie said. "Marshall was going to tell me about them when you walked in."

Marshall was leaning, not quite sitting, against the back of his desk, his palms on the surface.

"That's right," he said. "Colton has two. His son with Pamela is probably about seven. And his new wife just had a baby last summer. I honestly can't remember if it's a boy or a girl."

I could see Stephanie struggling to reconcile her interest in blood siblings with her understanding that meeting Colton's children would be complicated and challenging for reasons she hadn't even considered.

"Do you think they would want to meet me?" she asked Marshall.

He rubbed the back of his neck, and his tone turned apologetic.

"To tell you the truth, I don't know." He folded his arms professorially. "He doesn't talk about you." He said it gently, like he knew it was hard to hear. "He's always known you existed, but I've never heard him wonder about how you're doing."

Stephanie looked crestfallen.

"But I can approach him if you want me to," Marshall continued, when he could see how dismayed Stephanie was. "It wouldn't be the strangest deal I've ever brokered."

Stephanie pursed her lips.

"Maybe," she said hesitantly.

"For what it's worth," Marshall said, "he's a better person now than he was back then. What he did to your mother was by far the worst thing he's ever done."

Stephanie looked at me, and I could tell that it was her loyalty to me that prevented her from requesting an introduction.

"Do I have to tell you right now?"

"No, no. Of course not." Marshall picked up a small business card from a tray on his desk and handed it to Stephanie. "Think about it," he said. "You can call me any time."

Stephanie stared at the card, as if she were trying to install Marshall—his name, his office, and the morning she spent with him—in the hard drive of her mind.

While she took in the information, I asked Marshall the one question that had nagged at me.

"Did he ever get called up?"

Marshall brushed it off.

"Nah. The army wanted babies, not old men," he said. "It was our age that saved us."

Marshall turned toward Carter.

"How about you?" he asked. "Did you serve?"

"I got a deferral because I was teaching math in Roxbury. I'll let you decide if that counts as serving or not."

Marshall nodded. "I would say so," he said.

"Turns out I loved teaching," Carter said. "No regrets."

★ ★ ★

When we were outside again, Stephanie took Carter's arm.

"That was crazy!" she said. "For a few minutes there, I had, like, *three* fathers."

The two of them were dazed and giddy, like survivors of a freak accident.

"That's too many," Carter said, shaking his head and putting his hands in his pockets.

"I know," she agreed. "One is enough."

This was all he wanted to hear. He looked at me. "How was it seeing him again?"

It was nice of him to ask. Nice of him to remember that this was my drama too.

"Strange," I admitted. "Like meeting a new acquaintance and visiting my younger self all at once. I don't know how that happened."

He wasn't being dismissive or unsympathetic when he said, "Time passes, Bonnie."

"Yes," I agreed. "That's all it ever does."

★ ★ ★

When we got back from New York, it was almost Christmas, and Stephanie wanted to spend time with friends. For the holiday, I went to see Carol and her family, which I do every few years. For all her self-deprecating jokes about cooking, Carol is more than capable of producing a festive and satisfying holiday meal and serving it at a beautifully set table. Carol's sister's family was visiting, and they tried vigorously to convince Randy to open a branch of his firm near them in Houston. He humored them by claiming he would consider it if I would agree to join the practice. I listened to Topher and his cousin discuss the relative merits of racquetball versus squash, and I watched Emily dig into her Cornish game hen with no apparent memory of her summer vegetarianism. But mostly I waited until I could have a few minutes alone with Carol.

Finally, over stacks of dirty plates, I told Carol that there was something I had been keeping from her. If she was surprised, she didn't show it. On the contrary, she looked at me patiently, attentively, while I told her the interconnected stories of losing Hollis and finding Stephanie.

You know how every good heist movie has a scene at the end, when the entire film is replayed, sped up? And this time you get to see the maneuvers that were hidden on the first run-through, and you learn the secret of how the thief distracted the guard, impersonated the manager, penetrated the vault, and eluded the detective? Well, that's what it was like. I could see Carol's brain trying to replay our years of friendship, trying to understand the mechanics of the deception. She put down the plate she was rinsing, because her hands were shaking too much to be trusted with her wedding china.

"Oh, Bonnie," she said, but it was almost like a moan. "That's why you were so sad in college?"

"Did I seem sad?" I really didn't know what my classmates had been able to see in those years. We were new to each other, and everyone was constantly trying on new personalities. There was no way of knowing which ones were affected and which ones were real.

"No, not at first. But then when Hollis was gone, you seemed so bereft. I don't think I saw you smile for a year and a half. Every time her name came up, you looked like you were going to cry. I wanted to ask you what really happened. But when you finally seemed better, I was so relieved, that I decided to just let it go."

26

I saw Stephanie again at the end of January. She had mustered the courage to leave her apartment after all, and she asked me to help her move out. I arrived on Saturday morning, and parked across the street from Steph's soon-to-be-former home. At the curb in front of the house, Carter was standing by his car, tying a mattress to its roof. Stephanie had not told me that he would be helping with the move, but I was greatly relieved to learn that I was not expected to do any real heavy lifting. At least that's what I told myself about why I was so happy to see Carter. As soon as he noticed me, he put me to work. He tilted his chin toward a couple of suitcases on the sidewalk.

"Can you take these inside to Steph, please?"

I picked them up with an awkward jerk, not realizing they were empty. As I headed into the apartment, I passed Stephanie carrying a fan out to Carter's car. I wasn't sure which sight made her happier: me or the empty suitcases.

"Oh, great," she said. "There's a stack of sweaters on my floor. Can you toss them in there?"

Her bedroom was practically empty, except for some clothes, some trays of cassette tapes, and a futon frame. I packed the clothes in the empty suitcases and put them in my trunk. Carter put a box of books in my car, and then he and Stephanie broke down the futon frame. They tied it to the top of my car, while I grabbed a few more miscellaneous objects. I was pleased to see that Stephanie had claimed both the popsicle molds and the lanterns I had bought for her and Carina. Carter insisted that the box with Stephanie's mugs, cereal bowls and CDs was too heavy for anyone but him to carry. Once he slid it onto the trunk of my car, we were done. I followed Steph and her dad to the new apartment, all of four blocks away, and we started unloading.

Stephanie's new roommates, Katie and Kristin, were excited to show her which bedroom would be hers and where to post the phone messages and how to label the groceries she didn't want to share. It was nice to see Stephanie fussed over, even though it meant Carter and I didn't get much help from her. He carried most of the boxes, and I took the lighter things. I tried to get Stephanie to focus on the decisions at hand, like what to do with her music and her toiletries, but she was caught up in making plans with her new friends. It took about an hour to get the boxes and furniture and luggage inside, and then we were done. Stephanie didn't want our help setting up the futon bed, and she didn't want to go to Church Street for lunch.

"I need to knock out a sociology paper so I can go out tonight. You two go ahead," she said. "Dad, maybe Bonnie wants to watch the field house construction. I know that's your favorite thing." Then she turned to me, "That's what a provost does, you know. Talks about construction costs and labor contracts until everyone around them has practically died of boredom."

Then Kristin came into the room, and Stephanie poured two packets of sugar into her tone.

"Thank you so much for helping me move," she said, clearly for her roommate's benefit. "I'll see you soon, right? Maybe you can take me and my friends out some time." She said goodbye with an unsatisfying hug, too much elbow, and her head turned too far away from mine. Her farewell to Carter wasn't any better.

"Who was that girl?" I joked to him as soon as we were outside. His lips curled up, but I couldn't tell if he was smiling wryly or wincing from the cold.

I waited for him to say something reassuring. This was the perfect time for him to observe that Stephanie was mercurial but lovable. I figured we would find a diner, order omelets, and laugh about the way Stephanie had mocked us when it was just us in the room then showered us with gratitude when her roommates were watching. I would grumble good-naturedly about driving an hour and a half just to move a few boxes. Carter would assuage my resentment by reminding me that when young people are forging their independence, they need to test their parents. They demand your attention one minute and reject your company the next, he would tell me. We would drink our coffee and shake our heads and marvel at our daughter.

But Carter was already getting into his car. He rubbed his hands together and started the engine. He lowered the window and called out to me.

"Thanks for your help," he said. "That was surprisingly efficient."

I couldn't blame him for driving off. If I already knew everything he was going to say, there was no need for him to say it. And yet my visit felt incomplete without a debriefing with Carter. I wanted to talk about Stephanie, and, more importantly, I wanted to talk about her with him. He was the person who knew her best, the only person who gave her as much cognitive real estate as I did. And I had begun to feel that he was also, at this point in my life, the person who knew me best. To him, I had always, from the first moment of our meeting, been the woman who gave up a daughter and then found her. I had never had to pretend to be anything else.

27

A week after Stephanie moved, she called to tell me how much happier she was.

"Katie took us to a party where we met a bunch of med students, and I spent, like, an hour talking to this one guy. He asked for my phone number, and by the time I got home he had already left a message on my answering machine. Isn't that cute? He wants to meet me for a drink on Saturday. I guess that's something that people do, right? Meet for a drink? It sounded so grown up when he said it. What's a good drink to order that will make me look like I know what I'm doing?"

"Vodka gimlet."

"Thanks, Bonnie," she said brightly, appreciating both the speed and the specificity of the suggestion.

"What are mothers for?" I said flippantly. The time was long passed when I would have worried that the quip was too presumptuous. I knew Stephanie would let it go. She never minded jokes at Maureen's expense.

And then I didn't hear from Stephanie for a few weeks while the romance with the aspiring doctor ran its course.

"He was too serious," she told me, which was the closest I would get to an explanation for why she had stopped seeing him. "After graduation, I'm going to travel with my roommates. We're going to get Eurail passes and stay in youth hostels. My parents said the plane ticket could be my graduation present."

When she talked about the summer, she sounded just like the young woman I had hoped all along to find, from the moment I began my search. She was confident, hopeful, secure. I thought about how much I would miss her.

"That sounds like a great trip," I said. "What countries will you go to?"

"I think we'll start with England and Denmark. We've heard too many stories about creepy Mediterranean men."

"Good plan," I said. "And what about after that?"

"I don't know. Maybe Holland or Norway."

"No, I mean after your trip." It was already March. I thought it was time for Stephanie to start thinking about life after college, and this moment of expansive optimism seemed like an opportunity we shouldn't waste. "What are you thinking about for your life?"

But Stephanie's elevated mood could not withstand an inquiry into her post-college life plan. She tried to sound buoyant when she said, "Kristin says San Francisco is really nice. We were thinking of moving out there." But there was no conviction in her voice.

"I've heard it's a beautiful city," I said. "What kind of job would you get?"

She exhaled loudly, signaling a warning that I was asking too many questions.

"There are no jobs, Bonnie," she said with false forbearance.

She wasn't entirely wrong that 1992 was a terrible year to look for work, but there was nothing to gain from leaning into pessimism.

"People get jobs, even in a recession," I said. "And things are starting to get better. Why don't you come into my office one day soon, and we can work on your résumé. We'll print a bunch on nice paper, and Joyce can take them to the post office."

Stephanie didn't respond, and I wished she would accept my offer, so we could at least have this conversation in person.

"I wouldn't know where to send them," she finally said, sounding defeated. The brash young woman she had been just a few minutes ago had been replaced with an insecure girl.

"So let's talk about it. I'll help you figure it out."

I don't know whether it was the career guidance or the free office supplies that convinced her, but Stephanie agreed to come to Hopkins the next Friday.

★ ★ ★

She seemed overwhelmed, too small for her coat, the moment she walked in the door. Her backpack slid off her shoulder, down her arm and onto the floor like a dislodged boulder. Maybe I shouldn't have pushed her, I thought. Why couldn't I have just let her enjoy being young for a few more months? So what if she didn't have a plan? Just because I did when I was her age didn't mean she had to. But I had lured her down here to be optimistic, dammit, so optimistic we would be.

"Can I see what you have?" I asked, after she'd helped herself to a Tab and sat down at my conference table. She still wore her coat, as if she lacked the physical strength to remove it.

She bent down out of view while she fished a floppy disk out of her backpack. She handed it to me.

"Here," she said, anxious to be relieved of the offending plastic square, and convinced, it seemed, that her ineptitude was etched within its black casing.

I fed the diskette into the computer on my desk and opened up the file named *résumé*. The first thing I noticed was that she switched fonts, from Times New Roman to Courier, in the middle of her employment history. But I tried to focus on the content instead. I liked the description of her summer job, in which she had given herself a promotion from price tag scribe to assistant sales manager. I even learned a few things I hadn't known about Stephanie, like that she volunteered at a shelter for battered women, and that she recruited subjects for studies in the psychology department.

"This is a terrific résumé," I said, maybe a little too quickly. "You'll definitely want to fix the fonts and say a little more about your jobs. But, once you've done that, I think it will look great."

"What's wrong with the font?" Stephanie was sullen.

"You have more than one."

"Which one should I use?"

I had never seen Stephanie so passive.

"It doesn't matter which one. Just be consistent." I was trying to sound supportive, but my impatience was probably coming through. "The more important thing to think about is what you want to do. Who is going to be looking at this résumé?"

"I don't know," she said.

"Well, what did you imagine yourself doing after college?"

How was it possible that she didn't have an answer?

"Honestly? I always thought I would work for Governor Kunin. The coolest thing about Vermont is that we have a woman governor. But she's not even running again."

"So? Send her a résumé anyway. Isn't she going to work for Bill Clinton? He could be the candidate. Maybe you'd like to work on his campaign?"

"Maybe."

The truth was that I didn't know where the good jobs were either. I couldn't picture Stephanie on Wall Street, even if they would have her. And I couldn't name a single industry that was hiring or growing. And this was the irony. For so long, I had envied Stephanie for maturing in a time of quietude. When I was in school, there had been so much turmoil, not just over important things like sex and war, but over minutiae like haircuts and curse words. It often seemed that I had started college in one America and finished in another. The country in which Stephanie had matriculated was so much more stable, I thought. Practically boring. But when I watched her struggle to find her place in it, I realized that, actually, in the years that she had been on this earth, our entire nation had gone to sleep. My peers' howls of protest had been muffled by a blanket of money. And now even the money was drying up. Just a few years ago, Wall Street financiers were our cultural heroes. And now those very same corporate raiders were chalking up the walls of prison cells. What was an idealistic young woman to do?

"There's a new cable channel just about criminal trials," I offered. It was all I could come up with. "It's called Court TV. You could apply to be a production assistant there." I didn't want her to give up before she had even tried.

"What does a production assistant do?"

"Whatever the director tells you to do."

"Huh," she said, like she was actually considering it. "I wonder if I could work for a female director."

"Why not? You can do anything." How many times would I have to say this before it became true?

"I saw a movie recently that I think was made by a woman," she said, beginning to daydream. "It was about an Indian family from Uganda that owns a motel in Mississippi. I really liked it." She seemed to be emerging from her cave of despair, though I wasn't sure whether she was propelled by a newfound sense of agency or by the memory of going to the movies.

"Do you know the director's name?" I asked. "Send her a résumé."

"I never pictured myself in Hollywood, but at this point I would do anything to get away from here."

"March is like that," I agreed.

And then, to my surprise, Stephanie was crying softly.

"I'm sorry," she said. She dropped her face into her hands, in an unnecessary show of embarrassment.

"It's okay," I said, and stopped short of telling her how much I loved it when she let her guard down in front of me. "Graduating from college is stressful. It was even stressful for me, and I knew exactly what I was going to do next."

Stephanie stopped crying, but she slumped even farther down in her chair.

"It's not just that," she said. That was all she could get out at first, so I waited until she was ready to continue. "It feels like everything is ending. Not just school."

"What else?" I asked.

Her lips trembled and she began to cry again.

"My family," she finally said softly. "My family is ending." We were both surprised at how much grief the words unleashed.

"What do you mean?"

"Just what I said. It's over. My mom's leaving, and my dad doesn't even seem sad about it. Drew just wants to stay out of their way, and he might not come home for the summer. I feel like I don't have a family anymore."

I ignored the sting I felt at the demotion, and tried to be comforting.

"That's not true," I said. "They're still your family."

"Not really," she said. "We're like random stars in space. A family is supposed to add up to a picture of something, like the Big Dipper. You know what I mean?"

"Yes."

"I know I never said anything nice about my mom to you, but that was because . . ."

"I know," I interjected. "You don't need to explain."

"She's not that bad."

"You never said she was."

"I complained a lot. I know I did. You're too nice to say so. But now I feel like I drove her away."

I guess every kid thinks she's responsible for her parents' divorce, even a kid who's almost twenty-two years old.

"I've seen a lot of couples divorce," I said. "Trust me, it's never because of anything their kids did. I hate to break it to you, but you don't have that kind of power."

This must have helped a little, because she was able to lift her head and look me in the eye.

"If you say so."

"How is your dad?"

It wasn't until after I asked the question that I realized what I wanted the answer to be. I did not want to hear he was giddy with freedom, assembling a calendar bursting with dates and events. But nor did I want sweet, solid Carter to be broken or disconsolate. No, the image of Carter I had in my head, the one I wanted to hold onto, was of a man afflicted with just enough melancholy that he would welcome a phone call from me.

"He's okay," she said, and left it at that.

A few days later, I did reach out to Carter, sort of. Which is to say that I phoned his home in the middle of the day and expressed heartfelt emotional support to his answering machine. He did not return the call.

★ ★ ★

I tried to talk to Theo about Stephanie's pre-graduation ennui. I thought he might have some helpful insights.

"I don't entirely understand it," I said. "She's so fierce when it comes to ideas. She's been sending me pieces of her senior thesis, and

I'm so impressed. Apparently, there is something called Difference Feminism, and something called Equality Feminism, and there's enough tension between them to fill forty double-spaced pages. I mean, really. Who knew? But when it comes to taking control of her own life, she's really struggling. Her job search is so unfocused. We made a list of random people we admire and sent them her résumé."

"That's what kids are like these days," he said. "They're lazy, and they have no idea how to get anything done. You know who else is like that? Remember the woman you met who said she wanted to find her son?"

"Constance. Of course," I said.

"Right. Constance. She turned out to be useless. No drive. Like your daughter."

There it was, I thought. *Theo's sharp edge.* He was like two different people, I realized: one generous; one harsh. I was sad for him, because I knew what it was like to compartmentalize your different selves. I hoped Theo would someday realize, as I had, that he didn't have to do it anymore.

★ ★ ★

Every time I spoke to Stephanie in the next few weeks, she seemed shell-shocked. Until one day at the end of April she called me in a triumphant mood.

"Guess who just hired me."

"The Oakland A's?"

"Ooh, Bonnie. So close, but no. Try again. Think East Coast."

"Why don't you just tell me?"

"Okay. Are you ready?"

I didn't even get to signal my readiness before she said, "Your friend Marshall."

That was not the answer I had expected.

"What did he hire you for?"

"I'm going to be a paralegal at his law firm. I start on September 8th. How great is that?"

"Congratulations," I said. "How did that happen?"

"I just called him. About two weeks ago. Remember he gave me his card? He told me to call any time. So I called."

"Good for you," I said, truly impressed. "Good for you."

28

I HAD ONE GRATIFYING VICTORY AT WORK that spring. The district court decided that our restaurateur client could sue the owner of the old dry cleaner over the chemicals that were leaching into his wine bar. We had not, the judge ruled, missed the deadline to file our complaint. When I got the good news, I wanted terribly to share it with Stephanie. I knew she would congratulate me and then instantly lose interest, but I wanted to go through that ritual anyway. It took a few tries to reach her, but when we finally connected, she seemed, if anything, a little too happy about these developments.

"I'm so glad you have something to celebrate," she said, as if she were about to tell me something I didn't want to hear.

"Yeah," I agreed. "The case is going to be a lot of work, but that's better than the alternative."

"So, you're going to be really busy anyway?" she asked, and I didn't know what she meant.

"Is there something going on?" I finally asked.

She inhaled through her teeth.

"Don't be mad," she said.

"What?"

"I can't spend Mother's Day with you." She said it really fast, as if she didn't want me to take it in, as if the statement would trigger a deadly explosion.

"That's hardly the big deal you seem to think it is," I said, almost laughing.

"Are you sure you're not just saying that? I feel really bad. It's just that Drew and I have to spend the day with my mom. It's the first Mother's Day since, you know. Drew says we can't let her be alone."

Her contrition was so cute. I considered laying on a little guilt just to see what it would get me. But instead I assured her that I wasn't angry.

"Stephanie, it's fine. It's a holiday invented to sell greeting cards. I wasn't planning on it in the first place."

I didn't admit that I was happy just to know she had thought about spending the day with me.

"And my graduation is just the week after." She was still trying to placate me. "I'll see you then, right?"

This was the first time she had requested my presence at that particular milestone, and, despite the graceless invitation, I was thrilled.

"Of course," I said. "I wouldn't miss it."

★ ★ ★

I bought a new dress for Stephanie's graduation and made an appointment to get my hair done the day before. But mostly I focused on what to give her as a gift. The weekend before commencement, I took my mother's jewelry out of my upstairs closet and set about choosing a piece that Stephanie would find meaningful but also wearable. There was a brooch in the shape of a leaf, inlaid with tiny gems, and a string of pearls. The leaf was beautiful, but, really, no one wears brooches anymore. It was hard enough to picture Stephanie going to work in a suit jacket with shoulder pads. The addition of a giant pin on the lapel was just too much. She was likelier—barely—to wear the pearls, though I was less inclined to part with them. I was mulling it over when I heard a knock on my door.

When I opened it, the person smiling sheepishly on my threshold was Carter.

"Happy Mother's Day," he said. "There's no reason for us both to be alone."

I knew by the way he was looking at me that everything was about to change. He wasn't there to offer advice or consolation. He just wanted to be with me. He looked relaxed, light, free. I beckoned him in and moved aside to make way for him to enter. He stepped across the threshold, closed the door behind him and stood in front of me. We had never been this close or looked at each other so long.

"I'm glad you're here," I said. But I barely finished the sentence before he was kissing me. He kissed me hungrily, as if he had waited too long, as if he needed to make up for lost time. I leaned in and lost myself in his mouth and neck and shoulders. I thought only of him and what it would be like to kiss him like this forever.

We held hands as we walked into town for lunch. Carter wanted to know everything about me. We talked about my childhood on the farm and my mother's MS. I told him about building my own practice and buying my own house. I didn't have to talk about Stephanie, but I didn't have to pretend Stephanie didn't exist. He told me how lonely he had felt in his last few years of marriage. He told me about how right it felt to be with me. He didn't have to pretend that Stephanie was perfect, but he didn't have to explain why she was loveable. He told me he was sorry he could not sit with me at Stephanie's graduation.

"I have to sit on the stage," he explained. "I'm the provost, remember?"

★ ★ ★

By the time I sat in my plastic folding chair and watched Stephanie clutch her diploma, Carter and I had already spent three nights together. We saw each other every weekend that June, and by the time Stephanie left for Europe, we were looking at houses halfway between our two jobs. And at the end of the summer, when Stephanie started working at Marshall's firm, when Carter and I moved her into her tiny rental apartment on Avenue A, I was, for the second time in my life, pregnant.

About The Author

Ellen B. Rockmore was born and raised in Manhattan. She was once a New York lawyer, but now teaches expository writing at Dartmouth College. She lives in Hanover, New Hampshire, with her husband, children and golden retriever. She recently began a two-year term as a state legislator in the New Hampshire House of Representatives. Her essay titled "How Texas Teaches History" was published in the New York Times.

Acknowledgments

I am grateful to so many people who gave their time and support to *The Given-Up Girl*. I want to thank the many women who shared coffee and memories of their college years: Kris Aulenbach, Marilyn Breselor, Mary Jane Clark, Susan Damon, Deb Lievens, Maria Mossaides, Barbara Stern. I am indebted also to several doctors and social workers who educated me about the rationing of reproductive care: Phyllis King, Dr. Marilyn Levine, Dr. Carmel Cohen. I was lucky to have wonderful friends and students to read my drafts. Their comments and encouragement made me a better writer. Thanks to Lara Balick, Lisa Bornstein, KJ Dell'Antonio, Rachel Kleinbaum, Caroline Levy, Jennifer Mirsky, Amy Rifkind, Levi Roseman, Carole Schiffman, Sara Stemen And then I found the amazing women of Sibylline Press, who know so much more than I ever could: Vicki DeArmon, Julia Park Tracey, Maureen Jennings, Suzy Vitello. And, of course, I would be nowhere without the love of Dan, Alex, Shayna and Rachel.

Study Guide Questions

1. Bonnie encounters people who think it is immoral for her to search for her daughter. What do you think?

2. Both Bonnie and Constance, a birth-mother Bonnie tries to help, encounter people who think it is wrong for a young, unmarried woman to raise a child. Given the time and place of this novel, were they right?

3. At Halstead orientation, the college's president advises the new students to focus on their studies and not get distracted by turmoil over the Vietnam War and racial inequality. Do you think that was good advice?

4. Why does Bonnie have sex with Colton the first time she meets him?

5. Given Hollis's and Bonnie's different backgrounds, what makes their friendship work?

6. What are the costs and benefits of the feminist revolution for the women of Halstead?

7. How is Stephanie's personality shaped by her experience of being an adoptee?

8. What are the strengths and weakness of Bonnie's and Stephanie's relationship?

9. How well does Bonnie navigate her relationship with Stephanie's birth family?

Sibylline Press is proud to publish the brilliant work of women authors over 50. We are a woman-owned publishing company and, like our authors, represent women of a certain age.

www.ingramcontent.com/pod-product-compliance
Lightning Source LLC
Chambersburg PA
CBHW021038310726
48969CB00006B/1707